One-Woman Show

Kayla Parent

Copyright © 2017 Kayla Parent
All rights reserved.
ISBN: 1544770723
ISBN-13: 9781544770727

This book is dedicated to Jimmy Cannon, who was by my side as I wrote this through the good, the bad, and the ugly.

1

Eloisa

"Eloisa!"
"Eloisa Rae, over here!"
"Eloisa, to your right!"

I groan inwardly but make sure to keep the fake smile plastered on my face. Fame, and everything that comes along with it, never appealed to me. It still doesn't.

"Why did you pick Hartford, Connecticut, to kick off your tour?"

"What's going to be your next single?"

Ignoring their questions—questions I already answered during my announcement—I turn to go. I stop when I spot a small face in the crowd trying to get my attention. Making my way over, I bend down to address her through the metal bars.

"What's your name?" I ask, smiling at her wide-eyed expression.

"Marie," she replies. She thrusts a small Post-it note and marker in my direction. "Can I have your autograph?"

"Of course you can." I scribble down my name and hand it back over. "It's so nice to meet you, Marie."

"Thank you so much; she's such a big fan." I meet the eyes of a woman standing behind Marie and nod. Cameras flash around us, taking in the moment. I try not to roll my eyes. "You made her day!" the woman continues brightly, kissing the top of the little girl's head. Marie is now beaming as she stares down at the paper with my signature.

"She's made mine, too," I reply truthfully. The woman gives me a thankful smile but probably doesn't realize how much I mean that statement. Fans like Marie are the only reason I do this. My fans have saved my life. Literally.

I brush down the front of my dress to straighten it as I stand and take a quick peek around. I hate leaving any fans disappointed if they have gone to the trouble of hiding among the media. No doubt my manager, Rob, will try to force me into more interviews if I linger, but I just have to make sure.

A red hair ribbon catches my attention, and I lock eyes with a small woman who looks to be about my age. She pushes the errant bow away from her face when we lock eyes and smiles before aiming her phone to snap a picture. I smile widely and make sure she gets the photo she wants before looking away. A few more cameras go off after that, and I hold still.

"Eloisa, I love you!"

The declaration comes out in a shockingly aggressive shout, and I turn to the left, waving to the screaming fans who are lined up across the street as far as the eye can see. The turnout is much bigger than I expected for a last-minute press conference.

As expected, I feel a warm, slightly clammy hand at my elbow. "Ellie, we've got *People* mag for five minutes."

Without waiting for an answer, Rob steers me back toward the middle of the red carpet. Keeping my annoyance in check, I smile at the eager young woman in front of me. She doesn't waste any time.

"'Unsteady' is going to be your first tour—are you nervous?"

My body tenses up. If she only knew. I make sure my smile is still in place. "Yes. If I wasn't nervous, that would mean I had no business doing a tour."

She takes a quick peek down at her pad before meeting my eyes again. "Did you ever expect your first album to do so well?"

I give her the PG version of the truth I could recite in my sleep. "Writing *Hold on to Me* was an incredible experience and very therapeutic. That my fans have embraced it is an absolute blessing, and I owe all my success to them."

Her eyes narrow, and I know which question is coming next. "What do you have to say about the snub? Word is you've gotten on the wrong side of Martha Mathers."

Rob tenses behind me. He was hoping the snub wouldn't come up today. I, of course, am naturally cynical and knew it would. For such a clever businessman, Rob can be incredibly naive. Besides, I don't see the big fuss about refusing to work with Martha Mathers. By all accounts, she's a manipulative, angry, overly ambitious woman, and I don't trust her. She also happens to be the most sought-after, successful producer in the country, but that doesn't mean anything to me. My music is my own, and it always has been.

Rob steps between us. "We're only answering questions about the announcement of Eloisa's tour. That's what we're all here for, right?"

I place my hand gently on his arm and answer the woman anyway. Hiding from this has gotten old. "I'm not worried about Martha. I appreciate her interest and think she has made some incredible music, but for right now, I'm working solo. I'm just starting out and hoping to carve my own path."

"So it's true that you write all your own lyrics and music?"

Before I can answer that question, something off to the right catches my attention. I only have a split second to lock eyes on the object hurtling toward me before everything fades to black.

2

Xavier

Tap. Tap. Tap.

A voice sounds from within. "Come in."

I open the door and step inside, making note of my boss, Colonel Jackson, tapping furiously away at his keyboard. He doesn't look up from his laptop as he says, "X. On time as always. Please, have a seat."

I sit myself down in one of the utilitarian chairs across from his desk and wait patiently. The colonel is on his own schedule and won't begin talking until he's ready. Usually it doesn't bother me, but I'm anxious to get this meeting over with. I've been sitting with my thumb up my ass for a week now, waiting to get back to work. I don't do well alone with my thoughts.

After exactly seven minutes, the colonel sets his pen down and rubs his eyes. He's looking more tired than usual these days. But forty years of running the secret service security office will do that to you.

The colonel crosses his arms and looks up at me for the first time. "X, how has your week off been?"

"I'm ready to get back to work, sir."

He laughs loudly. "Eight years with the president without one vacation, and you're antsy after seven days?"

I shrug. "When can I head back to DC, sir?"

I'm positive I'll be assigned to the White House again. I revolutionized the security system there and have a perfect safety record. I know that building and the grounds inside and out, and the—now former—president himself told me I was the most trusted member of the team. Which is why I'm surprised when my question is greeted by silence.

The colonel's lips are pursed as he swivels in his high-backed chair. "You're not going back to DC just yet."

My body immediately reacts, but years of training transform my features into a look of disinterest. "Oh?"

The colonel sighs. "Something came down the pike this week, and you're the only man I trust for the job." His expression puts me on high alert. Reading people is my specialty, and right now, if I didn't know any better, I'd say the colonel looks—wary.

He grins when he realizes I'm not going to respond. "You always have been a man of few words, X. Here, I'll just show you the video."

I lean in, and he turns his laptop on the desk so it's facing me. The video gets going, and I see a gorgeous woman speaking in front of the camera as if in an interview. I quickly catalog the facts. She's short. Height about five feet three, give or take half an inch. Long, dark-brown hair. Green eyes. But before I can wonder about why I'm watching this, an object—my guess is a rock, from the size and velocity—flies in from the side of the screen, and the woman drops out of the frame.

I lean in closer as shouting erupts in the background, the whole scene turning chaotic. The camera guy pans down to focus on the woman who is now sprawled on the ground. I squint, and I'm able see a small but nasty wound just starting to bleed above her ear. Missed her temple, so she probably walked away with only a mild concussion. Lucky.

The video shuts off, and I lean back in my seat, crossing my arms over my chest. Tough luck for the woman, but why am I being shown this video? The colonel presses his fingers together and watches me as if he's waiting for me to figure it out. One second goes by—two—

Oh, fuck.

"No." My response is immediate. He wouldn't dare ask this of me.

"Her name is Eloisa Rae Morgan. She's a singer."

I'm not surprised when the name doesn't ring a bell. The safety and security of the president of the United States has been my only focus for the past eight years. I'd still be there now if I wasn't forced to take a vacation. There's been no room for trite celebrity drama in my life, and I certainly don't stay up-to-date on the who's-who bullshit. "I'm not doing personal security for some prima donna."

"There was a note attached to the rock she got hit with," the colonel goes on to explain. He drags a photocopied version of a crumpled letter up on screen. My hackles rise as I scan the words. A sick, sick person wrote this. There are even creepy hearts as the dots in a few of the *i*'s. I give my head a small shake in an effort to rid myself of the gruesome, violent prose. I meet his eyes, both of us thinking the same thing. Whoever wrote this letter is extremely dangerous. And clearly not afraid to make contact with her. Probably got a thrill. Did anyone see anything? As soon as the question enters my mind, I quickly banish it. It's not my problem, and it's not going to be.

"Rob's thinking she's got a stalker," the colonel says, rubbing his eyes again.

"Rob?"

"My little brother and Eloisa's current manager. Called me a few days ago. Said she's about to go on tour and needs her security detail completely revamped. You know, just in case this guy decides to show his ass again."

"Absolutely not. I didn't sign up for the secret service to do private security."

"X, listen—"

"No offense, sir, but you're way off pulse here. I don't even know who the woman is."

"I think that will work in your favor," he responds curtly. His hands are folded on his desk, a sure sign he's settling in until he gets what he wants. Not this time.

An image of me trailing after some hardheaded, narcissistic Barbie doll with a microphone has me grinding my teeth. "I don't have the patience for a job like this, sir. You know that."

He shrugs, knowing it's true. My efficiency is legendary in this business, and I don't wait on anyone. "It would be a small, temporary leave of absence. My buddy runs a private security company that can help you out with any equipment and transportation you may need. Four months for the tour, and then I'll assign you back to DC."

I leisurely brace my hands on the arms of the chair and give him the eye. Anyone else would wither under this expression, but the colonel holds tight. He comes across as a softy to those who don't know him, but he can be hard as nails. Both he and I know I don't really have a choice in the matter—not if I want to keep my job—even if he's making it seem like he's trying to convince me.

Despite that, I sigh and rub both hands over my face, not wanting to give in. This job is a nightmare materialized. I refuse to go from protecting the most important man in the nation to some entitled princess. "Why me?"

The colonel leans across the desk. "Look. This is my little brother, and I owe him the best I've got. You're the only man I trust to get this thing done right. You'll be working with the police if need be. I need you, X."

Fuck. There's just no way. Clamping my jaw shut, I stare at him in silence.

His eyes narrow. "Home base would be Stamford, Connecticut."

My stomach flips over. There's only one thing that would make me accept this asinine career detour, and he just landed on that hidden square. I have to wonder why he didn't just tell me this from the beginning. He knows where my father lives.

The colonel nods his head and picks up his pen, which means he's done with the conversation. "All the paperwork and your plane ticket are waiting for you in your PO box. They're expecting you by tonight."

3

Eloisa

I scurry down the hall, late as usual. My socked feet skid on the floor in front of my dining room, and I just catch myself on the lip of the doorway. Scowling, I straighten and take a deep breath, staring at the closed patio-style doors in front of me. Everyone is probably already inside. These weekly team meetings we have are a necessity. My inner circle needs to be on the same page, and with the tour starting in three weeks, there's much to discuss. This week, however, is the first meeting since my accident, and I'm dreading the fallout. I can't even imagine the restrictions they are going to try to put on me. Well, they'd better be ready for a battle.

I stride inside with a lot more confidence than I feel. My personal assistant, Sandy, the quiet but incredibly organized superwoman in my life, waves in greeting. I smile back before taking the seat beside her at the head of the table. I compliment her glasses—she seems to have a new pair every day—as I settle in.

Looking around, I can see there are only a few of us here. Perhaps I'm not as late as I thought.

"Good morning, *ma petite*. You look awful." Jacques, my talented and infuriatingly honest makeup maven and hairstylist, is sitting on my other side, wearing a large grin.

Rolling my eyes, I accept the small plate with a doughnut that he slides in my direction. Glazed. Yum. My favorite. I can never refuse a good treat—my dog and I have that in common. "Good morning to you, too."

"Should you really be eating that with a tour in three weeks?" Rob says as he walks in from a side door. He glares at me before taking his seat across from me at the opposite head.

"Oh, leave her alone," Michonne, my wardrobe stylist, growls at Rob. "Eloisa was just named the sexiest woman alive by *InStyle* magazine. Can you say the same, squishy pants?" A few crumbs fall out of my mouth as I choke on my first bite. Michonne, with her long dreads and bright lipstick, always has my back. She also has more venom than a cobra when provoked. Usually it's aimed at Rob.

She winks at me, but I wisely suppress my laughter when I see the look on Rob's face.

"Where are Joe and Big?" he asks impatiently, ignoring Michonne's comment.

As if on cue, the heads of my security team appear at the door.

"Sorry we're late," Joe chirps. "We got caught up on a call." He swings his big, blond, muscled body into the chair next to Sandy and nudges her with his shoulder. Sandy sniffs and doesn't acknowledge the greeting, per usual.

"Oh, Sandyyyyy," Joe sings under his breath, in a terrible impression of *Grease*. Sandy continues to ignore him.

Big takes the seat on his other side and makes a grab for the doughnuts. He's the strong and silent type—the introvert to Joe's extrovert.

I lick my fingers, enjoying the last bite of my own doughnut before locking eyes with my manager.

"Well, now that we're all here—" Rob clears his throat and rises from the table. "I see no reason to waste time. Ellie, we've made a couple maneuvers regarding your security."

I tense up, bracing myself for the conversation ahead. "What kind of maneuvers?"

"We're bringing in a new head. He comes highly recommended, and I have full confidence that an incident like last Friday's will never, ever happen again."

"Damn right it won't," Joe mutters. Both he and Big spent the night at the hospital with me, furious they didn't catch the threat in time. It wasn't their fault; it all happened so fast.

"OK, that's fine. But just a heads-up, I don't want any drastic changes," I say in response. "I can't work with someone constantly breathing down my neck."

"Ellie, be reasonable," Rob retorts. "If you read that note—"

"Please, stop bringing up the note," I plead for what feels like the fiftieth time. I haven't read it, because I don't want any negative words swimming in my head. Watching my team's reaction that night at the hospital as it was discovered, I gathered that those words were pretty ugly. The only thing I unintentionally overheard was that it was signed "Your biggest fan." And that hurt. I love my fans more than anything; everyone close to me knows that. Going above and beyond for them is one of the only things that brings me any joy. It hurts so much that one of them would do this, and I have no problem pretending that it never happened. I'm sure it's a one-off incident anyway.

"Ellie, *ma petite*. You are in danger," Jacques says, resting his hand over mine. "This security is needed. For you, for all of us."

"But I already have Joe and Big and the rest of the guys we hired for the tour," I say with an imploring look in their direction.

Joe regards me seriously. "This tour is going to be massive, Ellie. We don't have the experience for something like this. Last Friday proved that. You're...too famous now for just a few meatheads like us."

Big nods and leans toward me. "He's right, Ellie. X is going to bring in the big guns. We just spoke with him, and he's on his way; that's why we're late."

"Who is X?" I ask impatiently. And really? X? What a stereotypical moniker for someone in the security field. That can't be his real name.

"His real name is Xavier Cannon," Sandy whispers, answering me with her wizard-like mind-reading powers.

"He's highly qualified," Rob puts in. "He was the head of security at the White House and revolutionized the procedures there." His eyes light up as he describes what he no doubt feels is a most admirable quality. "He's a no-nonsense type of individual. He means business! My brother recommended him as the best they've got. And after reading that note...we need the best."

I look down at my hands, my mood taking a nosedive. I get it. I really do. I also recognize that I'm putting on a tough act to hide how hurt I am, but this is exactly what I was afraid of. I don't want to lose the closeness with my fans. I don't want to seem untouchable to them, being whisked away or unable to interact on a whim. "I refuse to go on lockdown," I respond. "If you guys want to amp up security, fine. But I'm not punishing my fans for this."

"Sunday brunches are out," Rob says next, his hands grabbing the back of his chair as if preparing for blowback.

The hairs on the back on my neck rise. "No."

"Come on, Rob," Michonne puts in. "You know how much Sunday brunches mean to our girl here. Can't this X guy make it work somehow?"

Every Sunday, two fans are invited over to the house to enjoy brunch with the inner circle and me. I look forward to it more than anything else that I do. All the different faces and backgrounds, all with a different story to tell: Squiggy, who climbed Mt. Everest three times; Darla, who made doggy treats that my Bella loved so much I started ordering two boxes a month from her shop; Pierre, who'd beaten childhood leukemia. They are all special to me.

I haven't missed a Sunday brunch in six months.

"This is nonnegotiable," Rob continues in a stern voice as he shoots Michonne a warning look. "I hate to be the hard-ass here, but we're not taking any chances."

"Everything is negotiable," I say loudly, refusing to back down. "Most of the time the fans are children anyway. What harm can they do?"

"Eloisa, be reasonable!" Rob says in exasperation. "How can you possibly want to continue to open your home to fans when one of them wants to kill you?"

His declaration is met with silence. Jacques reaches out to put his hand over mine. I give him a weak smile despite the turmoil coiling in my belly over the harsh words. I'm not stupid. I figured it was something along those lines, but hearing it out loud burns. *Why?* Why would someone want to kill me? I look around at the faces of my team. My closest confidants, the only people in the world I can trust. Everyone is subdued.

"Eloisa, I'm sorry," Rob says. "But you need to know the truth. Your safety is our number-one concern."

The deep frown lines around his mouth are prominent, which means he's really upset. Rob may be a conniving, manipulative jerk, but I know deep down he has my best interests at heart. I sigh, pushing out my chair behind me.

"Where are you going? We have a lot more to discuss. The band, a few hiccups in the tour dates...Eloisa!"

Don't cry. Don't cry in front of them. I suck in a breath, trying to stave off the telltale prickle behind my eyes.

"Sandy can catch me up later," I call out, disappearing around the corner. When I reach the music room, I immediately grab my guitar and settle into the worn couch by the window. Music is the only thing that can calm me when I feel this unsteady.

4

Xavier

I roll my car window down, more than a little surprised at what I see. This can't be where she lives. Granted, it's an oceanfront property in New England, so the price tag must be hefty, but—it's small. Not a house I would expect some fancy-pants singer to own. It's probably just one of many. Rolling my eyes at the thought, I ease forward.

An older gentleman with a long white beard waves me down from the driveway. Who is this?

"You must be X," the man chirps as he shuffles over. I see a set of jailer's keys in his hand, the sight immediately setting my nerves on edge. If Grandpa here and an old wrought-iron gate are the only means of security, then we're going to have a huge problem.

"Call me Harold," the old man says as he reaches my window. For some reason, he seems delighted to see me. I can't imagine why; no one is ever delighted to see me. "We've been expecting you. Come on in." And just like that, he starts walking back toward the gate.

I watch his retreat in silence. Stunned silence. I'm nearly speechless, in fact. Nearly. "Harold!" I call.

The man halts in his tracks, spinning to face me. I give a little wave outside the window, beckoning him back to the car. He starts to walk back toward me, and I notice a bit of confusion marring his otherwise friendly face. He has no idea.

I make sure to look him in the eye. "Harold, aren't you going to ask me to identify myself?"

The old man frowns. "Rob gave me a description of you and what time you'd be arriving. You are X. Aren't you?"

I run a hand over my face, trying to rein in my temper. This is worse than I thought. "Harold, as I'm sure you're aware, the mistress of this house was violently attacked last Friday."

"Of course I'm aware," Harold says defensively. "Terrible, nasty thing it was."

"So you understand my concern that you're not, at the very least, checking IDs when unidentified strangers pull up to the property."

Harold cottons on to my meaning and puffs his chest out. "I can assure you, young man, I take the guarding of that gate very seriously. No one gets by me!"

I glance back at the gate, noting the layers of rust and the single padlock sitting in the center of two bars that look like a strong gust of wind could take them out. "That gate will be the first thing to go," I tell him seriously.

"What was that?" Harold asks. I can tell he genuinely didn't hear me. Which is another problem. Christ.

I decide then and there not to argue with him until I can fully assess the situation and get all my ducks in a row. "Nothing. Can you please open the gate and direct me to the security office? I want to take a look at the camera systems."

"Camera systems?" Harold gives me a funny look. "We don't have any of that fancy stuff here."

I'm going to kill the colonel. I grind my teeth and look out the windshield. "Just open the gate, Harold."

The old man crosses his arms over his chest. "Well, now, I'd like to be seeing your ID first."

~ ~

Once I get the car parked in the circular driveway, I begin a cursory assessment of the grounds. Besides Harold and his trusty gate, there's really nothing to deter an eager intruder. The stone wall surrounding most of the property could easily be scaled. And the trees dotted around the quaint yard would provide excellent cover. This is the only house for at least a quarter of a mile on either side. Does anyone even live here with her? What a fucking joke of an operation.

Frustration mounting, I walk around toward the backyard. Miles of blue ocean spread before me, and I notice that the house is built on an inlet. Large rocks piled haphazardly together form a natural border on both ends of the yard, spreading out toward the beach. I watch the waves crash against the sand for a moment before I hear a slight noise behind me.

A carbon copy of the colonel—just ten years younger—is stepping outside onto the back deck. He gives me a small wave before heading in my direction. I don't wave back while I wait for him to come to me. I'm afraid if I do move, I'll shake him so hard his teeth will rattle. Clearly he doesn't give a shit about his client if he's allowing her to stay here.

"Xavier," he greets me as he gets closer. "Harold just rang and said you'd arrived. I'm Rob."

"X." I hesitate for a moment before grabbing his hand in a firm grip, making sure to give it a good squeeze. It doesn't really do much for my frustrations.

He pales a bit once I release him and gives his hand a shake. "X, yes. We're all very happy you're on board."

I don't respond. Just give a short nod. There's no time for pleasantries when there is clearly a lot of work to be done.

After a moment of tense silence, he laughs. "My brother did say you were a man of few words. How is the colonel, by the way?"

"He's fine," I answer shortly—then decide to change the subject. "Can you please direct me to the security team? Joe and Big. The men I spoke to earlier."

Rob stands his ground at my rudeness in a surprising show of will. "Of course. But there are just a few things I'd like you to know first."

I raise a brow and don't break eye contact as I wait for him to speak. He clears his throat.

"There will be about 180 people under Eloisa's employ for this tour. That includes her band, her hair and makeup team, her costume designers, the caterers, the truck drivers, production assistants, roadies, and lighting crew."

"I read all that in the file," I say impatiently. "I also asked for background checks on every one of them, e-mailed to me in PDF format by end of day tomorrow. Also—"

"Yes, but—"

I decide to bulldoze over him and get to my point. This is taking too long. "This property is a security nightmare. She might as well be standing with a target on her back for all the protection this place lends."

"I know, but—"

"I'm calling a private team recommended by your brother. They'll have a new security system installed by nightfall. The locks will all be touch sensored, and we're reinforcing that stone wall out front. And moving forward, there will be no visitors coming in or out unless they're on the master list, all of which is approved by me. The security is deplorable out front."

Rob sighs, running a hand through his hair. "I know. The gate has seen better days."

"So has Harold," I respond coolly.

Rob's mouth forms an O shape as he catches my meaning. "Eloisa will have a fit if you try to fire him."

"Eloisa isn't in charge."

Rob barks out a quick laugh. "Right. Well, X, I'm on board with all your decisions. I've been wanting to make some changes around here for a good long while. Just let me know how I can help and if Ellie gives you any trouble."

I give him a sharp nod. "One more thing," I ask. "Who else lives here?"

Rob shrugs. "There's always people around, but just Eloisa."

Fucking hell. As I figured. I turn toward the house. But, come to think of it, the fewer people milling about the better. I've always hated living in crowded quarters.

5

Eloisa

Sticking my pencil back in my bun, I narrow my eyes at the sheet in front of me. I haven't been able to write a new song in weeks. I could chalk it up to lack of inspiration, but I know that's not what's been bothering me.

I reach down and scratch Bellatrix—my little Bella—under her chin. She pants loudly, and her eyes start to close as she basks in the attention.

"What a life, eh?" I mumble.

The sound of thundering footsteps in the hallway breaks the peaceful silence. Bellatrix and I both freeze, listening as they get closer.

Without warning, the door to the library is whipped open, causing me to rear back into my pillows.

Oh, wow—

The breath is sucked out of my chest as I take in the formidable monster of a man filling the doorway. It's like he walked out of a nightmare, wearing all black and looming over the room with his arms crossed over his mighty chest. My eyes run from the shit-kicker boots to the cargo pants and long-sleeve Under Armour shirt, the latter two encasing what

I know right away is a long, lean, insanely muscled body. *He must be the new security detail—*

I clear my dry throat and force myself to look in the monster's face. He's scowling, but not at me. "Can you shut this thing up, or should I?"

Breaking out of my trance, I swallow and snap my mouth closed. It's only then that I notice Bellatrix yapping away at the intruder's feet.

"Bellatrix, stop that! Get over here," I scold. My voice comes out shaky to my own ears. *Get a grip, Morgan!* "Sorry," I continue. "She's hoping you have food."

He stares at me with a blank expression, so I try to explain. "She can't help but investigate every time someone enters a room. She loves to eat. In fact, she can smell her favorite treats from a mile away." And now I'm rambling. The yapping doesn't stop, so I clap my hands twice and raise my voice. "Bellatrix, now!"

A small series of growls emits from my twelve-year-old Pomeranian's mouth, but she listens and trots back over to my side. I make a show of petting her because I'm too overwhelmed to look at the captain of darkness in my doorway. I've never had any social grace around intimidating men.

Reaching into my pocket, I pull out one of Darla's treats to keep her busy. She takes it happily and settles into my lap. X still hasn't said anything, but his body language speaks a thousand words. Apparently he's in a bad mood.

Finally, after things are starting to get really awkward, he speaks. "I assume you knew I was coming today."

His deep, husky tone catches my attention, and I instinctively look up, noting his short brown hair and dark-brown eyes. But when I look closer, I can't help but marvel at his face. Chiseled, strong, with just a hint of stubble. Oh, I am way out of my element with this one. I remind myself that he works for me, so that automatically gives me the upper hand. "I was told just this morning."

He steps into the room at a leisurely pace and starts glancing around, picking up this and that as if he has all the time in the world. Both Bellatrix and I bristle. I get he's my part of the security team, but he's incredibly familiar considering we haven't even properly met. "Xavier, I think we should talk—"

"X," he replies, stopping about two feet in front of me. "And, yes, we should talk. There's much to discuss."

"I agree—"

"Starting with changes that are effective immediately," he interrupts, standing over me like a dark cloud.

I glare at him. "You sure don't waste any time, do you?" God forbid the man introduce himself properly.

"Why would I want to waste time?"

"Do you think two strangers exchanging initial pleasantries is a waste of time?"

His eyes narrow menacingly, but I force myself to hold his eyes as he responds. "I already know everything I need to know about you. I read the file."

I tut and resume petting Bellatrix. "OK, X. Have it your way. Let's get down to business."

He nods, my sarcasm clearly going over his head. We're off to a great start. "As of now, there are several crews on their way over to install a new security system."

I shrug, figuring as much. "Got it."

"The locks will be changed, and no one is allowed inside unless on a master list that is regulated by me."

Now would probably not be the best time to bring up brunch. I'll go with the element of surprise for that one. "Got it."

X looks at me cautiously, probably surprised by my easy acceptance, before resuming his earlier pace around the room. "Furthermore, you must bring any and all concerns to me, no matter how trivial they may be. Moving forward, consider me the only person you can trust."

I scoff. He can't be serious. "Look, I appreciate you being here. My life has gotten a little crazy over the last year, and with the tour coming up, I could use the additional security. But it's really not all that serious—"

"The seriousness of your situation, and any that will arise in the future, is for me to decide."

His glacial response and husky tone of voice are a deadly mixture. No doubt he wields both to get his way. A small chill runs through my body, and I resist the urge to cross my arms. How dare he make me feel this way in my own home. "Are you always going to be this rude?"

"I like to call it efficient."

"Well, your efficient energy is really off-putting." I scowl at him and lean back into my pillows. "I've deduced that already, and we've only been in each other's presence for a few minutes."

His top lip curls into a small snarl as he leans forward. "Eloisa, I am here to make sure no harm comes to you. That's it. I couldn't give a damn about energy or whatever else the A-list is into these days."

His dark stare adds a figurative exclamation point to his sentence. Fighting against my natural instincts, I glare back. Who does he think he is? "This is my house, X."

"Wrong. For the next four months, it's our house. I'll take the guest bedroom upstairs."

He was moving in? Was he crazy? He turns away and heads toward the door as if that bold statement doesn't need further clarification. I get my voice back just as he crosses the threshold.

"You can't move in here," I sputter angrily, getting to my feet. "I prefer to live alone."

"I am moving in here and will be in close proximity to you every moment, barring three hours every Sunday during which I will need personal time. At that time, I will double your security until I return. You don't have a choice in the matter." I watch his eyes narrow. "And let's get one thing straight: for the next four months, I refuse to deal with your attempts to thwart me at every turn. That's not how this is going to go. I don't mean to come off abrasive. I was hired to protect you, and that's what I'm going to do."

Wow. It felt like the man hated me. He clearly had made conclusions about me and my lifestyle before he got here and couldn't care less about taking the time to get to know me.

After a dramatic ten-second staring contest, I sighed and looked away, deciding to let him win this battle. We were off on the wrong foot, and I was embarrassed at how childish he seemed to think I was. No one had ever riled me up that much within five minutes. Damn him. "Take the basement," I say, throwing him a bone. I'd learned over the course of my life it was best to kill with kindness. And that's what I'd do to throw him off guard. "It's bigger with its own bathroom."

Before he could respond, Sandy popped her head in. "I'm sorry to interrupt, but your father just called. He wanted to wish you a happy birthday. I told him I'd give you the message."

I ignored the churning in my stomach at the news and managed a quick nod. My twenty-fifth birthday had been a week before, but it was no surprise my father hadn't remembered. Why he still bothered to call me, I had no idea. I hadn't accepted one of his calls in a year—and a year ago had been the first time I'd heard from him in about twelve. We had nothing to say to each other.

X cleared his throat, bringing me back to reality, and when I looked up, I found him staring at me with a black expression. What the hell? "I need to know of any birthday plans immediately. No one informed me you were celebrating. Whatever grand plans you had in mind, you'll have to reschedule. I'd prefer you not leave this house until everything is secure."

And it was at that moment I decided I didn't like X. How. Dare. He. He didn't know me from Adam but was so damn quick to judge, just like all the others who thought they knew me. The information about my dad had me reeling, and now I had to deal with this storm cloud's shitty attitude.

And when killing someone with kindness doesn't work? Make that person feel stupid. "For your information, I don't celebrate my birthday."

Picking up Bellatrix from the floor, I turned my back on him and walked toward the window. Luckily, he took it for the dismissal that it was and left a few seconds later.

6

Xavier

Grumbling to myself, I tossed my duffel bag over my shoulder and slammed my trunk shut. Damn woman. The next four months of my life would no doubt be the most trying of my career—I had been right about that.

Perhaps I could have tried to be a bit more accommodating, dealt with her gently, but there was no time for that. After seeing that note—one I heard she had refused to read—there was no time for indulgence. I couldn't escape the nagging feeling, though, that my father would have been appalled with my behavior.

It's not like I wasn't used to being around celebrities—I was. It came with the territory of working for the president. And I'd found that unless you were forceful—stood your ground—they'd walk all over you.

That wasn't going to happen here.

Walking up the wide, wraparound porch, I took in the pots of flowers and general clutter that usually accompanied a home well lived in. No doubt Eloisa employed a gardener. Another thing celebrities didn't do? Their own chores.

I was thinking back to her comment about not celebrating her birthday when the sound of footsteps had me glancing up and inside the house. Two men dressed in black waved in greeting as they came down the stairs and exited onto the porch. They were almost as tall as I was, but a little bulkier in the arms and shoulders. Belying their figures, their faces looked to be about as menacing as a pair of college football players—which I already knew them to be.

"X, nice to meet you, man. I'm Joe, and this is Big."

Joe regarded me with a wide smile, as if he was excited I was here. With his blond hair and jolly expression, I couldn't help but be reminded of a golden retriever. Big, on the other hand, was more Saint Bernard.

They both would learn very quickly that I wasn't here to make friends.

I shook their hands and removed my sunglasses. When they got their first glimpse of my expression, their smiles dimmed. "The security upgrades we spoke about over the phone are set in motion. Several teams will be here within the hour. I want you two to familiarize yourselves with the equipment immediately and report back to me with any questions by EOD."

Joe looked taken aback, and I watched his blue eyes darken. "We thought we would give you a tour, show you the lay of the land and what you're going to be working with, but I guess you already have that under control."

Ah, sarcasm. Duly noted. The golden retriever had some bite. I expected the pushback, and I held my ground. "I've been here for nearly half an hour, something you two should have known immediately."

Joe raised an eyebrow. "Oh, we saw you all right. Giving old Harold the third degree. Just so you know, he's very important to Ellie."

As if that would change my behavior regarding the man. I stifled an irritated sigh. "What's important to *me* is her safety. Do you honestly think old Harold could stop an intruder?"

Joe crossed his arms and stood firm, but didn't answer the question. "Look, X, we're relieved that you're here. What happened to Ellie... shit...we feel awful about it. We need the extra manpower. Last week we were scoping out the scene by the limo when—"

"You don't have to explain," I cut in. "And you're right. Now that I'm here with extra manpower, it won't happen again. Now if you'll excuse me, I need to bring my stuff down to the basement."

I didn't wait for a response. Just maneuvered my way around Joe, who I knew was glaring at me with disdain. A potted plant fell over as I opened the screen door, and I made a mental note to right it once I put my bags down. Just as the door shut behind me, I heard Big speak up for the first time.

"Be careful with Ellie's plants. She takes a lot of pride in her flowers."

The finished basement was larger than I was expecting and nearly empty. The walls were a crisp white, and the only furnishings were a large wooden dresser and a king-size bed. A soft hum drew my attention to a humidifier in the far corner, and I saw that the shower was just large enough for me to be comfortable in. The stark design would suit me just fine.

I had just set my bag down on the bed when my phone rang. Seeing the 203 area code had me picking up immediately.

"Hey, Pops."

"Xavier? How are you?"

The relief I felt at hearing his voice was staggering. I never knew when I'd get my last call. "How are you feeling?"

"Well, I'm alive." He laughed at his own morbid sense of humor. "How are you? Are you in Connecticut yet?"

"Just got here. I am hoping to make it out to you on Sunday. Does that work?"

"Sunday? Sure. I have dinner at the boat club, but not until five."

My fists clenched at the news. "Should you really be going out?"

"I may have cancer, son, but I also have a social life. I don't know how many days I've got left, and I want to make the most of them."

I pressed my fists to my forehead and bit back a response. I'd convince him to stay in when I saw him on Sunday. "Don't talk like that."

"Talk like what? Come now. You heard the doc. I don't plan to spend my remaining time moping around feeling sorry for myself."

My heart pounded furiously in my chest, and my voice got lodged in my throat. I wanted to tell him so many things—mostly I wanted to apologize. I'd never apologized.

"So tell me about this singer you're working for. What's her name? I may have heard of her."

I doubted that, but I answered anyway, grateful for the subject change. "Eloisa Rae Morgan. I don't think she plays your type of music."

A gasp over the phone had me looking at it in confusion. "Eloisa Rae Morgan! Son! I'm a huge fan!" I didn't know what to say to that, feeling speechless at the revelation. He chuckled, and I heard his cane stomp on the floor. "You have to get me an autograph. Oh, I love that song of hers...what's it called? 'Bay of Lights.'"

"'Bay of Lights'?" I questioned. It seemed familiar, but I couldn't quite place it. But once he started singing it, the recognition clicked.

"Ah. I have heard that song. The first lady was a fan and would sing it nearly every morning for a month; it drove me crazy by the end." Now here I was listening to my dad sing the same tune.

"I love that song!" my dad exclaimed. "You have to get me an autograph."

"I hate that song," I grumbled, feeling annoyed. "And I won't be getting any autographs, Pops. I'm here to do my four months of hell with the pop princess, and then I'm getting the hell out."

A throat cleared behind me, and I whipped around toward the stairs. Eloisa stood there with an armful of towels, her expression suspiciously blank. She had clearly heard my comment, though, as my expertise with reading people was able to home in on the twinge of hurt in her eyes. A sliver of guilt ran through me, which made me angry. Why the hell should I care what she thought? But, man, she and I were not off to a good start.

"Eloisa, I put a high value on my privacy. Please knock or announce your presence immediately next time you come down here."

Ignoring me, she walked toward the bathroom. She was wearing shorts and a tank top, her long brown hair in a messy knot atop her head—her feet bare. I deliberately averted my eyes from the ample curves her outfit didn't do much to hide. As she passed me, her bright-green eyes met mine, and the twinge of hurt I saw earlier had transformed into detached resignation. Interesting.

She placed the towels in the bathroom and retreated toward the stairs, her steps fluid and graceful. She didn't say a word until she hit the middle step. "Dinner's in two hours. We're ordering pizza."

I watched her disappear from view until I remembered my dad was on the phone. I could almost hear his disapproval through the line. "Don't tell me she heard what you said! Xavier, you have to apologize."

"Liking her music wasn't a job requirement," I told him stiffly, hating that I even felt a little bit guilty.

"I bet you haven't even heard it," he chastised. He was right. "You haven't listened to music since Mom—"

"Don't go there." I cut off that line of conversation, as I always did. "I've had a long day, and it's not even close to being over. See you Sunday?"

He sighed. "Fine. See you Sunday. And try not to be such a hard-ass, X. You sound like a drill sergeant."

7

Eloisa

The night brought on a whirlwind of activity. I watched from my window in resignation as an endless stream of strangers made their way in and out of my house. Large, black steel boxes of God knows what littered my lawn, and all the while X stood there on the porch like a sentry, barking orders and talking through an earpiece.

It all seemed to be a little much. All this extended effort for me and my safety. I rubbed the small lump on my head that was finally healing and felt a now-familiar sadness overwhelm me. It was hard to believe that one of my fans was hell-bent on causing me serious harm. But as I looked back down into my front yard, glimpsing all the activity, I knew that some people here took the threat very seriously.

X stood with his arms crossed over his wide chest, his face unreadable. He wore all black, and even from a distance I could sense the heat and energy coming off his frame. I had never seen a man so—capable and in charge. If there was anyone I should trust with my security, I knew intuitively he was the man. But that didn't mean I had to like him. The man seemed to have the personality of a rock. An angry rock.

I mean, I don't know what I'd hoped for when he arrived, but I figured we could at least be civil to each other. We'd be spending a lot of time in each other's company, after all. It's not like I expected friendship or anything. Ha—just the thought was a joke. I didn't make friends easily. Besides my crew, I didn't have friends. Besides my fans, I didn't have family.

Growing up in the foster system wasn't exactly conducive training on how to form lasting relationships. Joe and Big had been the exception when I met them at my last house, when I was seventeen. We bonded instantly, but that had more to do with their personalities than mine. Yup. I was pretty much hopeless at relationships of every kind.

Shaking away the negative thoughts, I looked back at X, only to find that he was looking directly at me. A chill ran up my spine at being caught, but I held his stare, not wanting him to grab the upper hand.

The man had been incredibly rude earlier when I tried to bring him some towels as a peace offering. I'd decided then that I wasn't going to make any more effort.

I watched as he reached up and pressed a button on his earpiece. My phone started ringing a moment later.

At the sound, Bellatrix lifted her head from her position on my lap and barked. Scratching her tummy, I reached over to my nightstand to grab my phone. Huh? I stared at the screen for a moment in shock.

Oh, this was just going too far.

I stared in anger at the single letter—a letter that I hadn't stored—flashing on the screen. Swiping my finger to answer the call, I pushed the curtains aside to glare down at him. "So now you're breaking into my phone?"

"We had to exchange phone numbers, E."

"Don't call me that. And usually to *exchange* numbers two people have to be involved!"

"E, I was hired to protect you—"

"*Stop* calling me that! And does protecting me mean invading my privacy and personal space? Is that what they teach you over in the secret service?" I leaned into the glass, wanting him to see my face and how angry I was.

"Yes."

My mouth dropped open. Bellatrix felt the tension simmering in me and jumped off my lap. "This is unacceptable. I'm letting you take over my house. I'm letting you move in with me—"

"Letting?"

"The least you could do is respect me as a person. You can't just do things like that without asking." I stood up and tried to singe him with my eyes through the glass.

He stood there, calm as a damned cucumber, meeting my gaze. "For the next four months, you and I will have no secrets."

"No secrets? What does that even mean?"

"You heard me. I already told you. I refuse to deal with unreasonable pushback. This conversation is irrelevant."

I stood up straight. "So you're just going to run right over me?"

"If I have to. Now come down here; there are a few things I need to show you."

He hung up on me and turned around, directing his attention elsewhere. I fumed at the window for a few moments before stalking toward the door. Oh, I was going down there all right. Grabbing a sweatshirt, I stormed downstairs, intent on finding the arrogant jackass to give him a piece of my mind. I really, really didn't like him.

8

Xavier

I deliberately didn't turn around when I heard the front door slam open. The sooner she accepted the situation, the better for all of us. I wasn't going to hold her hand while she did it. "I'm going to need a visual feed for all outdoor cameras synced to my phone."

But the man I was speaking with was no longer listening; his eyes were locked on something over my shoulder.

I checked my annoyance before turning around to face the very small, angry, red-faced woman. *Try to be nice, X.*

She stood there in a pale-pink sweatshirt and the same white shorts she had on earlier, her feet once again bare. An angry expression on such a delicate face seemed wrong, and I felt another pang of guilt. I forced my eyes to stop scanning her face, not wanting to get distracted.

"We need to talk," she hissed, pointing a finger into my chest.

But before I could respond, the man pushed his way around me and stuck out his hand. "Eloisa Rae, it is such a pleasure to meet you. My wife and I, we're...we're huge fans."

Suppressing the urge to roll my eyes, I glared at the man in question, but he didn't notice.

E's face broke into a bright smile, and she took his hand. "It's a pleasure to meet you. And welcome to my home! Sorry I'm not a bit more presentable."

The man laughed heartily. "Think nothing of it! One should always be comfortable in one's house, should one not?"

E laughed. "One should!"

I stifled an annoyed groan.

The man himself looked positively tickled. "Do you think we could take a picture together? It would mean so much to me."

E cut me off just as I was about to refuse. "Absolutely. X will take it."

I watched with impatience as they moved to stand next to each other. The man handed me his phone, and it was all I could do not to snatch it from his fingers. What a waste of time. I held up the phone and focused the screen, unable to help noticing the sincere gleam of happiness in E's eyes. Probably basking in the attention, no doubt.

I snapped the photo and impatiently handed it back. Several of the other men started crowding around, their phones out, but I held them off with my hand. "All of you. Get back to work. We need everything up and running by sunrise."

E walked back to my side, her arms crossed over her chest. "Are you always this fun to be around?"

"So I'm told."

"I bet you are."

"If you would just accept that I'm in charge, everything will run smoothly."

"I don't want you invading my privacy, X. That's crossing the line."

I leaned closer to her face, not to intimidate, but to show her how serious I was. "Right now, your safety is my utmost priority. Nothing in my life takes precedence over that. Whatever I have to do to make that happen, I'll do. I regret to tell you this may not be the only time you feel your privacy is compromised."

"But it's not right!"

"You're a celebrity. Aren't you used to having limited privacy?"

"It's not the same, and you know it."

"You're right. The situation I'm here to deal with is much more serious." A flicker of fear passed over her face before glum resignation kicked in. Finally, a breakthrough. Since the conversation was now closed, I turned away and beckoned her to follow. "This way, E. I have a lot to show you."

"Stop calling me that," she snapped.

"Why? It's more efficient."

She sighed heavily, shaking her head, probably at my audacity.

Tired of the subject, I waved a hand toward the cameras cleverly hidden in the trees. "You need to familiarize yourself with the new security equipment."

For the next hour, I took E around the perimeter of the house, getting her acclimated to all the changes. Surprisingly, she took everything in stride. The sensored alarms, the new locks on the windows and doors, the 250-plus cameras, and a new, state-of-the-art gate.

"So, now all that's left is for you to give me a list of family and friends who may come to visit," I tell her as we come to a stop on the porch. She doesn't respond to my question right away, but I can see her face is turning red. What is that about? I watch curiously as she bends down and fingers one of the flowerpots in what I know to be an avoidance tactic.

After a few moments, she stands up, wiping her hands clean on her shorts. "That's easy. I don't have a list. Besides the people who work for me, I don't get any visitors."

My senses tell me she's ashamed of this but is trying to hide it. I don't push her. "Fair enough."

I watch as she surveys her front lawn, letting out a deep sigh. A few stray hairs have come loose from her bun, but she doesn't fix them. Every time I've seen her thus far, she's been comfortable, relaxed. Definitely not what I was expecting. She meets my eyes for just a moment before heading back inside the house.

9

Eloisa

"I want to try something new," Jacques muses. He runs a long brush through my hair before gathering it in his fingers.

"We've heard that before," mumbles Michonne from inside my closet. She comes out carrying a casual Balmain jumpsuit. Still too fancy. I shake my head, and she rolls her eyes but disappears to try again.

"What would you say to a lavender ombré?"

I catch Jacques's eyes in the mirror. "Seriously?"

"Why not? Let me dye you, doll!"

I look at my long, chocolate-colored locks and shrug. "Sure. Why not? As long as it won't take too long; the signing starts in three hours."

"I have the perfect outfit if you're going with lavender!" Michonne calls out. She has the gait of a fashion model and better style than I could ever hope to have. I have no doubt she will deliver.

"If we work fast, we can do it," Jacques assures me, already pulling out a drawer to grab the dye. "You're going to look fabulous!"

I wasn't one to be too concerned with my appearance, but I *was* known to change my look now and again. Being under the spotlight for the last year had taught me a few valuable lessons about yoga pants and T-shirts as an acceptable public outfit.

"After what happened," Jacques whispers, "we need to make a statement! Show them you're not taking that bullshit lying down!"

With all that had been going on lately—the infamous snub, the red carpet incident, and X's presence—I could use a change and a little more confidence. "All right, Jacques. Do your worst."

Two hours later, he spins me around toward the mirror, and I gasp. "Oh. My. God."

"You are a magician," Michonne squeals in glee as she runs over to stand behind me. "Eloisa Rae Morgan, you are killin' that color!"

She's right. The pastel color clashes with my brown locks, but somehow Jacques makes it look completely seamless and trendy. I love it.

"Thank you," I say a little breathlessly, catching his eye in the mirror. "As always."

He winks and bends over to kiss my cheek. "As always. Now let's get that makeup done."

As he applies my lip liner, Michonne shoves a black corset top under my nose. "This. With your new True Religion skinnies and Michael Kors open toes. Casual enough for an album signing, but edgy enough to make a statement."

Picturing the outfit in my mind, I nod.

"You are going to look fabulous," she agrees, rushing into the closet to grab my jeans. "X is going to lose his mind when he sees you."

I freeze. What the hell does she mean by that? "What does X have to do with anything?"

Michonne peeks her head out the closet. "Girl, that man is fine. I know he's only been here one day, but please don't tell me you haven't noticed."

"I have," Jacques chimes in, reaching to grab my lipstick. "And I don't usually go for the masculine type. But that rough, boyish face is near perfection." Jacques shivers comically, and I roll my eyes.

I picture X in my mind and reluctantly have to agree. Strong, corded muscle and scorching heat rolling off him in waves, and a gaze so intense it almost hurts to look at it. But there is no way I would admit to it. "So what? He's an arrogant, invasive pain in the ass. Did I tell you he broke into my phone?"

"Ooh, a man that takes control," Machine responds, walking out of the closet, skinnies in hand. "I like it."

"Then why don't you go after him?" I deadpan, joking, since I know Michonne is already in a happy relationship.

She gives me a look and reaches under my bed to grab my shoes. "I don't need a man. You do."

"I do not."

Jacques blows out a breath. "Don't tell me you're still hung up on that drummer. What was his name again? Jasper?"

I scoff. "You know his name is Joel. And no, I'm not. We haven't spoken in months." Which had done wonders for my sanity. Joel and I had dated for three years, and our breakup really hit me hard. In the beginning it was wonderful. It had been all about the music. The music brought us together, but the music also tore us apart. He changed—for the worse—when he got a small taste of fame. I finally had the courage to start ignoring his calls, and I hadn't looked back since.

"Thank God that's over," Michonne declares. "You don't need a man who's intimidated by your success."

That wasn't the reason we broke up, but I keep that to myself, the wound still raw. Luckily, my phone saves me from having to respond. A text message from X flashes on the screen, and I narrow my eyes as I read the words.

X: *We're leaving in ten minutes. Don't be late, or I'll come up to get you.*

I suppress the urge to growl in frustration. The man could use a lesson in tact. I don't know if it's me he is so frustrated with or if he's just like this in general. I suspect the latter.

"There. Pretty as a peach," Jacques says as he touches my face up with finishing powder. "Knock 'em dead."

I glare at the text message in my hand. Oh, I will.

10

Xavier

Downstairs in the foyer, I glance at my watch when I hear footsteps overhead. One minute late. I'm cynical enough to think she would do that just to spite me. I know my behavior has been extreme as of late, but she wasn't making it any easier on me.

Checking that my earpiece is in place, I push the curtain aside to survey the status of things out front. Joe and Big are getting into the black SUV behind the one waiting for E, and two other men I hired are getting into one in front.

Sandy, E's personal assistant, is waiting by the car door talking to our driver. I take in her bright-pink glasses and large backpack she uses to carry God knows what. I'd noticed over the past couple of days that she's very efficient, like me. Quiet, but I could sense there was a lot going on behind those colorful glasses.

I turn when I hear footsteps coming down the stairs and have to hide a small jolt. It's the most dressed up I've ever seen her. She takes each step slowly, as if she has all the time in the world. My eyes home in on the different hair color immediately. Her gaze meets mine, and I spot the flash of annoyance in her eyes and the small frown on her lips. My eyes travel quickly down her petite frame of their own accord, taking note of the tight top and jeans that I know will drive her fans crazy. She looks expensive and out of everyone's league. "You're late."

She's looking in her purse for something as she walks up to me. "I know."

Sandy suddenly appears beside me and gives E a big smile. "Ellie, I love your hair!"

"Thank you Sandy," E replies, a little flushed. I can tell she likes the new style, too, but I don't see any of the conceit I would have expected.

"Let's get a picture for social media," Sandy says, already taking out her phone.

"No, there's no time," I cut in.

"Good idea," E replies, as if she hasn't heard me.

I watch in annoyance as she fluffs her hair around her shoulders and smiles brightly for the camera. Sandy snaps a few photos and quickly gets to uploading them as we all finally walk outside.

"Are you on social media?" E asks, taking me by surprise, once she and I get settled in the backseat. Sandy sits up front with the driver.

"No." I look out the back window to make sure that the third car is following once we pull off.

Instead of the judgment I expected, she nods. "I wasn't, either, until I had to be. But it's a good way to connect with my fans."

Something occurs to me as I watch her enthusiastically wave goodbye to Harold at the front gate. "Have you gotten any messages on those accounts I should know about? Now that I think about it, I should scan them. Let me see your phone."

She grips it in her hands. "Sandy deals with all my messages, and there is nothing there you need to see. She would have mentioned it. Right, Sandy?"

"Right." Sandy turns around in her seat to face us. Her bright glasses fall down her nose, and she pushes them up before responding. "I promise, X. If I see anything remotely suspicious, I'll let you know right away."

I nod, agreeing for the time being. There are more pressing matters at hand. Along with my other observations about Sandy, I know she is a no-nonsense assistant who doesn't have any trouble doing what she is supposed to. If only E could read a page out of that book.

Out of the corner of my eye, I can see E wringing her hands together. "Are you nervous?" The question comes out before I have time to think about it.

She glances up at me. "No, just excited. This was my favorite music store when I was a little girl. It's...surreal that I get to sell mine here."

"You grew up in Connecticut?" I ask, surprised.

She frowns at me as if I should already know that information. "In Norwalk, yes."

Stunned, I turn to face her. "I grew up in Stamford."

Her mouth drops open. "No way! I guess we have something in common after all, huh?"

She gifts me with the first genuine smile I've seen from her since we met, and I'm so taken aback I stare for a few seconds longer than I normally would. Angry at myself for being distracted even momentarily, I turn to stare out the window and don't respond. After a few moments of awkward silence, she busies herself by talking to Sandy.

My phone suddenly rings, breaking the silence. After a short conversation, I lean forward to redirect the driver toward a set of side streets.

"Where are we going?" E looks at me in confusion.

"The front entrance is swamped. There's a larger turnout than expected."

Her mouth forms an O shape. "I hope I get to meet everyone. I thought this would just be a local crowd."

Sandy turns around. "I think we're officially at the point in your career where those days are behind you. Even unmarketed appearances like this one. You just sold out a four-month tour."

A stressed expression crosses E's face, and I feel compelled to reassure her. "Don't worry. We're prepared for every possibility."

I call the rest of my security team and inform them of the change in plan just as we pull into a narrow side street. I scan the sides of the road for any movement, and my eyes home in on a lone figure by the back door.

"That's Lynette. Her family owns the music store."

I nod. "Stay here."

I hop out and note that the two other security SUVs pull in behind us. I check in with the crew members already on the scene, and they inform me that everything is good to go.

Lynette eyes me warily as I approach—an expression I'm used to seeing on women. She has long blond hair and dark lipstick, and she is probably around twenty-five years old.

I stick a hand out for her to shake. "X. Head of Eloisa's security team," I say in way of greeting. My eyes dart around the back lot, looking for any sign of movement. Everything looks as it should be.

"Pleasure to meet you. I'm Lynette." She gives my hand a small shake. "We're going to open the doors in ten minutes. Is Ellie ready?"

"I'm ready!"

E hops down from the SUV. I guess it would have been too much to ask to follow my instruction to stay put. I make sure she sees the frown on my face before grabbing the handle on the back door.

The two women follow me inside, chattering away while I scope out the scene. I nod to the guards lingering by the front entrance, letting them know it's go time. The music store is nothing more than a quirky storefront. A small, boxlike room with rows of used CDs and even a section for cassettes. Old posters of eighties rock bands and folk artists dot the walls, and a worn red rug covers the floor. I'm unimpressed.

I turn toward Lynette. "We're going to let five people in at a time. No more than fifteen seconds with each person."

E frowns. "Fifteen seconds? That's barely any time at all."

Thinking quickly, I play toward her emotions. "It's the only way we'd be able to get through everyone."

She nods reluctantly and takes a seat at a table set up in the middle of the room. Sandy enters through the back hallway alongside Joe and Big, who are carrying two boxes filled with studio photographs of E.

"Showtime!" Joe says, bending down to give E a loud kiss on her cheek. I can't help but wonder at the nature of that relationship. I'll make it a point to find out. Joe goes over to Sandy and tries to kiss her cheek as well, but she ducks out of the way just in time. She glares at him and adjusts her glasses before taking the seat beside E. Hmm.

"Thank you so much for doing this," Lynette says, giving E a tight squeeze.

E leans back into the hug. "Thank you," she replies emphatically. "I only wish your dad was able to come. I miss him!"

Lynette smiles warmly. "He's hoping to stop by later. He wouldn't miss this for the world."

They continue to chat quietly as I conduct one final run-through to make sure everything inside the store is in place.

"Where's Rob?" E asks me.

"Not coming," I tell her. "He's hammering out some details for the tour." I peek outside and take a deep breath, noting the sheer size of the crowd. "Showtime."

11

Eloisa

Nothing in the world gives me more joy than sharing my music with my fans. Meeting them, however, is a close second. The noise was deafening once the doors opened and had barely let up for the past half hour as people filed in and out. I'm doing my best to acknowledge everyone, trying to make every person who showed up feel important. But the fifteen-second time limit is rough.

The whole thing is jarring, since I was alone for so much of my childhood. Abandoned. Forgotten. Music had been—and still is—a therapy for my troubles, and if I can soothe someone else's with my words, then I have a purpose. There's nothing more important than that. Especially when you don't have any real loved ones.

I smile into the face of a young teenager who's visibly shaken as he walks toward the table. His vulnerability floors me. So far there has been excitement, giddiness, a few happy tears, but nothing like this. As he gets closer and I wave hello, he begins to sob into his hands. Affected, I get up and try to walk around the table. X stops me with a hard grip on my arm.

"Let go," I hiss, meeting his hard gaze.

"No contact," he replies, clearly guessing at my motive to give him a hug.

"You can't be serious. He's upset!"

"You can take a photo or sign a picture, but no contact. I'm not wavering on that, E."

Frustrated, but not wanting to make a scene in front of my fans or the cameras, I sit back down. I send X a glacial stare, which he promptly ignores. The nerve of him. He's going to hear it from me later.

"What's your name, sweetheart?" I ask the boy.

"Trent. I'm your biggest fan," he sniffs, clearly trying to pull himself together.

I quickly sign the CD, thank him for coming out, and watch as the next group files in. There are three men, probably midtwenties like me, each of them shirtless and carrying signs. I can't help but laugh as I take in the words.

Marry Me, Eloisa!
No, Marry Me, Eloisa!
Be My Wife, Eloisa!

All three get down on one knee in front of the table as if they are actually proposing. Sandy giggles and takes a picture to put on social media. I place a hand on my chest in amusement. "Men, I am beyond flattered. Three proposals in one day!"

They all grin and start talking at once. They are sweaty and probably had a couple of beers before coming in, but all in all they're harmless. Sandy hands them each a photo, and I have a small laugh with each of them as I sign.

X mutters something under his breath as they file out. I turn to look up at him and notice his frosty glare.

"Did you say something?" I ask politely. From this angle I have a direct view of his insanely muscled bicep and lean waist. My eyes trail up that chiseled frame before landing on his eyes.

"They were drunk."

"So? They seemed of age."

"It does take a little liquid courage to propose to a girl!" Joe pipes in from where he and Big stand guarding the back hallway. "I'll probably need a whole bottle of the stuff before I pop the question to Sandy."

Sandy doesn't acknowledge the declaration and just continues writing something in her notepad. Poor Joe. Sandy barely gives him the time of day. Probably for the best, since they have to work together.

X is glaring down at me. "It makes them unpredictable. And it's dangerous."

"It's not against the rules," I respond, his irrationality making my temper rise. "And I listened to what you said—no contact."

"You toed the line," he replies, waving forward the next set of fans. "You have to remember, E. I'm doing this for your own good. I'm here to protect you because someone out there wishes you serious harm. Please don't forget that."

His little speech removes the passion behind my argument. As two guys and one girl approach the table, I feel a switch flip in my head. Could it be them? A sliver of fear runs through me. I'd never looked at my fans with anything but absolute trust. But now…man, it's depressing.

The signing lasted three hours, and I was exhausted. I'd met so many wonderful people, but my thoughts had been a bit morose by the end.

I helped Sandy and Lynette pick up some trash and errant photos once the doors were closed.

"You go on," Lynette insisted, bringing me in for a hug. "I've got the cleaning crew on the way, and they'll have everything back to rights in no time."

"OK. Thank you so much again. This was incredible."

When I turned back to X, he was ending a call. "Everything's secure outside. You ready?"

I nodded. Walking toward the back door, I realized he hadn't left my side the entire time. Did he even use the bathroom? It was like he was a bodyguard or something. I told him as much, and he spared me a quick glance before we walked outside.

"I'm your personal security detail. Everywhere you go, I go."

The words sounded strangely intimate in his deep, husky tone. Feeling a bit off balance, I made sure not to brush up against him as he helped me into the waiting SUV. It was impossible, however, not to be affected by his large presence. It was almost as if he was a superhero. You knew he was dangerous, but you trusted him at the same time.

"Eloisa! Eloisa, wait!"

The door suddenly slammed, and X went charging forward. Before I could blink, he had a man on the ground, his large forearm pressing the man's neck to the pavement.

Once I got a good look at the face, I gasped.

"X, no!"

12

Xavier

The man underneath me wasn't putting up much of a fight. At the lack of a struggle—and a look into his panicked and confused blue eyes—I let up. Slightly.

"X, no!"

I growled as I saw E jump out of the car and run toward us. "Stay where you are!"

Her face had turned bright red. "That's Lynette's father! His name is Gale, and he owns the music store!"

Joe and Big appeared beside me, but luckily they were smart enough not to try to hold me back.

"She's telling the truth; let him up," Joe said quietly.

The man beneath me was nodding furiously, and after a few seconds I got to my feet.

E was nearly hysterical as she ran to his side to help him up. "You can't just attack people like that!"

My temper rose. Didn't she get it? I pointed in the man's face, giving him my full attention. "You can't just run up on her like that; do you hear me? I'm trained to act first and ask questions later."

"I understand," the man replied, wheezing. I pegged him at midfifties. A faded Stones T-shirt and white jeans covered a thin frame. He set a hand on E's shoulder. "It's all right, my dear. He's right."

"I'm not the president of the United States," E fired at me. "Heck, I'm not even Beyoncé. You could have really hurt him!"

"I'm just doing my job, E. I'm getting really tired of having to explain myself to you," I snapped. I couldn't help but be surprised at the tone of my voice. I quickly reined in my emotions and chastised myself for getting so worked up. It wasn't like me.

She sighed and didn't spare me another glance as she said, "I'm getting tired of you, in general."

Looping arms with the man, she started walking him toward the back door of the music store. Joe and Big followed her wordlessly while I stayed behind.

I didn't speak to E for the rest of the night. The ride home was silent, and once we arrived back at the house, she holed up in her room. I could hear the gentle pluck of guitar strings, but otherwise no word. It was better that way. If she couldn't get into her brain the seriousness of her own situation, I was done trying to convince her. She would do what I said, and I didn't care how she felt.

God, these four months couldn't be over soon enough.

The next day dawned hot and humid. The fickle nature of New England weather was nothing new to me, but it did nothing to better my mood. I was still steaming over the events of the previous day when I made my morning rounds around the property. Rob met me out back, a clipboard in his hand.

"X, good to see you," he said briskly, typing on his cell phone. "I heard the signing was a great success."

I didn't reply until he looked up and made eye contact. "It was." Which was true. No one got hurt.

"Everything is coming along nicely here," he said, looking around. "I can't believe you got all this done so quickly."

I nodded, taking in the altered landscape. There was not an inch of Eloisa's property that was hidden from one of the security cameras. Faux red lights flashed here and there to deter a potential intruder, including along the windows, which were all secured with individual codes.

"Anyway," Rob continued when I didn't answer, "I'm going inside to find Eloisa. We have a few technical details to hammer out."

He walked toward the back of the house just as my cell rang.

"Hey, Pops."

"Happy hump day!"

The exclamation was followed by peals of my father's laughter. I felt a small smile touch my lips at his happiness.

"Get it, son? It's Wednesday."

"I get it, Dad." I decided to tease him. "I just can't believe it's the first time you're hearing that joke."

He laughed again. "I learn something new every day."

"How are you feeling?"

"Oh, I'm fine, son. I've got me a hot date tonight!"

Nearly choking, I stopped short on the sand. "Excuse me?"

"You heard me. Your old man's got a date—met her at the grocery store. Her name is Rose, and I'm taking her to dinner."

Different scenarios and implications ran through my head. "But... does she...how are you going to...a date?"

He made a sound of disapproval. "Stop overthinking it. All that matters is today—I'm alive. And today I've got a date with a beautiful woman. Everything else is just details."

I pinched the bridge of my nose. I had already been planning to talk him out of going to the boat club for dinner this Sunday, and now this. He never took anything seriously or considered the risk of his actions. He should be on bed rest, not gallivanting around on dates. Every question I had—even growing up—had always been answered with a carefree response. It was a wonder we were related.

"Now tell me. How's the beautiful Eloisa Rae Morgan?"

"A pain in my ass."

"Are you going to bring her here? I'd love to meet her."

I sighed, watching the waves lap against the shore. "No. But I'll be there on Sunday."

"You be nice to that girl, Xavier James Cannon. I didn't raise you to be so indifferent to women."

I raised a brow. "Ah, yes. I remember your advice. Don't judge a woman...from one hundred feet away."

That sent him into another round of hearty chuckles. "That one never gets old," he wheezed.

"See you Sunday?"

"Yes, enjoy your hump day. I know I'm going to enjoy mine!"

He hung up amid another round of laughter, and my mood couldn't help but lift. It was bittersweet. Hearing him laugh, enjoying life. But the familiar guilt I felt after almost all our conversations hit me hard. I owed him so much. First and foremost, an apology that I just couldn't seem to get out.

13

Eloisa

Taking a large bite of egg whites, I observed X through the kitchen window. He was staring at the water, his big body seemingly crackling with heat, as always. I almost wanted to go out there and apologize. Almost.

I was embarrassed about what I'd said at the signing, but he really needed to learn how to compromise. What he did to Gale yesterday couldn't happen again. Now that some time had passed, I could see his side, but there had to be a better solution.

"Ah, there you are."

I turned at the sound of Rob's voice. My watch told me it was 8:00 a.m. Rob looked like he had been up for hours.

"Here I am," I said with forced cheer, bringing my plate to the sink. "Let's have the rundown."

Every morning Rob came to me with a list of things that needed to be accomplished. My days kept getting busier and busier.

"You have two phone interviews in the morning, followed by a photo shoot for *Le Dame*. After that, the set list, Eloisa."

I sighed. The set list for the tour was 90 percent complete. There was just something—missing. There were eighteen songs right now, all of them representations of my life and the things I'd gone through. Each a piece of my soul. But something about it didn't feel right. Rob had been courteous and given me time to figure it out, but time was running out.

"I'm working on it."

He didn't look convinced. "I've got the band down my back, Ellie. By the end of the week, please."

I nodded, running a hand through my hair. I needed a shower. "I'm going to get ready. First interview is at nine, right?"

He nodded absently, texting on his phone. "Sharp."

I wasn't looking forward to the interviews. The thought of how selfish that was made me adjust my perspective, but I just really missed anonymity. Back in the day, it was so much easier. Playing music for small crowds and then walking home to my apartment. Those nights were perfect. Just me and the music. But how does one say no when given the opportunity to share with even more people? That feeling was priceless.

I took a quick shower and hopped in bed, just as my work phone rang. Settling against my pillows, I pulled Bellatrix into my lap as I listened to the woman on the other end introduce herself. After a few pleasantries, she cut right to the chase.

"Do you have any leads about your attack last week?"

"I don't. But I've taken measures, both for myself and the upcoming tour, to make sure that everyone who attends will be safe."

"What, exactly, were the contents of the note attached to the rock?"

"I have no idea, and I don't want to know."

"You haven't read it?"

"No."

She made a sound of disappointment. "Well, how are you feeling?"

A question that should have probably been asked first, but I didn't comment on that. "I feel better than ever. We've got some really fun surprises planned for the tour's opening, so I've been concentrating on that."

"Are you still unwilling to work with Martha Mathers?"

I nearly growled. She was one of the ones out for blood. "I already addressed that last week."

"Do you think upsetting her ruins any chance you have of winning a Grammy?"

"Winning a Grammy would be an incredible honor. I don't expect it, but I would hope that if I ever did win, it would be because of my music, and not who I rubbed elbows with."

"You're already notorious for snubbing quite a few offers from industry leaders. Why is that?"

"Music often becomes...diluted in this industry. I wanted this album to one hundred percent reflect me and my vision. I guess you could say... I'm a one-woman show."

I knew she wanted something a bit juicier, but she wasn't going to get it. There were celebrities out there—socialites like Joel—who knew how to create drama for drama's sake, eager for press, but that wasn't me. Keeping myself separate, as anonymous as possible, kept me safe.

I answered several more of her questions before Sandy came in and held up a hand. My other interview was starting in five minutes. I ended the call and took the water bottle she handed me.

She shifted from foot to foot, seeming nervous about something.

"What is it?" I asked.

She shrugged, smoothing her skirt. It was clear she didn't want to tell me the news. "Your father called again."

I felt my cheeks go hot. "What did he want?"

Sad eyes met mine. "He said he got tickets to your second show."

"Of course he did."

She blew out a breath. "We can try to find out where he's sitting...try to see if we can buy them off him?"

She didn't sound confident. But when it came to my father and how I felt, I wasn't, either. On one hand, I wanted to show him how successful I'd become, but on the other hand, I didn't want him anywhere near me. "Thanks for the suggestion, but let's hold off for now. See how I feel as it gets closer."

She nodded, scribbling something down in a pad she pulled out of her back pocket. She had on glasses with circular frames today. "Don't take this the wrong way—because they're awesome," I told her, "but those glasses make you look a bit like Harry Potter."

She laughed. "Joe told me the same thing this morning."

"Man, he really likes you."

"I know. He tells me all the time."

"And?"

"And what?" she asked, pretending not to understand what I was getting at.

"Are you interested in him?"

She sighed. "No. He's out of my league. I need to date someone more my speed."

"Out of your league? Don't be silly. You're smart, beautiful, and incredibly ambitious. I have no idea what I'd do without you."

Which was true. After a few days of working with Sandy, I'd known I'd made the right choice in hiring her. She had become more than my assistant. She was a friend. It had taken a while, but she was slowly coming out of her shell. I couldn't blame her, as I'm sure she could say the same about me.

"You have to say that," she said, blushing.

"No, I don't," I told her. "I'm the one paying you, after all."

My phone rang again, interrupting our laughter, and I resigned myself to yet another interview.

The day passed by in a blur of activity. After my second interview—which went remarkably better—I was whisked off for another one of the tour's photo shoots. Luckily, the set location was only about ten minutes from my house, so no large security measures were needed.

X and I barely spoke. He shadowed me during the photo shoot, standing off to the side of the green screen. It felt awkward, and I don't think we made eye contact once. Not on the way home, either.

I changed into my bathing suit first thing, thinking about the events of the day. I really did want to get back on the right foot with him. Ha! That would imply we were ever on the right one. This was a very exciting time in my life, and I didn't want to walk on eggshells with someone whom I'd be spending a lot of time with.

Determined, I threw a white cover-up on over my bathing suit and made my way downstairs. I would start by making a concession and including X in my plans for the night. I texted him when I was on the back deck.

E: *Meet me out back?*

He responded almost immediately.

X: *On my way.*

A few seconds later, he entered the kitchen. He was in his usual all-black outfit, but I could tell from his wet hair that he must have showered recently. A five o'clock shadow that looked like it never left covered his strong, square jawline. The man was incredibly attractive. A prime specimen if I'd ever seen one. Someone like him had to have a girlfriend or a wife—or a harem.

I pushed the thought out of my mind and stood tall and confident as he stepped outside and closed the patio door behind him. He towered above me by at least a foot, so I'm sure the effort was wasted.

He searched my face. "Is everything OK?"

"I want to start over."

Looking baffled at my request, he raised a brow. "What does that mean, exactly?"

"Look, I'm sorry about what I said yesterday. I'm not used to this sort of thing. The past year has been a roller coaster, and I'm still getting used to all the changes. I know you're just trying to protect me, and I'll try to be more understanding of what that entails."

My little speech *must* have taken him by surprise, but he hid it well. "I am glad to hear you've come to that conclusion."

I waited for him to say something else, and when he didn't, I gave him an exasperated look. "Don't you have anything to say to me?"

"Like what?"

"Like you are willing to compromise on certain things, or you're sorry for assaulting one of my oldest friends."

"I am not willing to compromise on your safety, and what happened yesterday was his fault. Not mine."

I threw my head back to hide an eye roll that I knew he probably saw anyway. "Never mind. I'm going for a swim." I took off toward the shore.

"Now?"

I looked at him over my shoulder. "Yes, now. The ocean is calmer at night."

"It's not safe."

That stopped me in my tracks. I turned around and glared at him. "Do you think someone is going to crawl out from the depths and grab me like a sea monster? Besides, this place is now more secure than Fort Knox. Give me a break, X. Please."

"X, huh?"

"You call me E. It's only fitting."

He was silent after that, and I took it as a good sign. Then finally he said, "I'll stay out here with you."

Hmm. I thought he would put up more of a fight. Perhaps everything wasn't a lost cause after all. Maybe it would just take baby steps to get us on the same page.

The slight breeze felt wonderful on my skin when I took off my cover-up. Normally I would have felt self-conscious about being in a bikini around a stranger, but X made it a point to look at me only when he absolutely had to. That, and I knew he didn't really like me that much. I took a curious peek, and just as I thought, he was scanning the dark water.

Feeling safe, I dived in. Growing up in New England, I had a soul-deep connection with the ocean. Which reminded me of something X had told me the day before. He had grown up here, too. I couldn't help but wonder if he had spent his childhood at the beach, like me.

I turned toward shore, looking at the large figure unmoving at the water's edge. "Want to come in? The water's fine."

I couldn't see his expression, but his tone was condescending. "No, thank you."

"Don't you know how to swim?" I teased, splashing a bit of water in his direction.

"Of course I do."

"Well, it's sort of weird—you just standing there watching me in here."

"I'm not watching you. I'm securing the perimeter."

A chuckle escaped. "Securing the perimeter? It's a beautiful night, and there is no threat to my safety."

He didn't reply to that, and I took a few moments to dunk myself and float. The stress of the day seemed to melt away, as it always did during my midnight swims. But the silence felt heavy. I looked toward X and noticed he was leaning against a large rock to my right.

The question was leaving my mouth before I thought twice. "Are you married?"

He barked out a laugh. "Married? No."

I shrugged. "Girlfriend?"

"No. I'm not involved with anyone at the moment."

"Why not?"

"I don't have time." He sounded exasperated with the line of questioning. "Why are we talking about this?"

I didn't want to admit my earlier thoughts about how good-looking he was, so I went with the obvious. "I was just thinking that if there was a woman in your life, she wouldn't be happy about your new job position. You'd never have time to see her."

Well, only the three hours he requested on Sundays. Surely that wouldn't be enough time.

I could see his shoulders shrug, but he didn't respond. I understood in a way. I knew what it was like to be married to your job. But for some reason, it made me wonder if X was lonely. I knew what that was like, too.

His next question took me by surprise. "What about you? Any boyfriends I should know about?"

14

Xavier

The second the question came out of my mouth, I wanted to take it back. I knew how it sounded. I was sure she didn't have a boyfriend, or I would have known about him by now.

She didn't look perturbed by the question as she skimmed the water with her fingertips. "No. There's no one."

"Good."

Her eyes danced with laughter as they met mine. "Oh, yeah? Good for who?"

"Me. One less person to worry about."

She didn't reply to that comment, seemingly lost in her thoughts as she looked out into the ocean. The stars weren't out, but the moon was full and cast a glittering reflection on the water. I watched her hands for a while before resuming monitoring the perimeter.

"How old are you?" she asked.

I paused for a moment but didn't see any harm in telling her. "I just turned thirty-two."

She looked surprised. "You're younger than I thought."

"Gee, thanks," I teased, surprising myself.

She laughed, the husky sound fading into the night before she took a step toward me. "I didn't mean you look old. It's more about the way you carry yourself. You seem so...secure."

I shrugged. "I'm an old soul, I guess."

She stared at me for a moment, smiling, and I felt the air change between us. For some reason, it put me on alert. "How old are you?" Wait, I already knew the answer to that question. What was wrong with me?

"Twenty-five," she replied. "As of a few days ago."

"Ah. Right."

I remembered her saying she didn't celebrate her birthday. I almost asked her why before I forced myself to stop asking irrelevant questions.

"It sounds so old, but I know it's not."

"You're right. It's not."

"I just thought I'd feel different at this age, I guess."

"Different how?"

She shrugged and waded farther into the water. "I don't know. I just thought I would *feel* like an adult, ya know?"

"Are you saying you feel like a kid?"

She ran her hands through her hair and put it over her shoulder. "No. I haven't felt like a kid for a long time."

I actually knew what she meant, but I didn't say so. I was starting to get a little unnerved. It was hard to match the girl in the ocean with the one I'd seen the past two days. Had I been looking at her all wrong?

"So are we friends now?" she asked. "Are we starting over?"

I honestly had no idea what to say to that. We weren't friends. I was head of her security team, and it was inappropriate for us to have anything more than a professional relationship. I made sure to keep my eyes averted as she slowly got out of the water. It was harder than I thought it would be.

She smiled as she grabbed her cover-up from the sand. I guess she stopped waiting for an answer, because she gave me a pat on the shoulder and started heading back toward the house. "Baby steps."

I was making a protein shake in the kitchen the next morning when I felt a small nip on my leg. I looked down to see Bella looking up at me with her beady little eyes.

"What do you want?"

She looked back at me, panting. I remembered Eloisa's words from a few days before about her eating habits and frowned. "Scavenging for food, no doubt?"

I decided to ignore her and went back to making my protein shake, but the damn thing got my attention again with a bark.

"Go away!" I told her.

Another bark.

I sighed, making my way over to the pantry. I found the dog food quickly, but when I pulled it out, I heard a growl.

"What? Not good enough for you?"

Wondering what had come over me, I made my way to the fridge. Inside I saw a box of doggy treats with a bow and a few hearts on it. When I pulled it out, the little rascal went nuts until I threw a treat to her. "Damn dog."

Just then a call came through from one of the men I'd hired to patrol the area. "Eloisa's got a visitor."

"Who is it?"

"Some guy named Joel. He's in a limo outside the gate right now talking to Harold."

"I'll be right out."

I took in the long black limo as I strode toward the gate. The man standing outside it had dark hair that went to his shoulders, dark sunglasses, and a ripped denim jacket over a flannel shirt. He looked homeless, but I could tell right away that wasn't case. I would have bet money that he dressed that way on purpose.

I typed in the code and exited the gate, my eyes still on the stranger. He was taller than I thought, and as I approached, he took off his sunglasses. His eyes were a clear blue, wary as they took me in.

"Joel Stanton," he said, reaching out his hand for me to shake. Not wanting to start a scene so early in the morning, I shook his hand and visibly sized him up.

"X. Head of security. Can I help you with something?"

He gave me a smile, but it seemed condescending. "I'm here to see Eloisa. Can you tell her I'm here?"

His tone grated, and I turned to the old man. "Did you ask for an ID, Harold?"

Harold smiled fondly in Joel's direction. "No need. Joel and Eloisa here go way back. He's been here plenty of times before."

I looked back into the smug eyes of the man before me. "You weren't on the visitors list E gave me."

He blinked at that and rubbed the back of his neck. "That doesn't surprise me. But trust me, she'll want to see me."

Putting his sunglasses back on, he made to walk by me. I stopped him easily with a hand on his shoulder. "As I just said, you weren't on her list. You need to leave."

"Don't you know who I am?"

I studied his face carefully, but his features didn't ring any bells. Not that I cared. My instincts told me this man was a grade-A bastard. "Am I supposed to know who you are?"

"Jet Five." He looked at me incredulously but took a step back.

When I didn't respond, his jaw went a little slack. "We had three number-one hit singles last year."

I schooled my face as comprehension set in. This guy thought he was somebody special. Too bad I didn't know, or give two shits about knowing, his damned band. I remained silent. After a few seconds of awkward silence, he cursed and whipped out his phone.

"I'll call her now. You'll regret this."

Harold and I watched as he dialed E's number with no success. His annoyance was clearly morphing into anger, and it instantly put me on alert. Red flags rolled off this douche like a bad smell. He wasn't getting anywhere near E until I figured out what was going on.

He ended the call, and I could tell he had more to say, but the look on my face must have quieted the urge. Pushing his shoulders back, he turned toward Harold. "It was nice to see you, Harold. If you could tell Eloisa I love her, and to call me, I'll owe you one."

Surprise had my eyebrows lifting as he turned back in my direction. "I'll see *you* later," he spit out. We watched as he got back into his limo and drove away.

"I can't believe you did that," Harold said as he shielded his eyes from the sun. "That man is a rock god. Most people—men included—fall at his feet."

Before I could respond, loud chuckles sounded from the front yard. I turned to see Joe and Big in the throes of laughter. Joe had his massive hands on his stomach as he met my curious stare. "Thanks, X. That just made my morning."

The normally quiet Big wiped at his eyes. "The look on his stupid face. Priceless."

Harold grumbled something and walked off back toward his post while I went up to them, intending to get some answers. "Why would he think he could just walk in here?"

"That's Ellie's ex-boyfriend," Joe replied. "They broke up about a year ago. Guy thinks he's the shit."

Ex-boyfriend. The phrase rankled. I didn't know anything about any famous ex-boyfriend. I thought about what she had told me at the beach just last night. *There's no one.* "Why would he be showing up here if they broke up?"

"It's public knowledge he wants her back," Joe explained. "He tells it to anyone who will listen. I don't feel sorry for the rat, because it's also common knowledge he cheated on her. God knows how many times."

"And he never showed up to her album-release party or wanted anything to do with her career," Big put in. "Too concerned with his own." I gave the large, muscled man a once-over. He normally relied on Joe to do the talking, but it was clear he had a lot to say on this subject.

"She's better off without him," Joe continued. "I can't stand to see her with any more heartache."

That reminded me. I was more than interested in how Joe and Big seemed to know so much about her. It was clear they had a relationship beyond the professional scope. "How long have you known Eloisa?"

"About eight years. Big, Eloisa, and I are shining products of the foster care system."

This time, I couldn't hide the surprise on my face. I had wrongfully assumed she had come from money. I should have read her file a bit more closely. "How long was she in the foster care system?"

Joe shook his head sadly. "Since she was about twelve years old. She was shipped from house to house over the years, never finding anything permanent. When she was about seventeen, she was brought into our family. Kids were always rotating in and out there, but the three of us managed to become pretty tight."

A million questions assailed me, and I felt my perspective of E shift in a totally different direction. "What happened to her parents?"

"Mother died at birth," Joe told me. "Father...I'm not too sure exactly what happened. She doesn't like to talk about it, so I just assume he's a deadbeat. That's another one that's been sniffing around here lately. Couldn't help himself once she got famous."

The conversation I heard between Sandy and E the first day I arrived came to mind. It was clear she didn't want to talk to him. A few more puzzle pieces fell together. It was humbling.

"She saved us," Joe said, looking me in the eye. "She's always been kind and selfless. Big and me here, we were...trouble. She motivated us to get into college, encouraged us to play sports, and then gave us jobs. We wouldn't be where we are today if it weren't for her."

I had a feeling if I dug any deeper into that, I wouldn't like where it went. But my gut instinct told me I could trust the two men, especially when it came to Eloisa. I nodded, acknowledging their comments. "Where is she now?"

Joe pointed to the backyard. "By the water." He frowned. "She won't be happy to hear that Joel showed up."

I couldn't be too sure of that yet. She could just as easily be upset with me for interfering. Either way, I was prepared for a fight. I gave both men a nod before going to seek out E.

15

Eloisa

I was trying and failing to come up with a new song for the tour when I saw X coming toward me. The man was clearly on a mission. His gait was purposeful, dark eyes focused solely on me. The strong lines of that jaw were locked tight, and I couldn't help but feel like a cornered rabbit under the seeing eye of the wolf.

Trying to lighten the mood, I began to play "Bay of Lights"—the song X claimed he couldn't stand. Meeting his eyes, I belted out the lyrics and played my heart out. I could have sworn I saw his lips twitch, but it was gone by the time he reached me.

He blocked the sun completely as he loomed over me, arms crossed. I couldn't help but notice that his crotch was right near my face. I felt the blush spread over my cheeks, and as if he was reading my mind, he cleared his throat and moved to sit on the rock beside me. "You had a visitor just now."

"Really?" I asked, surprised. "There's someone here?"

"It was Joel Stanton. And no—not anymore. I sent him away."

My whole body tensed as my stomach rolled over. "Joel was here? And you...sent him away?"

X nodded, his eyes roaming over my face. "He wasn't on the master list. I told you the rules about that."

I could tell he thought I'd be angry—could see his body braced for it. He only relaxed when I let out a sigh of relief. "Thank you. I don't want to see him."

X nodded. "I'll make sure to let the guards know. If he shows up again, I'll personally kick him off the property."

I gave X a fond smile. He didn't know what had happened between Joel and me, but it felt a little bit like he was on my side. Which was nice, because, according to the media, I was a terrible heartbreaker. "I'd appreciate it."

A tense silence fell over us before X turned to me again. "You know, I didn't mean to insult your song."

Laughing in response, I picked up my guitar and began to play a low melody. "I know." I knew that was probably the most I'd get out of him on the subject. I was proven right when he got up in the next moment and gave me a small wave.

"OK, then. Call me if you need anything."

He strode away before something he'd said earlier popped into my mind. "X, wait!"

He turned around, a small frown on his lips.

"Did the first lady really sing my song?"

"Yes."

I beamed. And this time, I knew I saw his lips twitch.

The whole team and I—including X—had a nice dinner together that night. We ordered in from my favorite mom-and-pop Italian restaurant down the road, and conversation flowed easily. It was a nice change from the usual tense and frantic atmosphere we all had become accustomed to as of late. Even Rob was in a cheerful mood as he oohed and ahhed over his pasta. It made me happy. I was anxious to put the accident behind me and concentrate on the tour and what it meant for my career. X was a constant reminder of the danger, of course, but I was even starting to get used to him hanging around. As long as I didn't think about crazy fans who wanted to kill me, I was OK.

Everyone headed home at around 11:00 p.m. I went upstairs to clean up before bed, looking for Bellatrix on the way. Searching through a few rooms, I called for her, but there was no sign she was even in the house. Thinking it odd, but figuring she would show up soon, as she always did, I hopped into the shower. After nearly thirteen years, I knew her habits like the back of my hand.

I soaped up my hair, humming the tune I couldn't get out of my head, when I heard the click of toenails on the bathroom floor. Ah. There she was.

"Where have you been all night, girl?" I called out. The clicking continued, as if she was running around in circles or was excited about something.

I smiled as I washed the soap out of my hair. What was she up to now?

Wiping the water of out my face, I drew back the curtain to see what was going on.

It took only one second for the grisly image in front of me to sink in before I screamed.

16

Xavier

I had just gotten off the phone with the colonel when I heard a loud, piercing scream. There was no doubt in my mind it came from E.

My heart thundered in my chest as I raced up the basement steps toward the source of the sound. A million scenarios ran through my head. Was someone in the house? How did that person get in? What did I miss?

I had just reached the second flight of stairs when E screamed again. I managed to scale each flight in two bounds, ran down the hallway, and burst through her bedroom door. The room was empty, but the shower was running in the adjoining bathroom. Adrenaline pumped purposefully through my blood as I stormed into the bathroom, nearly tripping over that damn dog.

I looked to the floor and reeled back at the macabre sight. A large and mangled bird was clamped in the mutt's jaws. Then my eyes landed on E. She was standing alone in the tub, soaking wet and completely naked. Her eyes were wild as she looked down at Bellatrix. Her gaze flew toward me, and I felt my eyes widen in shock.

I looked away immediately, unsuccessfully trying to blink away the image of all that golden skin. The sound of shower-curtain rings sweeping over the bar rang out in the small room as she gasped.

"Are you OK?" I bit out, my pulse hammering. My eyes stayed glued to the ceiling.

"I'm fine," she squeaked. "Bellatrix just scared the crap out of me! Can you get that thing out of here?"

I was already moving to do just that. Grabbing a spare towel, I knelt down beside Bellatrix and gripped the bird's body, tugging on it slightly.

"Bellatrix, drop that right now! That's not food! Bad girl!" E shouted. She was now peering out from behind the curtain.

The dog jumped at the sound of her voice and dropped the bird on the rug. I carefully picked it up with the towel and left without another word. A little dazed, I headed to the stairs. A few of the security crew who patrolled the grounds were just heading up. I assured them everything was OK, ordered them not to go upstairs, and headed outside to the trash can.

The fresh air was welcome against my heated skin. I quickly threw out the bird and the towel before taking a few deep breaths, trying to get my bearings. From one minute thinking E was in danger, to bursting in on her in the shower, the episode had me more than a little rattled.

An image of her standing there flashed through my mind again, and for just a split second, out there in the dark, I allowed myself to picture it fully. Long, wet hair plastered to her body. Big, watery green eyes. Sun-kissed skin and a few freckles sprinkled over flawless curves—goddamn it, I'd seen everything. I shook myself out of the musing and headed back inside. I could not allow myself to linger over such thoughts.

I wondered if I should check on her, but I decided to give her a few more minutes. She was probably embarrassed. Grabbing a bottle of water, I headed toward the basement.

My phone dinged as I was making my way down the stairs.

E: *I am so sorry. I didn't mean to worry anyone. If it helps, know that I am mortified.*

Scratching the stubble on my jaw, I typed out a reply.

X: *OK.*

My phone dinged again.

E: *I can't believe Bellatrix brought that thing into the house! She's never done that before. I'm so surprised.*

Talk about being surprised. My head was still reeling.

X: *No harm done.*

E: *Easy for you to say! You didn't just flash an unsuspecting employee!*

I don't know where the notion came from, but I decided to tease her a little bit.

X: *True.*

There was silence for a bit before she sent me a yellow face that looked to be rolling its eyes.

E: *Very funny. You want a nightcap?*

X: *Not going to drink on the job.*

No need to mention I didn't drink at all.

E: *Well, can you at least meet me in the kitchen? I need to face you again so the awkwardness doesn't get any bigger in my head.*

I didn't know what she meant by that, but I typed an affirmative and headed back upstairs. A few moments later, I heard her feet overhead. She walked in the kitchen a few seconds later, and I nearly smiled when I saw her cheeks were bright red. Bellatrix was cuddled in her arms.

However, she bravely met my gaze and stood before me. "Bellatrix would like to apologize for the trouble she's caused."

The dog panted happily between us, not looking the least bit sorry, in my opinion. Before she could say anything else, the mutt jumped from her arms and into mine. I barely caught her before she hit the ground.

E looked shocked. "I don't know what's gotten into her! I've never seen her do that before. She must like you."

"The feeling is mutual," I mumbled sarcastically. The damn dog snuggled into the crook of my elbow. I wanted to hand her back, but E was already fixing herself a glass of wine. "Probably because I gave her food the other day."

"Probably," she said after she took a big sip. Her eyes suddenly went wide. "Wait, I hope you don't think I planned that!"

"The thought hadn't even crossed my mind." Which was true.

She looked relieved. "OK, good. I'll try not to overreact like that again over something so stupid. Let's just forget it happened."

As if her words conjured it, the image of her standing there in the shower flashed like a fantasy I couldn't escape. I cleared my throat and shifted, settling Bellatrix on the other side of my arm. "Already forgotten."

"Good, good."

The silence stretched between us before E snapped her fingers. "Oh, I forgot to tell you. Rob scheduled a last-minute sound check for Sunday. I know you take some time off, so just wanted to give you a heads-up."

"What time?"

"We have to be in Hartford by two p.m."

I nodded. "I'll be back before noon."

I could tell she wanted to ask where I was going, but I also knew she wouldn't. And even though she'd tried to avoid it, there was a tension between us now. It was subtle, but it was there, bubbling under the surface. It made me distinctly uncomfortable. I looked down at Bellatrix. Rascal.

E finished her wine and came toward me, reaching for the dog. "Thanks again."

Our eyes met briefly before we turned and went our separate ways.

I didn't see E much on Saturday. She was locked away in her room working on her music, so I took the opportunity to check on all my security upgrades.

Harold waved at me when I came outside. I gave him a small nod. He was nice enough, but he wasn't the type of man I needed guarding that gate. I wanted someone...well, frankly, someone younger. Faster. Less trusting. At least there were cameras and reinforced locks now, but something about having him there just rubbed me the wrong way.

After doubling security, I left E's house at around 7:00 a.m. that Sunday to head for my father's. He lived pretty close by, and the convenience was a huge weight off my shoulders. I hadn't been able to see him nearly as much being in DC for as long as I was. I wanted to spend as much time with him as I could before—

I shook myself out of the dark thoughts and pulled into the driveway of my childhood home. I didn't have good memories of the place—that was certain—but my dad refused to move. So every time, I had to push past the terrible, sinking anxiety I got from being there.

With my salary, he was able to have around-the-clock care if needed and the best treatment money could buy. He still had to go to the hospital for his chemo, but I made sure he was as comfortable as possible. I owed him that much.

The front door swung open, and my old man came out with his arms wide open.

"Xavier! You're a sight for sore eyes."

"Hey, Pops." I came up the steps and pulled him into my arms, trying to ignore how weak he seemed. "You look great."

He pushed his chest out. "Of course I do. Now get inside. I have that buffalo chicken dip from Stew Leonard's that you like."

We headed inside, and I waved to Georgette, his Sunday nurse.

"Ask him about his hot date," she teased, heading upstairs with a laundry basket.

I turned to my father, who was rummaging through the fridge. "How was the date?"

"It was marvelous!" I grabbed a couple of plates while he put the dip and chips on the table. "Rose is a good ol' gal. They don't make 'em like that anymore."

I raised a brow. "Oh, yeah? What did you guys do?"

He took a large bite of a chip. "We wanted to go dancing, but there wasn't anywhere to go that time of day. So we settled for feeding the birds down at the beach."

I took in his hunched shoulders, balding head, and skin that had so many more wrinkles than I ever remembered. He was smiling at me, and seeing his grin eased the pain and anxiety in my chest slightly. That was still the same. He had a genuine smile that just made you feel good.

"Sounds like fun."

He was still smiling at me. "I'm so glad you're close to me again, son. I know I'm not as important as the president, but I've missed you so much."

My dad was always so free with his emotions. Another way he was opposite from me.

I decided to try to let my guard down for him. "I've missed you, too. The only reason I took this job is so I could be close to you."

He took a sip of water and gave me a sardonic look. "That can't be the only reason."

"What do you mean?"

"The beautiful Eloisa Rae Morgan didn't have anything to do with it?"

"You know it didn't."

I stuffed my mouth full of dip. If he only knew what had happened the day before. It would probably give the old man a heart attack.

"Did you apologize for those comments you made about her music?"

I shrugged. "We worked it out."

"Good. So now you can invite her over here. I would love to meet her."

Sighing heavily, I gave him a look. "Maybe."

"I'll take it," he said, munching. "How's the dip?"

"Best in the world."

"Second to your mother's," he said, his eyes twinkling. "Do you remember that salsa she used to make? I would do anything to have a bite of that again!"

And just like that, the heavy weight descended back onto my chest. The anxiety came rushing in, and it felt like the walls were closing in on me. He knew I didn't like to talk about Mom. Knew it was hard enough for me to live with the guilt of what had happened to her.

After a few moments, he took pity on me and changed the subject. But the sadness in his eyes only made me feel worse.

17

Eloisa

I was tending to my plants when I saw X's black SUV make its way around the circular driveway. Back from his mysterious three-hour Sunday sabbatical, I noted.

I stood up as he got closer and noticed he had something tucked under his arm. "What's that?" I asked.

He didn't answer right away, shifting the bag to his other arm. He kept looking between me and the plants. What was that about? But it was then I noticed that he had a bag from Stew's.

I gasped. "Oh my God. Next time you go to Stew's, let me know! I love that place."

"I have some buffalo chicken dip. Have you ever tried it?"

"No, but it sounds amazing."

"It is. Follow me."

I followed him into the kitchen and watched as he pulled out a bag of Tostitos and opened the top of the dip. Stomach rumbling, I dug in right away, the wonderful taste of buffalo sauce and cheese exploding in my mouth. "Oh my God. This is incredible!"

X grabbed a chip himself. "It's my favorite. I could probably eat a whole tub of this if I let myself."

He seemed more at ease than I had ever seen him. Maybe all the man needed to let off some steam was a good snack. It was also possible whatever he had spent the last three hours doing was responsible for the change. I was more curious than I had a right to be.

"I may do just that," I answered.

I noticed something else sticking out of the bag. It looked like three dog toys. "What do you have there?"

"They're for Bella."

I paused, a chip halfway to my mouth. "My Bella?"

His eyebrows knit together as if he was embarrassed. "Well, I figured she could use something...non-bird-like...to chew on."

My cheeks warmed, but surprise and gleefulness warred for space in my brain. He bought toys for my dog? "Oh...yes. She's going to love those. Thank you."

I couldn't keep the wide grin off my face.

"What?" he asked.

"I'm just surprised. That's all."

"About what?"

"That you'd think of Bella. It doesn't really seem like an X thing to do," I teased.

He frowned. "I was nearby. I got the toys. Case closed." He turned toward the door. "Be ready to leave for rehearsal in an hour."

He left the room in short order after that, but it took a while for me to stop smiling.

We arrived at the Hartford Civic Center twenty minutes early thanks to X and his efficiency hurrying us along.

Rob looked positively tickled, as I was usually several minutes late to most things. "You guys made it on time!" He rubbed his hands together, a big grin on his face. "How are you feeling, Eloisa?"

"Nervous and excited," I told him truthfully. "Are we doing a full dress rehearsal?"

"Not for a couple of days. There are still a few kinks in the costume lineup. Just checking sound today."

"Sounds good."

We made our way into the arena, meeting up with a few crew members along the way. Everyone was working so hard to put this together, and I couldn't have been more grateful. Never in a million years did I think I'd be in this incredible position. All the nights alone, just me and my music. Now I got to share it with the world.

I noted a few security guards I hadn't previously seen stationed around the arena. Each gave X a nod when he passed. This man didn't miss a beat.

After the mic check and a few preliminaries, I walked to the center of the stage, where my guitar sat propped up against a stool. My pulse felt erratic, and my stomach squeezed and knotted. There was not a single person in the audience, but I suddenly felt very nervous.

Sandy and X stood together offstage, and an idea struck me.

"Can you two go sit in the audience? I'm getting a case of the butterflies here."

After a moment, they both nodded. They reappeared moments later on the arena floor and took two seats right in the middle.

Sandy gave me a thumbs-up while X seemed to be watching me carefully. Could he tell I was nervous? I felt bad asking this of him, but I already felt loads better just looking at a few familiar faces.

"You all set, girl?" Joe called out from somewhere.

I nodded, and just like that, the chords of the song "Dream of Me" began to play.

This was one of my favorite lullabies, and I'd wanted it on my first album. If I had gone with someone like Martha Mathers, or another major studio, this type of track would have never been allowed on. It was simple and haunting, and it held a lot of meaning for me.

Let me sleep,

For when I sleep, I dream that you are here,

You're mine.
And all my fears are left behind,
I float, on air...
The nightingale sings gentle lullabies,
So let me close my eyes...

And just like that, I got lost in the music. Song after song, I lost sight of everything else; the feelings took over inside me. Music touches me like nothing else can. It's the only thing that gives me a true and genuine sense of joy.

The sound guys call a halt after about seven songs, and I go for some water. Sandy, like the lovely assistant she is, gets on her feet and claps for me. X, to my astonishment, remains seated but claps, too.

I give him a big smile, and he gives me a small one back. Two steps back, one step forward.

After a few tech adjustments, I get started on the second set. This time, I can't seem to keep my gaze off X. Partially because I can feel his intense stare. It's intimidating to be caught in his sights to begin with, but I'm definitely not used to this pointed regard. I take a chance and meet his eyes, still singing, and for a few moments, we just look at each other. The tension that's been building still lingers between us, but for some reason, it doesn't feel awkward anymore.

I wonder what he's thinking about. He's rubbing a hand over his jaw, his eyes still not leaving mine. I close my own for a moment, getting lost in a high-pitched note when I hear a phone ring. A few seconds later, X is striding out of the arena. Even from here, I can tell he's upset.

Another song goes by, and he doesn't return. I figure he has something important to handle and don't think much of it until Rob comes onto the stage, looking distressed.

"We have to cut things short."

The panicked look in his eyes gets my heart racing. "Cut things short? Why?"

"There's been an incident."

Sandy comes up onstage and puts her hand on my shoulder. Her voice comes out low and soft. "Incident?"

"It's a...there's..."

I can't take the hedging. "Rob. What is it?"

"There's another note."

His words take a second or two to register. Sandy gasps from beside me, and the sound brings me back to the present.

Swallowing my nerves, I meet Rob's eyes. "Where?"

"At the house."

X's response has me looking his way. I hadn't even heard him return. Without warning, he grabs my hand and starts dragging me offstage.

"Wait!" I cry out but allow myself to be dragged all the same. "I want to know what's going on. What do you mean, at the house?"

He doesn't answer, but his grip on my hand seems to tighten more and more as we wind our way backstage. My thoughts are scattered, and I barely notice the crew staring at us as we race by. It seems they take one look at X's face and know to get out of the way.

The late-afternoon sun is blinding as we quickly exit out a side door and make our way toward the waiting SUV. Sandy runs up behind us and barely gets in as X slams the door and bellows at the driver to take off.

I rip my hand out of his and turn to face him on the large seat. There's hardly an inch between us, and I can feel the boiling anger emanating from his body. "X. Tell me what happened."

After signaling to the driver, his eyes meet mine for a moment before looking away. Outwardly he appears calm, but I see as well as sense the fury sizzling underneath the surface. My pulse picks up, and my hands start to tremble. What could have happened?

He turns to me again. "A note. Taped on the front door of your home. It was found fifteen minutes ago."

I put a hand against my heart to try to calm the erratic pounding. "But...with all your security measures? How?"

His jaw locks. "I don't know. But I intend to find out."

Sandy leans in closer, her eyes wary and full of tears. "What did the note say?"

X shifts in his seat. "It's from the same person."

The same person who tried to kill me. Somehow that person was able to get to my house and tape a note on my door. The seriousness of the situation sinks into my stomach like a brick. "What did it say, X?"

"Do you want to know?"

"Of course I want to know!"

"You didn't before, did you?"

His accusation stings like a lash. No. I didn't before. But having this person come onto my property, a place that has always been sacred, levels me like nothing else has. "No, I didn't. Don't make me feel guilty about that."

"This is something that can't be ignored. I need you to face that fact and understand that there's someone out there who is literally stalking you. Cleary this person has been watching the house," he says.

His words burn through me. Of course I understand that fact. He doesn't understand my side, though. He has no idea what my fans mean to me. He has no idea how much it hurts. "What did the note say?" I manage to squeak out.

He lets out a huge breath and runs a hand over his jaw. "It was short, unlike the first one. It said, 'Come find me, Eloisa. I'm waiting for you.'"

Sandy and I exchange loaded glances but stay silent.

"There was a butcher's knife with it."

I'm unable to control the hand that leaps up to cover my mouth. Unable to control the tear that drops down my cheek. X watches its watery path as he responds. "The cops are on the way and are going to dust it for prints. But my guess is they'll have as much luck with this as they did with the rock."

"What did the first note say?" I ask, hearing myself say the words as if through water. "On the rock?"

"You finally want to know?" X confirms.

"E, no," Sandy whispers.

But I nod to X, feeling as if I have no other choice. I have to rip off this Band-Aid. It's time for me to stop running scared. Every fiber of my being fights against it, but I dig deep in my gut for strength and ignore it.

X scrolls through his phone and pulls up a photo of the first note. I take a deep breath, and read.

Why don't you see me?

I am nothing to you.

I love you, but I'm nothing to you.

That doesn't stop me from watching you.

I want to kiss you.

I want to watch you undress.

I want to see what your insides are like...

Do you love me?

Say you love me.

You forgot me.

You're just using me...

You don't fucking deserve me!

I FUCKING HATE YOU!

DIE!

DIE!

DIE!

Your biggest fan.

My hand is trembling as X takes the phone gently from my fingers. I have no idea how much time has passed since he handed it to me. Fear, sorrow, and disgust lance through my heart like a deadly spear.

His phone rings, interrupting the silence. I reach out to Sandy, who is sniffling into her hands, as he picks it up.

A minute goes by until X finally responds to whoever is on the line. "Fire him."

I glance at his profile at the declaration, but his face gives nothing away.

"Fire the entire outdoor security crew and get them into questioning. I want a new team by nightfall." At this he hangs up and stares out the window, seeming oblivious to stares from Sandy and me.

"Fire who?" I ask weakly.

"Harold."

Shock nearly closes my throat. "You can't fire Harold!" And just like that, my fear from reading the note transforms itself into rage.

"Yes, I can."

"He's my employee, and he works for me. You have no right!" I swear I could reach out and punch the man in his arrogant face. How dare he? "Harold is a part of my family. He lives for his job because it's all he has."

"Harold shut down our entire security system."

That gives me pause. "Why would he do that?"

"Because he wanted to learn how everything worked and be able to turn things on and off himself. The whole system was off for hours."

I think of poor Harold, and my heart beats in empathy. "He probably figured it was OK if I wasn't there. You can't blame him for that. He didn't know!"

"I can't have someone on the team who doesn't follow orders. Who knows how long your stalker has been waiting for this opportunity? You don't understand how these things work. These fuckers are patient."

The phrase *your stalker* bounces around my brain, but I ignore it. "Where was the rest of your team?"

"The five I had stationed outside were inside eating lunch. Harold's the one that was supposed to guard the gate. It would be impossible to get in anywhere else on the property."

His tone gets under my skin. "Sandy, where's my phone?"

I put my hand out as X goes to respond, cutting him off. Sandy hands me my phone, and I read several apologetic texts from Harold. Rubbing my forehead in sadness, I hand it back to her. "I don't know what I want to say yet. Can you please tell him he can have his job back once this is all over?"

X grunts beside me. "You think this is a joke."

His words tumble me over the edge. "A joke? One of my fans wants to kill me. Stab me. Do other horrible things to me! And you think I'm laughing about it? This fucking hurts me, X! You have no idea, and you don't know me!"

His eyes widen slightly at my outburst, but he doesn't respond. I will the remaining tears away, blinking rapidly. But a sudden thought has me nearly jumping out of my seat. "Bellatrix! Is she OK? Has anyone seen her?" My heart gallops as I think of her little face and—

"Joe and Big are on their way to get her."

His declaration puts a halt to my escalating panic. "They...are?"

"Yes. We're going to meet them in an hour."

Surprised that he thought of Bella, I take a moment to gather myself and sit back in my seat. I violently shove away any thoughts of the notes, of my fans, and of X as I concentrate on taking deep breaths. I have no idea how long we drive in silence until I feel the car roll to a stop and realize it's dark outside.

"Where are we?"

In usual X fashion, he doesn't respond. He's out of the car and back within moments. In his hands are a small duffel bag and Bellatrix. She immediately leaps out of his grasp to lick my face.

"Sandy, you'll say goodbye here."

Sandy's face pales as she looks back and forth between us. Timid by nature, she doesn't argue.

"Where is she going?" I ask, trying to keep my temper in check.

"Wherever she wants to go."

I put a hand on Bellatrix's back and turn to look X in the face. "Sandy stays with me."

"Not right now. Sandy is going back with Joe and Big. We're giving her a couple days off until we get all this figured out."

"But what if—"

"She'll be safe. Members of your immediate circle are going to each get a small security team. Whether they choose to go back to your house is up to them, although the police are there now."

Sandy's shaking her head in disbelief and speaks for the first time in a while. "I'll be OK, Ellie. We...we have to do whatever we can to catch this guy."

Her words do little to calm me. And it makes me realize I have no idea where we're going. "Where *are* you taking me?"

"Somewhere safe."

I grip Bellatrix tighter. "Who are we going with?"

"No one. It will be just you and me until I confirm a few things. I don't trust anyone, E."

Sandy bristles, and I want to stick up for my team, but I feel drained and exhausted from trying to push the negative thoughts out of my head. X gives Sandy a look, and she hurries to unbuckle her seat belt.

"I'll text you later, Eloisa. You take care of yourself."

I put a hand on her arm right before she climbs out of the car, trying to convey what I can't with words. I manage a light smile. "I'll be OK. You keep Joe and Big in line and make sure they don't do anything stupid."

She laughs tightly, and then she's gone. The silence of just X and the darkness outside is stifling, broken up only by Bellatrix panting on my lap.

Neither of us speaks again as the car starts moving. For some reason, I'm furious with him. Firing Harold, taking away Sandy and my team. But another part of me, a part that I feel deep in my bones, instinctively knows that with X, I'm as safe as I can be. And after reading those notes, being safe is what's most important.

18

Xavier

My fists clench for the hundredth time as I stare out the window and try to conceal the immense rage that's rushing through my system. I failed. How could this have happened? How could this have happened under my watch? The situation is clearly more serious than even I first anticipated. I'm not used to someone getting a leg up on me, and it's almost more than I can bear.

Eloisa has finally fallen asleep beside me, her head resting on my shoulder. Normally I would've made an attempt to move her, but her weight has a calming effect that I didn't expect. Nonetheless, I tell myself it's because I don't want her to wake up, hoping she'll sleep off the myriad of emotions she no doubt went through this afternoon.

Familiar scenery whizzes by outside, and I become a bit nostalgic about our destination. I'm taking Eloisa to my father's old fishing cabin. It's secluded, far away from civilization, and the perfect place to regroup after what happened. I guess we could've stayed at a hotel, but...I don't want her around anyone right now. I also don't want to look too deeply into that, as I'm sure that notion is fear based.

E shifts a bit in her sleep. Bellatrix pops her head up at the movement from her place on E's lap, her dark, shiny eyes meeting mine. Without preamble, she gets up, stretches, and walks her furry little behind onto my lap. Goddamn it. I scratch her ears just as a text comes through on my phone.

Rob: *You can't just disappear with her, X. Her tour is days away!*

I ignore the text, having already explained myself to him. He'll just have to deal. Doesn't he realize there won't be a tour if I don't do everything in my power to keep her safe? E has a legit stalker. Someone who wouldn't hesitate to hurt her if given the chance. The thought sends a small shiver through my body that I'm sure Bellatrix notices. I've dealt with some loony tunes before, working at the White House, but that was to be expected. E doesn't deserve this. She hasn't asked for it. But is that the price of fame? A week or two ago I would have said yes.

E stirs awake as we pull onto the dirt road that leads to my father's cabin.

"Where are we?" Her voice is a little husky from sleep.

"My father's cabin. We're going to stay here for a little bit while I secure things at home base."

She suddenly sits upright, as if just noticing her head was on my shoulder. Her throat clears, and Bellatrix jumps back into her lap. I sense the embarrassment coming off her in waves and have to resist the urge to tell her it's fine.

"How long is a little bit?"

"I don't know yet."

Sighing, she leans back in her seat as the house comes into view.

The driver stops, and I immediately get out of the car to meet the man who's currently walking out the front door.

"Colonel," I say in way of greeting. "Thanks for coming out so quickly."

He nods and eyes the SUV. "Place is secure. New locks are in place."

I quickly give him a rundown of what happened this afternoon. His teeth grit, and he shakes his head. "I'll call the unit and make sure they're doing everything they can to nail this bastard down."

"They're swarming the place now. Police, too."

Colonel Jackson eyes me carefully, no doubt able to see my fury bubbling underneath the surface. "You all right?"

Pride has my chest puffing out, but I tell the truth. "No. I'm livid. I knew Harold should have been let go the second I arrived, but…"

Just then, the SUV door opens, and Eloisa climbs out. She's staring up at the house in what looks like awe. After a few steps, she notices the colonel and does her best to smile. It's a smile she wears often—one that attempts to put on a show of bravery that she's not feeling. I saw it onstage today before she began singing. I startle a little that I know that about her, but then I comfort myself with the fact that it's part of my job to know these things.

She walks over slowly and looks at me expectantly.

"E, this is the colonel." I pause for a moment. "My boss."

That brings a genuine smile to her lips. "The man who keeps this guy in line. It's nice to meet you. And, wow, you look just like your brother."

The colonel gives her a grin I haven't seen the likes of before. It's typical for men—and women—to act differently around E, but I never expected it from the colonel. "It's a pleasure to meet you, Eloisa," he says. "And yes, we've gotten that a lot. He's just got fewer gray hairs than I do."

They both laugh, but for some reason I just can't get myself to find anything funny. After their laughter dies down, the colonel looks at her seriously. "Are you all right?"

E deflates a bit and cuddles her dog to her chest. "To be honest, I don't really know. I'm trying not to think about it."

The colonel gives me a look. "Well, either way we'll make sure we keep you updated. I want you to know that my team and the local cops are doing everything we can to resolve this quickly and quietly."

E nods. "I appreciate it."

She glances back up at the house. "I love this place."

Warmth settles in my chest at her assessment. Going to this cabin is one of my best memories from childhood. I turn back to the colonel. "Food?"

"You'll survive," he responds, rubbing a hand over his belly. "I did what I could."

Everything is settled, then. The only people who know we're here are me, E, the colonel, and the driver. We shouldn't be bothered out here. Unsurprisingly, it does nothing to ease my fears.

E puts Bella on the ground, and the mutt immediately takes off to explore her surroundings.

"Cute little thing, isn't she?" the colonel says unexpectedly. I give him a strange look, and he shrugs his shoulders.

"She's my world," E responds in a lighthearted tone. I catch her eye, and I'm grateful for the small miracle of remembering to tell Joe to grab the thing.

"I understand that. I used to have a greyhound back in the day. Best friend I ever had," the colonel replies, surprising me yet again. It seems E has learned more personal things about my boss than I have in the past several years. Another unfamiliar emotion runs through me, but I can't pinpoint what it is. All I know is that I'm starting to feel unsettled... unsteady.

"Well, I best get going," the colonel continues. "You two stay safe and call me if you need anything."

We both nod and watch in silence as he gets in his SUV and drives away. Bella begins to nip at my feet, and E chuckles.

"Surprise, surprise—I think she's hungry," E says with a smile. "Mind if I head inside and check the cabinets?"

The question stirs me into motion, and I lead the way up the wide wooden porch to the front door. The colonel left it open, and I quickly grab the key he left for me on the side table. E gasps when I turn on the first light.

"This might just be the coziest place I've ever been."

I turn around and take in the familiar surroundings. Neutral colors, a large stone fireplace, dark wooden floors, thick woolen blankets strewn here and there—yeah, it is cozy. A thin coating of dust reminds me that my dad probably hasn't been out here in a while, and the heavy weight of that knowledge settles on my heart. He'd always make sure to come up at least once or twice a month, but clearly he hasn't been able to make the trip in quite some time.

E drops onto the nearest couch in a hilariously unladylike fashion. She opens one eye and peers up at me. "Thank you for choosing here and not some hotel. I think a little fresh air is exactly what I needed."

Her eyes close, and after a few seconds of silence I clear my throat. "I'll go see if there's something for the dog to eat."

I walk to the kitchen without waiting for a response, Bellatrix on my heels. Scouring the fridge, I find a jar of peanut butter and some turkey cold cuts. They're not her favorite treats, but they'll do.

As I'm scooping out the peanut butter on a Dixie plate, I hear E enter the kitchen. "She loves peanut butter."

"So do I."

E laughs quietly. "That makes three of us."

I grab some wheat bagels off the counter and hold them up. E nods and makes her way over. "I haven't had a bagel in so long. Rob is always telling me I need to watch my figure."

An image of E in the shower comes to mind, and I quickly shove the vivid image away, swallowing hard. But the scoff comes out of my mouth without warning, and I decide to just go with it. "Rob is an idiot. You don't need to watch your figure."

"Be still my heart; is that a compliment from Mr. X?"

Feeling uncomfortable, I busy myself with the food. "It's the truth."

"Yeah, well, I don't usually listen to what Rob says anyway," she jokes.

"You don't listen? That's hard to believe." I feign innocence and fight back a smile.

"A compliment and a smile?" I turn to see her eyes alight with mischief. "What has gotten into you?"

I honestly have no idea. "Must be the cabin. I haven't been here for years. It's nice to be back."

As soon as the words come out of my mouth, I regret them. We're here because there's a psychotic stalker who wants to kill her. I let out a breath as I finish spreading the peanut butter. E hasn't said anything.

And just as I thought, when I turn around, she seems to be staring into space.

"I'm sorry. I didn't mean anything by that."

"No, don't be sorry," she says. "This isn't your fault."

"It isn't your fault, either."

She sighs. "The price of fame."

I'm shocked to hear the words I had just been thinking about earlier. "No one deserves to be stalked or scared into hiding."

I bring her the bagel, but she doesn't reach for it. "I can't believe this is happening. That note was so…scary. I don't know what I'm supposed to do."

"Let me worry about that. And for right now, forget the note. I want you to eat."

She smiles and lifts the bagel off her plate and takes a large bite. "It's good," she says with a full mouth.

I watch her closely as she eats, trying not to stare at her soft, pink lips. God, perhaps it's been too long since I've had a woman. I've never been distracted on the job like this. It really must be the cabin that's bringing out all these unfamiliar emotions. I need to get my head back in the game; the situation is too serious.

E yawns in between bites and gives me a self-deprecating look. "Can we do the grand tour tomorrow? I'm exhausted."

"Yes. The bedroom is upstairs on the left. We'll go up together."

"Bedroom as in…only one bedroom?"

"Yes."

Her eyes are wide as she gives me a once-over. "We're going to sleep in the same bed?"

"I'm not going to sleep much." There was no way in hell my eyes were closing. There was too much to be done. I'd sleep later.

"What do you mean you're not going to sleep? Are you human or not?"

"Don't worry about me. I only need a quick nap."

"You need to sleep, X."

I sigh loudly in exasperation. "This is what I'm trained for. There's a lot to do before sunrise. It isn't your concern."

Grumbling, she scoops up Bella. "Doesn't sleep. Bah."

She sends me a fake sunny smile as she saunters by and out of the kitchen. "No wonder you're such a grump all the time."

I let out a sigh and look to the heavens before following her out of the kitchen.

Grump indeed.

19

Eloisa

I open my eyes in the middle of the night, feeling groggy. For a moment I can't remember where I am, but after a few moments of blinking away the sleep, it all comes back to me.

I feel a prickle of fear travel up my spine as I stare out the window into the darkness. Someone out there wants to kill me. Someone out there, for some reason, wants me dead. Why? The word echoes in my head as shapes in the dark room slowly come into focus.

I gasp, suddenly noticing the dark figure in the corner. Just as I am about to sit up, he holds up a hand.

"It's just me. Go back to sleep."

X. He's sitting in the old wooden rocker that's diagonal from the bed I'm in. That can't be comfortable to sleep in—well, nap in—and I marvel over how seriously he takes his job. He's watching over me.

I'm safe with him.

I close my eyes, exchanging that thought with the dark ones.

When I awake the next morning, X is nowhere to be found. It worries me slightly that I don't feel uneasy about him watching over me while I sleep. The fact is, I can no longer deny that I need him.

I yawn and reluctantly crawl out from under what I'm sure is a hand-knit quilt. There are lovely ones all over the house, and I wonder where I can get one.

As I make my way into the adjoining bathroom, I also wonder where Bella is. She's usually right by my side the second my feet hit the floor. I get into the shower, still wondering, but when the warm water washes over my skin, I groan aloud, all outside thoughts fleeing. Nothing like a shower to clear your mind.

After I get dressed, I head downstairs in search of food but pause when I pass the living room. My guitar is leaning up against the couch. X must have thought of that, too. Something about seeing it makes me uneasy.

How long are we going to stay here?

After a quick breakfast, I go in search of X and Bella. They're both out front—X on the phone and Bella panting up at him and scurrying around his feet. When I open the door and come outside, she bounds over.

"Hey, girl. Where have you been?" I coo.

X turns around, and we lock eyes. The man doesn't look tired at all. Dressed in blue jeans and a black Henley, he looks comfortable and formidable all at the same time.

"Good morning," I say as I make my way over. "Any news?"

"Not yet." He gives me a once-over. "There were no prints on the knife."

"Ah," I say quietly, stroking Bella's soft fur. The conversation feels so wrong out here in the bright morning sun and crisp air. "So what now?"

He squints his eyes and looks off into the trees. "We're going to stay here for a bit. It's going to take a while to replace the team and get things back in order at the house. As of now, it's a crime scene."

I think about going back there and fight back a shiver. "Sandy? Joe and Big? Are they OK?"

"They're fine but mad as hell at the situation. This..." He pauses to shake his head. "They're worried about you."

"Well, they shouldn't worry. I'm with you."

I don't know where the words come from. Probably all my pondering about feeling safe with him near, but I automatically know they surprise him.

"I'm glad you feel that way."

"Oh, yeah? Why?"

"Because it's true."

I laugh loudly, and Bella barks in response.

X glares at the dog in my arms. "The thing won't stop following me around."

"So what? She likes you."

He growls and rubs a hand over his short hair. "You give a dog a little food and look what happens."

I smile. "The change of scenery is probably exciting for her."

His phone rings, and we both startle. He glances at it. "Do you want to talk to Rob?"

I shake my head. For some reason, I don't feel like talking to anyone. He nods, screens the call, and shoves the phone in his back pocket.

"I have some work to do. Let's head inside."

Nodding, I follow him in and grab my guitar. He sets up in an alcove off the living room, and I sink onto the couch. I should definitely be using all this free time to get that last song written. Determined, I close my eyes and hum a few melodies. But a couple of hours later, inspiration still hasn't hit. I'm bored and restless, a terrible combination for songwriting.

Peeking in the alcove, I notice X typing away on his laptop. He looks extremely busy. I wander into the kitchen and get something to eat, then go in search of a television for a little mindless distraction. After a perfunctory search, I realize there isn't one. I also realize I don't have my own laptop with me.

Great.

I'm just about to head back down when I notice a wooden chest across from the top of the stairs. It's gorgeous. Light, washed-out wood held together with cast-iron locks. Old-fashioned with intricate, swirled carvings dancing up the sides. I run my hand over the top lightly before opening it.

There's another quilt lying on top, this one made from bright blues and greens. I move it out of the way and smile when I see a pile of picture frames. A little boy holding a woman's hand as they walk on a forest trail. Another one of the woman throwing the boy in the air and laughing. I get lost in dozens of memories of the boy and the lovely woman.

I know immediately it's X. He had the same serious stare back then as he does now. But his eyes were lighter and happier in these photos. What could have happened to take that light of out of his eyes? How did he get to be the serious, no-nonsense man that I know now?

There are pictures of him with a man I presume to be his father scattered here and there on the walls now—I'd noticed that earlier—but this woman is nowhere to be found on those walls. She's been hidden in this chest.

"What are you doing?"

I whirl around, gulping as if I'd just gotten my hand caught in the proverbial cookie jar. "Nothing."

He walks around me, and when he sees what I'm looking at, he slams the chest shut.

I jump back. "What the hell?"

"Why are you snooping around my things?" His voice is louder than I've ever heard it.

"Snooping? I was bored, so I—"

He narrows his eyes. "Bored? I brought your guitar and your dog; what else do you need?"

My mouth drops open at the rude comment. "Well, excuse me for opening up your secret chest. I suppose you think I'm supposed to be cowering in a corner right now instead?"

"Don't start with me," he growls. "Just get back downstairs where I can see you."

I grit my teeth as I watch him walk away. He is so dismissive and clearly treating me like a child. Will I ever get past his first layer? It's a first layer that seems to be made of black steel. Does he even have anything underneath? Something inside me decides to push him. Maybe it's the fear I'm keeping at bay, the frustration that's clawing to push to the surface or the helplessness that sits hot in my gut, but I want something more from him. "Is that your mother?"

He stops cold on the third stair. Obviously, I've completely shocked him with my question. A few seconds tick by. I've never, ever seen him so uneasy before. His large shoulders are tight, his spine a tight rod, the back of his neck bright red—something must have happened. Something that made the memory of his mother painful. So painful he hid her away in a beautiful chest at the top of the stairs.

Loud pounding footsteps echo throughout the hall as he makes his way back downstairs, ignoring my question.

I cross my arms tightly over my chest, wondering why I feel so stung. Shifting from foot to foot for a few moments, I finally blow the pent-up air in my chest out through my teeth. "There'd better be a wine cabinet here."

20

Xavier

I end the call and fight the urge to throw my phone against the wall. They still have nothing. No sign of the sick bastard who is stalking E. He's smart; I'll give him that. Somehow he was able to waltz up to her front door—shitting all over my defenses—and deliver his gift. The desire to wring his neck is strong. I can't wait to find him.

A glass tinkling in the kitchen draws my attention, and I realize I haven't heard a word from E since the incident on the stairs. The shock of seeing her standing by my mother's chest is still there. I wonder what she'd do if she knew the truth. Would she pity me like my father? The thought sickens me and forces me into motion. The wooden chair scrapes against the floor as I push it back with all my might.

Yet another shock greets me when I walk into the kitchen. E is sitting on the countertop, sipping some sort of amber liquid from my dad's favorite whiskey glass. A light shade of pink highlights her skin, and her long hair is in tendrils around her face. She's drunk.

"Well, look who it is," she says in a slightly slurred voice. The ice in the glass tinkles again as she takes another sip. "My very own storm cloud."

I bristle. "What do you think you're doing?"

"You forgot to mention whiskey."

"What?"

"Upstairs. My guitar, my dog, and whiskey. Now *that's* all I need."

I keep quiet while she takes yet another sip. I do feel bad about that comment I made, but I'm not about to apologize now that she's three sheets to the wind. Since I don't drink myself, my tolerance for drunks is paper-thin.

"Somebody really hates me," she says in a scared, dreamy tone. "Someone out there, right now, is pondering my death." She raises her glass in an imaginary toast. "A violent death, too, if that knife is any indication."

I take a step toward her. "All right, I think you've had enough."

I see her lip tremble for just a second before she bites it. "I know you think I'm just some dumb prima donna who craves attention, but I never asked for this."

"I know you didn't."

Her vulnerable green eyes meet mine, and the air between us moves. The seconds seem to drag by as something passes between us, as it has been more and more lately.

The unbidden thought of how beautiful she is enters my mind, but I fight against it. The last thing I want is for her to realize I think that, but she has to be feeling that vibe from me, no matter how much I try to hide it. It's hard even to admit it to myself, but damn it, it's true. And watching her sit there, her eyes filled with tears, gives me an unfamiliar urge to wrap my arms around her. What is she doing to me? Why can't I get a handle on this?

She takes another sip before continuing. "My mother died during childbirth, so all I had was my father growing up. But he wanted nothing to do with me. He made sure I ate once a day and once in a while took me to the thrift store—when my clothes got too ratty—but he never loved me. And then when I was twelve...he left."

I took a step closer. "What do you mean, he left?"

"He just left. I don't know where he went. One day I got home, and he wasn't there. He probably went to live his own life, free from the burden of his shabby child. We had some good memories together when I was really young but...he stopped loving me."

I watch her wipe an errant tear, my heart thumping.

She clears her throat. "He'd stopped paying bills on the house, and it was repossessed after about a week, so then I lived on the streets for a while. Found an old guitar in a dumpster and taught myself how to play. After about a month, someone noticed me—dirty and starving—and I was forced into foster care. Bounced around..."

She trails off and bites her lip again. "I don't want pity...I...don't even know why I'm telling you this."

I didn't know, either. Maybe because I wasn't opening up about my family. But selfishly, I wanted to hear more. "And then what?"

She takes another large gulp, hiccups, and then looks at me again. "None of the families I was assigned were lasting. I met Joe and Big at my last house, when I was seventeen. After that I took odd jobs. Waitressing mostly. I was allowed to play a gig one night...and the rest is history, I guess."

Her confession is alarming. My first thought was how much I wanted to kill her father. How could he do that? It was unthinkable. Never in a million years would I have thought that was her story. It seemed incredibly lonely. The image I had of her—the one that had been crumbling before my eyes—fell to pieces at my feet. "You made something of yourself, E. You have what you always wanted."

"No," she says, laughing sadly. "I never wanted this. I never wanted to have to hide or not be able to walk down the street. I wanted to play my music, yes. But lately, that music seems to have a mind of its own. I can't control it anymore. It just keeps getting bigger. I can't even write a damn song." She pauses for a moment and clears her throat. "Music has been my lifelong companion. And my fans...they are always there for me. They never leave...not like...not like..."

Her words trail off again, and it's then I realize how close I'm standing to her. We notice our close proximity at the same moment, because her eyes widen and she leans back. "My dad showed up out of nowhere a year ago, wanting back into my life. He told me my aunt was supposed to have taken care of me. That when he left, he thought my aunt would be coming to pick me up. Whether that's true or not, I don't know. She never came."

The fucking bastard. I swallow loudly, unsure of what to say.

"Someone wants to kill me, X," she whispers then. "Who is it?"

"I'm going to find out." The slight waver in my voice scares me. "I promise you."

She smiles sadly, as if she doesn't believe my words. I stare at her face, willing her to believe me. I feel her body tense as if she's suddenly uncomfortable, and when she tries to jump off the counter, she slips. Before I know it, my arms are around her, just as I had imagined.

I know I should let her go. I shouldn't be holding her, not even if she's drunk—especially not if she's drunk. But my upper body seems to be encased in cement, my arms unable to move.

"I'm drunk," she states, her eyes roaming my face. "And you're beautiful."

The stark statement cuts through the rapid-fire thoughts running through my head, and I let out a staccato breath. She thinks I'm beautiful? I mean, I'd never had a problem getting a woman when I wanted one, but no one had ever called me beautiful. Damn it, she shouldn't think I'm beautiful. Or at least, she shouldn't be saying it out loud. This is wrong...the situation is careening out of my control.

"E, listen—"

But before I can get the words out, her mouth's on mine.

I don't think I've ever seen someone move so quickly before, and it takes a second to get my bearings. But the slight touch of her sweet lips begins registering, and my worrisome thoughts start flying out the window as I fall into the kiss. But when the hint of whiskey reaches my nose a few seconds later, I tear myself away. What the hell is happening here? What am I doing?

"No," I tell her, backing up. "You're drunk, and you don't know what you're doing."

Her face crumples, and she hides her face in her hands. "I'm sorry. I don't know what's gotten into me."

Without another word, she runs out of the room and up the stairs. I take a moment to gather myself, overwhelmed at all the feelings churning and pumping the blood through my body. What the fuck was I thinking! Something like that can never, ever happen again. I'd lose my job and everything I've worked so hard for over the years. She isn't even my type or anyone I could entertain starting something with, despite my recent thoughts about her beauty—about her vulnerability.

I'm disgusted with myself. Mostly because, no matter how much I try to fight it, I can't deny I wanted to kiss her so bad that it hurt.

After about fifteen minutes, I pad up the stairs to find her. We have to talk about what had just happened. No doubt she's feeling awkward—at least as awkward as I am—and with the situation at hand, there's no room for any weirdness between us. E is in a lot of danger, and I won't have her hesitating to call me or reach out to me because of some kiss. I sigh loudly, determined not to allow my thoughts to picture the kiss and what could have happened.

I hear snores as I make my way down the hallway to the bedroom. Hmm. She clearly isn't as rattled as I am. Must be all that godforsaken whiskey. I'm definitely hiding the rest of the bottles—one drunken night was enough.

As expected, when I push open the door, she's fast asleep. I walk over, slip her shoes off, and give Bella's head a small pat before taking a seat in the rocking chair. I close my eyes for a few minutes, knowing I'll wake instantly at even the slightest sound.

Sleep, however, was elusive. I was incredibly unsettled. Looking through hooded eyes at her small form on the bed, I wonder for the millionth time how in the hell I found myself in this situation. Fish out of water didn't even begin to explain things. For Christ's sake, I had been dealing with terrorist threats and shady politics for nearly a decade. Every day had been a planned routine. There was structure and discipline.

And now there was so much stuff I was unsure of. I mean, I wasn't exactly hired on as a bodyguard, but it seemed that was exactly what the situation was becoming. I realized then that I couldn't walk away from this if I tried. No one was getting anywhere near her. Especially not that damn stalker.

About ten minutes later, just as I start to drift off, I hear a light buzzing sound coming from the bed. E's phone. She doesn't stir, so I stride over and pick it up to see who it is. Unknown number.

My heart starts to race as I palm the phone and exit the room as quickly as I can. If this was the stalker, he had no idea what was waiting for him on the line.

"Who is this?" I ask roughly, walking toward the stairs.

"Hello? Ellie?"

"Who is this?" I growl.

"This is Joel. Who is this? And why are you answering Ellie's phone?"

I was both relieved and disappointed it wasn't our guy. I'd done a little research after Joel's first visit to the house, and the timeline didn't match up. He couldn't have been responsible for the rock. Plus, Joel didn't fit the personality profile, despite having motive. He was too concerned with himself and was too outspoken. I was sure E's stalker was an introvert.

I grip the phone hard. "I thought I told you to get lost."

Joel sighs on the other end. "Oh, it's you. Where's Ellie? I need to speak to her. It's urgent."

"What's so urgent that you have to call her this late?"

"It's none of your business."

I roll my eyes toward the ceiling. "Fine. I'm hanging up now. Don't call again."

"*Wait!*" he shouts, just as I knew he would. "I just...I heard there was an incident at the arena today. I wanted to make sure she was OK. Especially after what happened on the red carpet."

How the hell could he have heard anything? "I have no idea what you're talking about."

"Oh, don't bullshit me. It's all over the news. 'Eloisa Morgan races out of the arena in the middle of rehearsal.' A few arena workers spilled the beans, and I have to say, the rumors of why are getting quite nasty."

"Is that all?" I reply, keeping an iron grip on my temper.

"Some say the two incidents could be related…"

"Is that all?" I repeat.

"Look," he said, voice rising. "Eloisa and I go way back, and I want to make sure she's all right! You don't get to tell me that I can't talk to her. Now give her the damn phone."

"I've been given strict orders to make sure you two have no contact."

"You can't do that! She'd never say that!"

"Now, I'm only going to tell you this one more time. Don't ever let me catch you calling this number again, or you're going to have to deal with me. And I won't be so nice next time."

I hang up the phone and slide it into my pocket. My temper sizzles as I scroll through article after article of sordid speculation about what happened today. That damn rock-and-roll asshole was right. Word had leaked that Eloisa Rae Morgan left her sound check unexpectedly, and the gossip rags were all aflutter. There is nothing about the knife or note, however, which calms me down.

I take a moment to scroll through her texts, but there doesn't seem to be anything out of the ordinary. The grandfather clock ticks the hours away as I sit deep in thought about Eloisa and our current predicament. I also think a lot about the whiskey bottle in the kitchen.

Maybe in another life I could have enjoyed a casual drink like most adults. But in this one, the thought of taking even a small sip revolts me. I don't deserve it, and I never will. Not after what it took from me.

21

Eloisa

Coming down the stairs the next morning is an exercise in self-control. In other words, I basically have to force myself. How. Embarrassing.

Unfortunately for me, I am not someone who doesn't remember things while drinking. I remember every detail of last night. Particularly vomiting the sob story of my childhood, assaulting X, and making a fool of myself. I honestly don't know what came over me. I remember feeling so low over the events of the day and everything going on. I remember the whiskey went down really easily. I remember pressing my mouth to his without any warning whatsoever. Good God. How was I going to face him?

I hear dishes clanking in the kitchen, and when I walk in, his back's to me, and a towel's thrown over his shoulder. It's strangely domestic.

"Good morning," he says without turning around. "I left some Advil on the table."

"Oh, thank you." I feel OK, but I grab the Advil anyway to avoid talking, downing it with the glass of water he left beside the pills.

I watch him divide some scrambled eggs between two plates that already hold toast and bacon. It smells delicious, so I tell him so.

He doesn't answer. Just grabs the plates and places them on the counter. I follow without a word and sit down, taking another sip of water in an effort to avoid meeting his eyes.

X apparently has other plans. He shifts in his seat on the stool so he's facing me, and there's a small tilt to his lips. "You kissed me last night."

The man clearly needs a lesson in subtlety. "I know. I'm sorry. I have no idea what I was thinking. Well, I was drunk, so clearly I wasn't."

He holds up a hand to stop me. "It's fine. I just need your word that something like that won't happen again."

That gives me pause. *OK.* "Of course it won't. I wasn't in my right mind. I would have never, ever done that otherwise. Trust me. You're not my type."

He scoops some eggs on his fork and raises a brow at my overly emphatic statement. My hackles rise. "Did you have to mention that first thing in the morning? Can't a girl eat her breakfast before facing her humiliation of the night before?"

He ignores my comment. Then to my surprise, he leans down and gives my ever-hungry dog a few scraps of food. "We have to stay here another day. There's no leads."

My stomach drops, and I place the piece of toast I'm eating back on my plate. "Nothing?"

X chews his food for a moment before answering, and I watch his strong jaw work up and down. "Nothing. But I want you to know everyone is doing everything they can. And right now, I feel safest with you here."

I sigh. "I'm on *Crenshaw* tomorrow night. I can't miss it."

X grunts. "You think a talk show is more important than your safety?"

"Of course not. But I can't let this psycho ruin my life. What if it's just some troll living under a bridge? I...I've worked too hard to get where I am. This tour means a lot to me."

I try to mask the sadness in my voice and bravely meet X's eyes when he looks over. The brown orbs roam my face, and I have a sense that he's remembering everything I told him last night.

"I'll see what I can do," he answers roughly.

"Thank you."

"So what are your plans for the day?" he asks next.

"No idea," I say, shrugging. "Trying to write my song seems useless. I've got a serious case of writer's block."

He nods, standing up and grabbing our plates to bring to the sink. His next question comes out of left field. "Do you want to see one of my favorite places? It might give you a bit of inspiration."

If I didn't know any better, I'd say the question embarrassed him. He busied himself with the dishes and didn't look at me when he asked. The thought makes me smile, and I realize that is exactly what I want to do. Not only would it give me a look into his mind, but it would get me out of this house.

"Heck yeah! I'll get my coat," I say before jumping out of my seat and running out of the kitchen.

I could have sworn I heard a small chuckle, but that was probably just my imagination.

And then there I was, trekking through the woods with X on an unseasonably brisk morning.

The trees here are impossibly green and large, and an oversize, sweet-looking bunny bounds across our path, earning a laugh from me and what I think is a smile from X.

My troubles seem to melt away under the sun, and I lose myself in not just nature, but X's company.

He's different out here, too, his face not so tight with stress and worry as it usually is. But one glance at his hunched shoulders tells me he's still carrying something around, something that's weighing heavily on his mind. I think back to the woman in the chest and wonder what possibly could have happened.

Several scenarios run through my head. Is she missing? Did she pass away? Did something terrible happen and there was nothing he could do to stop it? I knew right away a man like X would not like to feel helpless. Perhaps the memory of being unable to save her haunted him.

I peek over at him from the corner of my eye. What other secrets does this big man keep inside? Does he have anyone to confide in at all? My curiosity gets the better of me.

"It's incredible out here. How long has this place been in your family?"

He purses his lips. "My grandfather bought it back in the forties. My father had been keeping up with the place, but it looks like he hasn't been out here for a while."

The question hangs in the air, so I decide to take hold. "Oh?"

"He's sick. Cancer."

I stop short. "Oh my God. X...I'm sorry."

He nods, accepting my words as he stops beside me. "He lives in Stamford. I've been visiting him on Sundays."

So that's where he goes during his three hours off. "Is it bad...is he...?" I don't know how to phrase the morbid question and stumble to find the right words.

To my surprise, he laughs. "They shorten his timeline every time he goes to the doctor, but each time I see him, he's in better spirits than the last. In fact, he went out on a date last week."

His eyes light up, and I grasp at the happier line of conversation. "That's wonderful. He sounds like a strong-willed man, staying positive like that."

"He is. And he's happy that I'm back in Connecticut. I didn't get to see him as much when I lived in DC."

He gives me a self-deprecating smile, and I imagine my location was probably one of the main reasons he decided to take this job. I try not to let that thought sting as I begin walking again.

"He's a big fan of yours, you know."

I can't help but smile. "Really?"

X nods, a small smile on his perfectly formed lips. "He really likes your music. I think he may be a little jealous that I'm working for you."

I laugh. "How nice. Well, let him know that I appreciate him as a fan. Maybe I can meet him sometime."

"Maybe."

X cuts in front of me with a mumble about leading the way, and I let my mind wander as I trail behind. So his dad is sick...and his mom, who knows? I hold these two small nuggets of information close as we make our way silently through the thick forest.

After another ten minutes, X stops in front of me. He waves me over without looking behind him, and when I walk up and peer over his shoulder, I stop short. *Oh my God.*

I bark out a laugh. "A tree house?"

He shifts on his feet. "I remember it being a lot bigger."

I take in the old, dilapidated fortress sitting high in the tree and picture a small X peeking out of its windows. A little boy's dream. I can't resist a little teasing. "It does look like the perfect thinking place."

He gives me a sardonic smile—then walks over to touch a piece of wood that's nailed into the trunk. "My dad wouldn't let me get one of those rope ladders, so he did this instead."

I reach out and touch the wood myself in response to his comment. "So what did little Xavier Cannon think about when he was up here?"

He shrugs, shielding his eyes from the sun as he peers up at the house. "Fighting off cops and robbers, Indians and cowboys, terrorists and corrupt government officials."

"So not much has changed," I joke.

He laughs. Dear God. He laughs. The sound is rich and deep, and a thrill goes up my spine. *Holy crap.* My eyes find his lips of their own volition and linger there, observing where that wonderful sound originated. He clears his throat, and my eyes jerk to his, caught.

Luckily X doesn't mention my staring. God, he probably thinks I'm wanton. Jumping him last night and then gazing at him like a lustful schoolgirl. I push all those thoughts out of my brain, not wanting to face the truth of what is really going on.

"Well," he continues, "I was hoping I could take you up there and check it out, but that's not happening. The place hasn't really held up over the years."

I click my tongue and give him a smile. "Too bad. I was hoping for some honest-to-God tree house inspiration."

Instead of taking the joke for what it was, he looks at me seriously. "What do you think the problem is?"

I shrug. "I don't know what's wrong with me. I've never really had a problem coming up with original love songs before, but since the attack, my creative brain has gone into hiding."

X looks at me thoughtfully. "Well, you're different now. Something like that changes a person. Why don't you write about something new?"

"What do you mean?"

He crosses his arms as if uncomfortable making the suggestion. "You have a lot of love songs. Why don't you switch it up? What do you hate?"

Instead of waiting for an answer, he leaves me standing by the trunk as he makes his way back to the clearing. After a moment, I jog over to catch up with him. "Something I hate?"

He keeps his back to me, but I see his shoulders jump up and down quickly. "Yeah, but don't take my word for it. I don't know anything about songwriting."

A smile crawls across my lips as we walk in silence back toward the house. How very wrong he was.

22

Xavier

I try not to hang up on one of my contacts as he relays the bad news. Still. Nothing.

I knew I should have gone to the house myself. Clearly my team is fucking incompetent. As soon as the words enter my consciousness, I know they aren't true, and I take a deep breath to calm myself down.

If I trusted anyone else to watch over E, I would have gone to her house myself. Maybe they overlooked something. Maybe the stalker left something behind that they weren't picking up on. I pride myself on my instincts, and they haven't really failed me yet.

How could one man attack a goddamned celebrity on a red carpet without being seen, and then break into her property without leaving a fucking trace? How was it possible? Who was he?

I down a glass of water and register E's presence over my shoulder.

"Rob called," she says quietly. "He said he tried to call you first but..."

"I ignored it." I knew Rob was just going to bitch about E's schedule, and my mind wasn't in the right place to listen to him right now.

E laughs quietly. "He wants to know what the deal is for *Crenshaw*."

It had been a few hours since we'd gotten back from visiting my old tree house, and while E had been upstairs locked in a room with her guitar, I'd been coming up with a plan to make that happen for her. I knew she didn't want to miss it.

"We'll be leaving here within the hour," I say, surprising her. "I've rented a room at the Radisson. The suite on the top floor. I don't want you going back to your house right now."

Something about that sentence makes her sad. Does she want to return home? Does the thought of staying at a hotel scare her? Her big green eyes blink a few times as if clearing tears, and then she nods. "I'll start gathering my things."

I watch her walk away, damning myself that I didn't ask her what was wrong. But besides my father, I wasn't sure that I had ever asked anyone about their feelings. I didn't think I had it in me. But if that was the case, why did I feel so shitty?

After locking up the cabin, I watch in amusement as E and Sandy run toward each other like long-lost lovers. I'd decided to have her, Joe, and Big meet us here as a surprise for E—to cheer her up—after I got some final clarification on a few things in their backgrounds. I'd been 99 percent sure they were innocent, but I had to be certain. Sometimes stalkers were hidden in plain sight, after all. So here they were—hopefully they were able to follow my directions.

The two friends laughed and gripped each other tight, and when they were done, Joe swooped her up and gave her just as big of a hug. I rolled my eyes. Did he really have to hold her for that long?

I walk over and clear my throat loudly to get everyone's attention, trying to hide the annoyance on my face. How would I ever explain that? The joy from their reunion simmers down a bit at my loud interruption, and an unfamiliar thrill spirals through me when E returns to stand by my side.

"Joe, did you bring what I asked?"

He nods, shrugging off a backpack. "Michonne already had one on hand."

"Had what?" asks E, trying to see what's in his backpack. Her eyes widen when she sees the long, blond wig. "You've got to be kidding me."

Sandy wrings her hands. "We're going to use it to sneak you into the hotel. As far as we know, no one knows that you've rented out the suite. X said we don't want word of your whereabouts to get out…"

Sandy's nervous eyes meet mine. "She's right," I say. "For right now, we still want to keep your location a secret." I eye the phone clutched tightly in Sandy's hand. "So that means no social media posts."

Sandy pouts, and Joe swings a meaty arm over her shoulder, which she quickly shoves off. Those two are so odd together.

E fingers her pretty lavender locks. "But won't people get suspicious anyway when they see three large SUVs show up? They'll start snooping around, and I'm sure they'll figure it out."

I shake my head. "It will just be one SUV, as you, Sandy, and I are the only ones staying at this particular hotel. And we're going to be entering through a back door. I'm confident we can go two nights uninterrupted."

The sad look washes over E's face again, but she doesn't comment.

Sandy notices, too, and links her arm through E's. "This is all going to be figured out, Ellie. Right, X?"

I nod stiffly. "We all just have to be diligent. And I don't think I have to remind anyone to keep me informed of any little thing that seems out of the ordinary." Sandy, E, and Big nod and start walking toward the waiting SUVs. Joe hangs back, and I wait patiently for him to get what he wants to say off his chest.

"Have you thought of drawing this guy out somehow? Making it easy for him?"

I cross my arms, knowing where this is going. "You mean using E as bait."

He pales a bit. "Or a lookalike. Just…make him come out of his damn hidey-hole."

I don't have time to discuss the full stupidity of that plan, and I force myself to keep my voice light. "There are probably many men across the country right now who have a desire to harm E. That's the sick, sad reality. Some because they have sexual fetishes, some because they hate women. Whichever category our bastard falls into, we wouldn't be able to distinguish him from the crowd just yet. He needs to show us his cards first."

I walk away, vowing that I'll do everything in my power to force his fucking hand.

I stare out the front window from the passenger side of the SUV as E scrambles around in the backseat, trying to arrange her disguise.

"You make quite the blonde," Sandy jokes in response to E's grunting. "I think it's a good look for you."

"This sweat suit is two sizes too big," I hear E say. "Not to mention it's the middle of July and a little hot to be buried in this thing. That in itself will draw attention to me."

We'd just arrived at the hotel ten minutes earlier, and so far we were the only ones parked in the lot behind the building. It was a good sign, but I wasn't going to be too careful. My eyes dart around as I try to spot any sign of life. There's nothing.

Why then, did I have such a strange feeling in my stomach?

With about forty floors, the hotel was one of the largest in the state. Not only was it smack in the middle of downtown Stamford, but it was home to a popular Brazilian restaurant chain, along with a few small vendors, which made it a buzzy spot for businesspeople and revelers alike.

I chose it so E could blend in, and I was hoping for just the right amount of busy. Too many people could be a problem, and too little even more so. That must be what had me so on edge. I check my phone again, waiting for a status update from the man I had inside the building.

"Whew!" E blows out a breath from the backseat. I take a look in my rearview mirror and see that she's fanning herself. I blink twice, suppressing a small chuckle. The outfit is nearly swallowing her whole. The blond wig, however, looks flattering. Although I can't help but miss the sight of her pastel locks.

Oh, God, what's happening to me?

My phone dings. It's one of the guys from the security team.

"All clear. There's some teenagers hanging in the staircase—take her through the lobby to the elevators. Room 4040."

I turn in my seat. "Ready?"

She nods. "Should I grab my bags?"

"I'll have one of the guys do it. We're going through the lobby to elevators on the south side. Act casual."

I jump out of the car and stride around to her side, opening the door and grabbing her hand as soon as she comes out.

"What the—? X, at least loosen your grip; this looks too obvious."

I try to do as she asks, but the churning in my stomach has my grip tightening even more instead. I sense E's questioning gaze, but I ignore it. Sandy closes the door behind us, and the three of us make our way across the parking lot.

After going through a series of empty hallways, we come out into the lobby. Scanning the room, I make a mental note that nothing seems out of the ordinary. Which doesn't mean anything. Feeling eyes on me, my gaze travels to the desk, where a man in a suit is whispering to a woman behind a computer. He lifts a hand in greeting. The manager.

The guys told the staff the bare minimum. They know a celebrity is staying in a suite over the weekend, but they don't know who. Right now, I can tell he's trying to discern who E is from a distance.

I let go of E's hand. "I'm going to go speak with the manager. You two stay here."

E's admiring a large, colorful painting and nods imperceptibly.

I stride away, keeping my eyes on the manager. He straightens as he watches my approach.

"Welcome," he says when I stop at the front desk. "Your room is ready for you."

"Have my colleagues discussed the circumstances of our stay?" I know someone had, but I wanted this man to see my face as he repeated it back to me. A lot of men stronger-willed than he have wavered under my stare, so why not use it to my advantage?

He nods. "I assure you, we are most discreet here. And I will personally deliver any meals—"

"That won't be necessary," I interrupt. "I'll be coming down to get any food we may need."

The man deflates a little, and I watch his eyes look over my shoulder, so I move a couple of inches to block his view. His eyes fly to mine, and I know then my message is clear. Maybe I'm overdoing it, but I can't take chances when it comes to E's safety. That's how I was trained, and I'm not going to examine any reasoning beyond that.

"Well, please let us know how we can assist you further," he says stiffly. "We here at Radisson put the comfort of our guests above all else."

I hand him a card. "Call me immediately if you see anything or anyone suspicious."

When I walk back over to E and Sandy, they're giggling and looking at Sandy's phone. E's eyes are bright with happiness, and an unexpected warm feeling settles in my chest. That's been happening a lot more lately. I chalk it up to knowing her a bit better now, but that explanation doesn't seem to sit right.

"Elevators are this way," I say. "Sandy, your room will be connected to ours."

"We're staying in the same room?" E asks.

I throw her an incredulous look, surprised she hasn't gotten the memo by now. She mumbles something under her breath as we walk toward the elevators, and I do my best to hide a smile. A part of me still likes pushing her buttons.

Our room is pretty luxurious, and E flops on the white leather couch as soon as we get inside. Sandy scurries off to her own room to settle in.

"I have so many e-mails," E moans as she scrolls through her phone. "And Rob is going to kill me for ignoring his calls."

"I've been keeping him updated," I tell her. "He's super busy with the tour. You two can catch up later if you don't feel like calling right now."

"I was looking forward to doing this talk show," E says sadly. "It was supposed to be about promoting my tour...but now..."

Everyone would want to talk about what happened on the red carpet. Everyone would be interested to know the truth about why she ran from the arena. "It's nobody's business. Just say you don't want to talk about anything but your music. If that doesn't work, say you were feeling a little lightheaded and had to call it quits for the day. A white lie never hurt anyone. Chances are our guy will be watching for any indication that he's gotten to you."

E closes her eyes as if she is gathering strength. "But he has gotten to me."

"Don't let him. We're going to figure this out," I tell her forcefully. "We just have to be on our guard until then."

She nods, reaching up and fingering the blond wig on her head. "Can I take this off now?"

"Sure."

I watch as she peels the wig from her forehead and places it on the coffee table. Her own hair underneath tumbles down, the pretty lavender strands a bit sweaty and a few shades darker. "I'm going to take a shower."

She gets up but then pauses before the entrance to the hallway. "Are you hungry?" she asks.

I give her a quick nod. "I'll order some food. Steak sound good?"

"It sounds amazing."

I take a moment to gather myself once E disappears down the hallway. There are so many thoughts stampeding through my mind. A part of me wants to give the duty of watching E to someone else, so I can concentrate on catching the damn bastard who's stalking her. But another part of me—a part I can hardly recognize—doesn't want to let her out of my sight. It's a hidden part that's beginning to cause me extreme anxiety. I have to be honest and admit that I want to be around her because I like her, and the icing on that cake is the fact that I'm shamefully attracted to her. Attracted to not only her looks, but also her bravery. Her story.

KAYLA PARENT

    I put my head in my hands, knowing that the situation is becoming complicated and there is nothing I can do to stop it. In a way, I'm losing focus. I'm losing objectivity. And in matters of life or death, there's nothing more dangerous.

23

Eloisa

Freshly showered, I exit the hallway and see X setting up a plates on the table. Sandy is sitting in the living area on the far corner of the couch, and when I meet her eyes, she gives me a meaningful look. I try not to laugh, but it's easy to decipher what she's trying to tell me.

Sandy is definitely not comfortable around X. Understandably so. He's pretty intimidating with his black attire, closely shaved hair, and considerable muscles. However, after our stay at the cabin, he doesn't intimidate me as he once did. There's a good person in there. A person who has been hurt, yes, but one I trust.

I admire said muscles as I take a seat at the table. My phone dings a text but I ignore it, already knowing it's Michonne—again—wanting to know if X and I have "given in to our base desires" yet. It seems not everyone on my team has been wary of my new bodyguard.

"Food smells amazing," I say once X disappears into the kitchen to grab waters. "Thank you."

"Yes, thank you," Sandy says, coming over to sit down.

X passes out the water and then seats himself at the head of the table, taking a large bite out of a considerable piece of steak. He reaches down and gives Bella one of her treats as well. "You're welcome."

It's hard not to watch him eat after that. The man went after his food like he went after life—full steam ahead. He had such a sculpted, enticing jaw, and I couldn't look away from the way it was moving up and down. I eyed the stubble on his face, remembering what it felt like on my cheek. He is such an incredibly attractive man. How many hearts had that face broken?

Sandy clears her throat, making me realize I had once again been staring. If X noticed, he didn't say anything. Sandy's eyes dance a little as she wipes her mouth with a napkin. "All your wardrobe is set for the tour," she announces, breaking the silence. "And we finally were able to hire that ballerina you wanted for the second set."

That brightens my mood. "She agreed? Holy cow, that's amazing."

Sandy nods. "Everything is really coming together. The wardrobe, the lighting, the schedule, the backup singers..."

She lets the sentence trail off, and I know what she's thinking. "I started my new song. I'm going to work on it in the next couple days and hand it over to the production studio this weekend."

Her eyes pop. "That soon? I thought you had writer's block!"

"I did, until a little birdie in a tree house gave me some inspiration."

If I hadn't been watching, I wouldn't have seen his lovely jaw pause for the tiny second that it did.

"I don't know what that means, but Rob is going to flip! Can I tell him?" Sandy asks, wringing her napkin in her hands. I realize then how nervous my writer's block had made everyone on the team. Apparently they could finally put everything into place once it was done.

"You can tell him," I say, watching her shoot up from the table. "And tell him I'll talk to him tomorrow."

Sandy skips into the connecting room, and I turn my smile to X. "If you didn't get that, the little birdie was you. Thank you."

"So you're writing about something you hate?"

I nod. "In so many words."

He grabs another slice of pizza. "Well, what's it called?"

"'Loneliness.'"

X's hand pauses, and he looks at me. "I see."

A thought occurs to me, and I can't help but wonder if he'll bite. "What would yours be called?"

To my surprise, he appears to give it some thought. What looks like a sliver of pain wrinkles the skin around his eyes. "'Guilt.'"

Curiosity sizzles beneath my skin, but we both fall silent. What does he feel guilty about? Does it have to do with his mother? I want him to elaborate, but it's clear he isn't going to say anything further on the subject. Baby steps.

The tension in the air is palpable. I can only wonder if he feels the pulsing energy, too, and if it is what I think it is. Because it feels a hell of a lot like chemistry. I'm drawn to him, picturing him in ways he'd probably be furious about—if the way he reacted to my kiss was any indication.

But how could I help it? Not only was he mysterious and incredible to look at, he was the man who was keeping me safe, the one I unwittingly bared my soul to. He was the man I was entrusting with my life. The man who was allowing me to be brave and face all this. And the mystery hidden behind the depths of his eyes attracted me like a magnet.

He gets up to clear his plate, and I watch him as he makes his way around the kitchen. Was he going to turn in for the night? I wasn't remotely tired, and I could admit to myself I wasn't really ready to leave his company, either. Which is probably why the next sentence came out of my mouth without much thought. "Do you want to watch a movie?"

"Now?" he asks. He was turned away from me, washing his hands at the sink, which was a good thing because my cheeks were definitely growing hot. It feels like I just asked the man on a date.

"I'm not really tired, so I figured I'd order one..." I trail off and take a sip of my water to fill the silence.

"Sure," he responds casually. His nonchalant answer is at complete odds with what I'm feeling inside, and I can't help but feel like a dumb schoolgirl.

His phone rings, and he dries his hands before picking it up. "It's the police chief. He's going to want to talk to you."

My stomach drops. "Why?"

"They want to talk about what happened at the house. I've been warding them off, but they want to see if you know anything."

"I don't. I talked to them extensively after the attack on the red carpet, and I really have no idea who it is."

He walks into the hallway and calls to me over his shoulder. "I'll take care of it. You pick the movie."

What would I do without him? Feeling decidedly charitable, I scroll through the movies, bypassing the romantic comedies in favor of something we both might like. I wonder how he feels about horror?

Five minutes later he comes back, his face tight.

"Is everything OK?" I ask.

He sighs loudly before taking a seat on the end of the couch. I notice he's changed into sweatpants, and I wonder when our bags were brought up. He really did take care of everything. I try not to stare too hard at the outline of his legs, because they still seem impressive despite the loose fabric. "I held them off for another day, but we have to meet with them sometime in the next couple days. Hopefully, they'll have some damn leads by then."

The ever-present fear simmering beneath the surface of my skin flares to life. Why couldn't they find anything on this guy? The thought was terrifying. "Well, I don't know what I'm going to tell them."

The door to the connecting room opens, and Sandy, followed by an eager Bellatrix, comes into the room. Bella jumps on my lap, and I cuddle her close, happy for her comfort.

"Rob is over the moon," she says happily, taking a seat beside me. "That missing song was the final piece."

All the relief I should have felt is overshadowed by bubbling fear. I try not to let it show on my face. "We're going to watch a movie," I say instead. "Everyone good with scary?"

Sandy makes a face. "Really? Can't we watch a comedy or something?"

"Horror is a better reflection of my mood these days," I half joke. I pull up the latest zombie thriller and raise a brow at my companions. "What do you think?"

"Looks good to me," says X, leaning back into the couch. His quiet solidarity makes me feel as if he understands my mood.

Sandy shrugs but ultimately settles in as I press "Play."

I've always had a thing for scary movies. I used to watch them in slight awe, a fascination born from being on the outside looking in at something terrible. But it felt different this time. Was I in my own horror movie? Was my ending going to be just as tragic?

Sandy makes it about half an hour in before tapping out. She gets a text and then stands quickly, her face red. "I'll see you two in the morning. I think if I watch any more, I'll have nightmares."

"Chicken," I tease. I wonder for a moment whether she's leaving because of the movie or because of the text she just got, but I don't say anything.

And then it was just X and I. I was getting used to the tension between us. I just couldn't decide if I was the only one feeling it, and it made me feel a little out of balance. The urge to stare at his strong jaw, built-for-sin legs, and powerful upper body was overwhelming.

Apparently I'm not the only one drawn to him, because Bellatrix jumps off my lap, trots over to the other couch, and crawls into his. The old traitor.

"Where is the loyalty?" I joke.

X shakes his head in resignation and pulls Bella into a more comfortable position. When he reaches out to stroke her head, I nearly melt into the couch. There's just something about a sexy man and a small dog. "What can I say? The women love me."

Was that a joke? I laugh more out of shock than anything. My heart skips a beat when I catch the boyish sparkle in his eyes. Latching on to the subject, I stretch out my feet to rest them on the coffee table. "Is that so?"

He looks as if he wants to take back his statement, but he responds quickly. "I was kidding, E."

"Somehow I doubt that." A sharp look is thrown my way as if to scold me, but I don't regret what I said. From the beginning, I've been wanting to push this man's buttons, wanting to get under his outer shell. And what did I get for my efforts? A goddamned crush. I feel it as I stare at him now, along with the desire to push him more. "What did I say? Why do you look uncomfortable now?"

"I'm not."

"You definitely are. But what's so wrong about what I said? You're a good-looking man, X. You must have women all over you."

His eyes flash. "Drop it, E."

"Can I just ask one question?" I plead. "Just one, I promise."

He rolls his eyes but doesn't say no, so my heart does a little victory dance. "When do you have time for women? I know you don't have a girlfriend or anything, but you seem to work...a lot."

"I'm not talking to you about my sex life. That's incredibly inappropriate."

I pout, and then inspiration strikes. "Mine is nonexistent at the moment," I share suddenly, shocking both him and me. "I haven't had sex in over a year."

He pauses in the motion of petting Bella and gives me a piercing look that nearly sets me aflame. He mulls over that statement for a while—long enough for embarrassment to creep in. He must think I'm such a loser! I have to redeem myself. "I just...haven't really had the opportunity, getting ready for the tour and all. And there's no one...there hasn't been...no one's been..."

"No one's been what?" he asks quietly.

I shrug. "Interested."

He gives me a look. "Somehow I doubt that," he replies, throwing my earlier words back at me.

Wait a second. Did he just admit he thought I was good-looking? I can't help my shit-eating grin, and I'm unable to form another sentence because I'm so pleased, but luckily he just returns my smile before turning toward the TV.

It doesn't escape my notice that he avoided my question. I doubt I'll ever figure out this man. But I know one thing: he thinks I'm attractive. I fall asleep a little while later with a smile on my lips, comforted by the thought.

24

Xavier

I'm a little surprised to see the credits roll, because I barely watched the movie. After E fell asleep, I shamefully hadn't been able to keep my eyes off her. I watched her now, mouth slightly open, curled up in a little ball against the large cushions.

To say that she shocked me with her earlier statement about sex was an understatement. That she would share something so intimate with me brought our relationship to a new level. Were we friends? I couldn't be her friend; I was her employee. Trusted to guard and protect her. Whatever this was, it was heading into territory I wasn't comfortable with. There was chemistry between us, and both she and I knew it.

But fuck if I knew how to stop it.

I can't help but think about how much I'd misjudged her. She's not a typical celebrity. She's a girl with a dream who had a tough life and made it big strictly off her own talent. She'd endured so much hardship and had clearly never coveted a life of fame…at least not one like this.

As quietly as I can, I get up and walk over to her couch, Bella trotting behind me. Scooping E into my arms, I carry her into the master bedroom, trying to ignore how warm and feminine she feels in my arms—how good she smells. I roll down the bed covers with one arm and place her gently under. I linger a bit, tucking her in and making sure she's comfortable—then force myself to leave.

I walk into the spare bedroom, which is right beside the master, and climb into bed myself, my stomach in knots. I haven't felt like this, so drawn to someone, in years—if ever.

What the hell was I going to do?

I get up early the next morning and shower quickly, wanting to get a few things done before the girls wake up. After grabbing breakfast from downstairs, I call our driver for a scope on the situation outside. He confirms that all seems normal, and I breathe a sigh of relief. No one knows she's here. We go over our plan for the day, and the doorbell rings just as I'm throwing Bella a bit of food.

I tense, even though I know who is on the other side. Bella barks happily at the door as if she knows, too.

"What is this I hear about a wig?" Jacques demands as he storms inside the room. "What am I supposed to do with her hair for the show? It will get ruined under that thing!"

"Nice suite," Michonne says as she glances around. "Where's Ellie?"

I cross my arms. "Still asleep." I ignore Jacques's question, and he throws me a nasty look.

At that moment the connecting door opens, and Sandy bounds through, clearly excited to see her fellow team members. "You two are early!"

"We couldn't wait to see Ellie," Michonne replies before turning to me. "I understand why you're doing what you're doing, though. The thought of everything that's happening makes me sick to my stomach. I'm glad you're keeping our girl as safe as possible."

Our girl. The phrase makes me distinctly uncomfortable, but it doesn't feel wrong.

Jacques clears his throat. "Yes, we all appreciate it! But can we do without the wig? Please? I had the perfect hairstyle for *Crenshaw*, and a wig will ruin it!"

"Wig stays on when she goes in and out of this hotel," I say, making sure my voice leaves no room for argument. "We leave in three hours."

I head back to the spare room to make a few calls as the three of them scurry off to E's bedroom.

I use the time they're getting ready to clean my guns. I haven't taken them out in front of E before, and I'm not going to start now. As I look down the barrel, I hope that I won't have to use them.

A couple of hours later I hear the door open, followed by excited voices coming down the hallway. I come out from the kitchen, hoping everyone is ready to get going, and nearly lose my breath. E is wearing a light-green summer dress that softly hugs her curves, and she walks in a pair of nude heels. Her lavender locks are piled on her head in a messy, just-got-out-of-bed look, and her lightly colored lips make her natural pout all the more enticing. Holy God, she's stunning. My throat feels dry, and I work hard to tamp down the image of her wet and dripping in the shower.

I notice then that she's trying not to meet my eyes, as if she's nervous about my reaction. I have no idea what to say to ease her mind, so I settle for a quick nod in Sandy's direction. "Ready?"

Jacques gives me a condescending stare. "As you can see, she has yet to put on that damn wig. Luckily, I bobby pinned the crap out of her hair, so it should stay in place while she runs to the car."

I watch as he picks up said wig from the counter and places it carefully on her head. E laughs as Sandy, Michonne, and Jacques fidget with it around her. "It's just for a second. I'll be fine."

I go to the hall closet and pull out a long trench I ordered from downstairs. "Wear this."

E stares at it. "What for?"

I look her up and down. "To hide your body. Your fans can recognize you in more ways than one."

"That's a little creepy," is her mumbled reply.

Michonne cackles in glee. "It's your ass, Ellie. You could balance a coffee mug on that thing."

I stare at her face, not daring to look down at the aforementioned body part as the rest of the room is doing. A soft blush lights her cheeks, and I wonder if she can hear how fast my heart is beating. I don't think I've ever been this attracted to a woman before. I need to get myself together—and fast.

We leave the hotel—E in all her gear—without trouble and get to New York in a little over an hour. We have some time before the show, so we do a little sightseeing in Central Park. I sip my coffee, keeping an eye out for anything unusual as I watch Sandy and E take in the scenery. I notice some people starting to stare, so I hustle everyone back to the car.

"I wouldn't mind staying to sign a few autographs," E says testily. "It's safe here; I'm out in the open."

"It's not safe anywhere," I warn her. "And there's only one of me. The last thing we need is a mob scene in Central Park." I know meeting and greeting her fans means a lot to her, but I'm still not going to take any chances.

She pouts a little, but ever since the note on her door, I haven't had much resistance from her. I picture her fiery face coming toward me on the front lawn the first couple of days and marvel at how much has changed since then.

"Are you going to talk about the stalker?" Sandy asks nervously from the backseat. "The general news media has no idea what's going, on but there have been some rumors."

"No," I reply, cutting E off. "You're not to talk about the stalker at all. He's going to be watching tonight and is hoping for a scrap of your attention. We aren't going to give it to him."

E bites her lip. "But shouldn't I try to warn him off? Or try to trap him somehow? Maybe say we have a lead on who he is?"

"No," I tell her sternly. "A man like this doesn't think the way you or I do. Anything you say about him would seem like validation. He'll twist your words in his mind until he hears what he wants."

"Wow," Sandy whispers. "And you're sure he's going to be watching?"

I nodded. "I am."

The car becomes quiet after that, and nothing else is said until we pull up in front of the studio. I curse under my breath when I see the large crowd of reporters and fans.

"Hide the wig," I tell her. "And let me get out first."

When the car comes to a stop, I step out and quickly go to E's door. The cacophony of sounds is deafening. Reporters and fans screaming her name, cameras going off, and studio security yelling for everyone to keep back. I block it all out, focusing on my route to the door.

Once the car door opens, I grasp her hand lightly, as if I have no care in the world. Her palm is soft in my hand, but I can feel a bit of pressure. She's nervous. I turn to lock eyes with Joe and Big, who are waiting by the large double doors, before I begin to push through the crowd.

E looks up and smiles as if she also doesn't have a care in the world. She waves to a couple of cameras as we walk past but thankfully doesn't stop to answer any of their questions. She's better at this than I gave her credit for.

"Eloisa, is it true your ex-boyfriend Joel is being questioned for the incident on the red carpet?"

"Eloisa, who is your new bodyguard?"

"Why did you run out of the stadium a couple of days ago?"

"Is your tour canceled?"

"Eloisa, where have you been the past couple of days?"

We make it to the double doors and race inside, shutting out the noise with a loud bang.

"Whew!" Sandy says. "Did you see how many people are out there? It's never been like that before, has it?"

Joe walks over to us and grins. "Ellie, I think we can officially say you're on the A-list."

E frowns. "Did you hear the questions they were asking? Is Joel really a suspect?"

Sandy shakes her head. "No. I haven't read that anywhere. They're just looking for a story."

ONE-WOMAN SHOW

"I'd rather have them think that than get wind of the real one," E says, looking up at me and remembering my comments from the car. It's then that I realize I'm still holding her hand, so I promptly let it go.

She locks eyes with me, and I can't help but wonder if her hand feels as empty as mine does now.

We're interrupted by a harried-looking woman with a clipboard. "Eloisa, we're so happy you're here!" she says. "Would you mind following me? Your room is ready for you."

And so it begins. A whirlwind of producers, assistants, makeup artists, and stylists file in and out of the room as if E is getting ready to put on the show of the century. And in between all of that, she practices scales to warm up her voice for the performance. I don't know how she does it. I'm agitated just standing there and watching. Then Johnny Crenshaw himself walks in, looking as jolly and professional as he does on TV. "Eloisa! You're a sight for sore eyes! How is this the first time you're on my show?"

They launch into a lively discussion after that, and even I laugh a few times at their back-and-forth banter. He leaves after telling E he has a surprise for her, and then the team is alone again.

"This is so exciting!" Sandy exclaims, staring at her phone. "Your picture with Johnny already has eleven thousand likes!"

E laughs. "The likes are probably for him, not me!"

How wrong she is. She's a beautiful woman, inside and out.

Near showtime, we walk toward the back, where E has to stand until she's called out. Sandy and the rest of the crew have gone to sit in the audience, so it's just her and me. I watch again as she bites that tempting bottom lip.

"Nervous?" I ask.

She nods. "Very. I don't think I'll ever get used to this part. I wish I was just going out there to play my song, and that's it. Then this would be easy."

"Music calms the soul," I muse quietly.

She turns to me with a thoughtful expression. "What's your favorite song, X? Of all time."

I debate telling her the truth, but for some reason I'm unable to help myself. "'Bridge Over Troubled Water.'"

Her eyes soften. "That's a beautiful song."

"I used to listen to the Simon and Garfunkel version before I went to sleep."

She moves in closer, her grin a mile wide. "Is that so?" I smile back, and there's a moment of silence before she turns to me again. "I like that I know that about you."

Looking down at her smiling up at me, the overwhelming urge to kiss her nearly blows me over. That chemistry between us sparks and sizzles until I forget where I am. I feel myself move closer. It's only her and me, lost in a hazy world of possibility.

"E, Johnny's ready for you now. Can you come with me?"

The loud, intrusive words nearly have me jumping out of my skin. Goddamn it! I was so far gone, and by the looks of it, so was she. What was I thinking? She's counting on me to keep her safe, and I'm behaving like a horny teenager.

We take a step back from each other, and without another word, she disappears behind the curtain. I see her put a hand on her chest as if to calm her breathing, and I can't help but wonder if her nerves are due to the show or if she feels what I just did.

25

Eloisa

I had about ten seconds until Johnny was going to call me to walk out. That meant I had about ten seconds to catch my breath and somehow pull myself together.

That moment with X was real. I know it was. There's something between us, and I can no longer brush it aside.

There's just something about him that touches me somewhere deep inside. Something about his tough exterior that makes me feel safe while at the same time luring me in with something so much softer underneath. So far I've gotten sneak peeks of his boyish grin, hearty laugh… and, sadly enough, his deep pain.

But what can I do about it? Nothing can happen between us. He's my employee. Not to mention he's only sticking around because there's a psycho after me.

As my entrance music blares through the speakers, I shake off my thoughts and paste a bright smile on my face. Everything after that happens in a blur. The audience members screaming and jumping. Me waving and laughing as I walk to my chair. All of it so surreal.

I think of X's words. *He's watching.*

I embrace Johnny in a strong hug as if we're old friends and laugh at a few of his opening jokes as I take my seat.

"Eloisa, I feel like you came out of nowhere! And now you're about to embark on the most anticipated tour of the year. To what do you attribute your superstardom?"

I take a deep breath. "To be honest, I don't really feel like a celebrity. I followed the music, and I was lucky enough for it to bring me here, where I am today. I know how blessed I am. But otherwise, I'm just along for the ride."

"Uh-huh. I've heard you're considered to be pretty elusive by the industry…"

I laugh. "I wouldn't say that. I just like doing my own thing. My creative freedom means a lot to me."

"I can understand. I lost mine years ago!"

The audience erupts in laughter, and I force myself to do the same.

"Now, let me ask you this," he continues. "What comes to mind when you hear the name Martha Mathers?"

Of course. The snub. I knew it was coming, but it still leaves a bad taste in my mouth. "Honestly, nothing really comes to mind. I know she's had a lot of success in her career, and I wish her the best."

"I hate to bring this up, but she hasn't had the best things to say about you."

I shrug. "I haven't paid attention."

Johnny laughs. "I can understand that, too! Have you seen her recently?"

"Not lately, no."

"Well, you're in for a surprise, because she actually called us last night and demanded we let her on the show!"

My stomach drops. "What?"

Before I can fully understand his meaning, the woman herself comes strutting out from behind the curtain. She looks like the devil wearing Prada incarnate. Flawless in her beauty, she has sleek, shoulder-length white hair and is wearing a bold, formfitting cerulean power suit. She looks nowhere near the fifty-nine I know her to be.

She also has a sickly sweet smile on her face that I'm sure matches mine. It looks as if she was coming right for me, and sure enough, her thin, pale fingers gently touch my shoulder as she air-kisses both of my cheeks.

After that awkward moment, we both sit down and look to Johnny for some sort of direction. I can't believe they would paint me into a corner like this. The woman whom I had so heartily offended by refusing to work with her.

"Great to have you back, Martha," Johnny starts, folding his hands on his desk. "And I have to say, you look incredible!"

"Thank you, Johnny," Martha says with a titter, reaching up to pat her hair. "You really do know how to flatter a lady."

"Don't tell my wife that," Johnny jokes, causing the audience to laugh again. It's all I can do not to roll my eyes. I can't believe this is the same man I met backstage.

"Anyway, anyway," Johnny continues, catching his breath. "Martha, I hear you've got tickets to Eloisa's first show?"

"I do," Martha confirms. "I have to see what all the fuss is about, of course."

I smile politely, trying to keep my cool. "Well, I hope you enjoy the show. It will be an honor to have you watching."

She accepts the compliment with a nod. "Although, I hope the tour is still on?"

Oh, no. She had clearly been reading the news and heard about my hasty exit. I decide to play dumb. "Why wouldn't it be?"

Her eyes narrow. "Well, you've seen the news, of course. Everyone is quite concerned about what happened at the arena in Hartford."

Johnny leans in. "Well, now that you brought it up. What happened, Eloisa?"

"Yes, what happened?" Martha croons nastily, her heeled foot bouncing up and down. "You've had quite a time of it lately. The red carpet incident—then this?"

I pause, unsure of what to say. I can't tell the truth—it would put the whole investigation at risk. An idea sneaks in, and I decide to go with it. "Stomach bug. I thought I was going to lose my lunch all over the stage."

Martha frowns. "Stomach bug?"

"That's all there is to it," I explain. "After getting home I had a bit of water, and now I feel much better."

"Hmm." Martha hums from beside me.

I can tell she doesn't believe me, but I don't care. The woman is out for blood, and I'm not going to offer a vein. "As we all know, the media is often full of fake news."

After that first blow, the rest of the conversation goes a lot smoother. I was able to combat any and all subtle blows that were thrown my way by both Johnny and Martha. I was a little surprised Martha kept her claws sheathed for the most part.

My performance also went off without a hitch. I chose a light, poppy song off my album, and the audience seemed to love it. I lost myself in the words, words that I remembered writing while sitting by the ocean at my house. This is why I did this. Nothing else in the world made me as happy as sharing my music. Hoping that I was making a difference in someone's world would also be my motivation, as music had done exactly that for me.

Midway through the song, I take a moment to glance at the crowd. A guy about my age was staring at me in what looked like adoration. Could it be him? Technically it could be anyone in this crowd. I had no idea. A shot of fear pierces my gut at the same time that a girl rests her head on his shoulder, both of them clearly enjoying the song. I let out a deep breath, relieved.

There's another girl in the audience who catches my attention. She has a large bow in her hair, and she's swaying her head to the beat as if transfixed. Somewhere a little behind her there's a child in her mother's arms, clapping along and smiling in my direction.

My fans. This is why I did this. I had to remember that.

When I finish, Johnny and the entire audience give me a standing ovation. Martha, to her credit, does clap lightly, but I see the tightness around her mouth as she stares at me. Why did that woman hate me? It's like no one had ever told her no before.

After the show, I walk backstage thinking, all in all, I got off pretty lucky. Hopefully, I had squashed all the rumors circulating about my abrupt exit from the arena and settled any lingering questions about Martha and me. No, we would never be best friends, and I sure as hell would never work with her, but we could be in the same room and be cordial. Maybe all the press would go back to normal and focus on my music and upcoming tour instead of all the manufactured drama.

I should have known better.

As X, Sandy, and I are leaving through the back door, I hear Martha call my name. I turn just in time to see the evil glare on her face change into an expression of detachment.

"Eloisa, I'm glad I caught you," she says, a little out of breath. She turns to look at X. "Fetch me a glass of water, please. My Evian is in that room just there."

My hackles rise, and I suddenly want to claw her eyes out. How fucking dare she talk to him like that? Like he was nothing but hired help to aid us "important" people through life. When I turn my angry eyes to X, I notice he looks perfectly composed, as if her order didn't bother him one bit. He raises a brow in my direction, probably at the severity of the emotion showing on my face. It's also clear he doesn't plan on going to fetch the woman any water. I take a deep breath. "Martha, we're all on our way out. Is there something you wanted?"

She sniffs lightly in X's direction when he doesn't move, and as I knew she would, Sandy scurries off in the direction of the dressing room after a few more tense moments. I'd have to talk to that girl about dealing with awkward silences.

"There is something," Martha begins. "Look, I know we got off on the wrong foot. That's regrettable. However, I am willing to forgive any past transgressions between us…if…well, I assume you've heard about Cher Kahn?"

Of course I had. Martha had just signed the most naturally talented emcee and DJ that I and the country had ever had the pleasure of hearing. He was incredibly creative and totally progressive in his approach to harmonizing. Secretly, I was dying to work with him. "I heard you scooped him up, yes. Congratulations. He's one of a kind."

"Yes," Martha says proudly. "And he's expressed an interest in working with you."

My palms literally begin to sweat. "Really?"

"Indeed. He's got some beats laid out he wants you to hear. Shall I tell him you'll be by the studio?"

Her studio, she meant. She was asking me to work with her...again. Maybe. *Maybe* I would have considered it if she hadn't just treated X like scum on the bottom of her shoe. Sure, she and I could make a hit record together. And with Cher Kahn involved, I'm sure it would be the hit of the summer. But I'm making hit music on my own, and I don't need someone like her. "Not just yet," I tell her, hedging. "I'll call you."

The beast's eyes flare, and her hands fly to her hips as if getting ready to scold me like a child. Everyone knew *I'll call you* was the industry signal for *fuck off*. "Eloisa, I'm confused. I'm offering you the opportunity of a lifetime here."

"I'm just not interested at this time," I say, moving to X's side. I hope he realizes that means I am ready to go. "Look, I need to run..."

"Don't you dare walk out on my offer again," she bites out, taking a few steps toward me. "I can end your career before it really begins!"

I back up into the double doors, more nervous than I should be. One door pops open slightly just as X moves in between us. "Hey, back off," he growls at Martha, pulling me into his side. I stumble on the doorstop, but X catches me instantly. He tries to close the door again, but it's too late.

Cameras start going off, catching me off guard. I know what it must look like. Me hiding in X's arms with Martha glaring at us.

"Shit," X curses under his breath. He tucks me in securely as we take off toward a waiting SUV. I hear Sandy run up behind us, and we jump into the car and manage to speed away fairly quickly.

"What a bitch!" Sandy cries angrily from the backseat. "I'm so glad you told her no."

I watch the reporters and journalists get smaller and smaller in the rearview mirror. "I wouldn't work with that woman if my career depended on it," I answer quietly, trying to get my breath after what had just happened. Did I think she was going to attack me? No. I'm clearly just on edge these days because of everything that's going on.

X is typing furiously on his phone. What has him so agitated? His strong jaw's locked tight, and his leg's bouncing up and down.

"What is it?" I ask nervously. "Did something happen?"

"I got her water like a little chump, that's what happened!" Sandy says, her voice full of anger.

I sigh, turning away from X, who doesn't seem like he's going to acknowledge my question. "Don't be too hard on yourself. She is Martha Mathers, after all."

"I don't care who she is," Sandy says with a pout. "And after the way she came after you on the show? I should have let her get her own damn water."

"Don't let it bother you," I say. "I'm not." I'm more concerned about why X is so upset.

I toe my heels off and put my feet up on the large seat. What a day. All I want to do is go back to my hotel room and watch another movie, preferably with X. Oh, God. With all the commotion, I'd almost forgotten what happened between us backstage. That was something else I'd have to deal with.

He's still typing on his phone, his eyes hidden behind a pair of black sunglasses.

"What happened?" I ask again, this time determined to get an answer.

He puts his phone down. "I'm texting Joe and Big, hoping they can stop the cameramen from releasing any of the photos they got."

"Why? I don't care if they have photos of me and Martha. If they think we're still arguing, fine. I couldn't honestly care less."

"That's not what I'm worried about," he replies, looking exhausted.

"Well, what are you worried about?"

As if on cue, Sandy gasps from the backseat. "Perez Hilton just uploaded a photo of you!"

X picks up his phone and starts typing as I turn around. "Of what just happened? It hasn't even been ten minutes!"

She shakes her head. "You know how fast the media works these days. You won't believe the headline! 'Is Eloisa Rae Morgan having an affair with her bodyguard?'"

My mouth drops open, and I snatch the phone from her. "No way."

Sure enough, the photo isn't centered around Martha and me; it's centered on me and X. My arms are around him, and my face is tilted up, looking at him in adoration. I remember that moment. At the time I was just looking to him to follow his lead. There are already tons of comments:

> *Holy sh*t that man is fine!*
> *Thank GOD she didn't go crawling back to Joel!*
> *Aw, I'm happy for her.*

My goodness. The media would seriously do anything for a story. I mean, I guess it could have been worse. And this was almost better than them harping on the story about Martha and me.

But when I turn to X, he looks furious.

I blink, confused by his expression. "What is it?"

"That damn story," he growls. "This is the worst possible thing that could have happened."

His words sting, and I bristle, crossing my arms over my chest. "I'm sorry that rumor is so distasteful to you."

He finally puts his phone down and turns to look at me. "What are you talking about?"

"Clearly you're salty because you don't want to appear as if we're romantically connected!"

"Salty? What does that mean?"

"You've been agitated since we got into this car," I tell him, unable to help myself from leaning in. "And now you look angrier than I've ever seen you."

"Because I was afraid this would happen," he snaps back. "Your stalker is going to see those photos—a photo of you connected to another man—and lose his shit."

Sandy gasps again, and the car falls silent.

"I didn't think of it that way," I say quietly.

"It may be a trigger for him. It may set him off. I was texting Joe and Big, hoping they could prevent what I knew would look like racy photos from getting out, but we were too late."

Sandy shrugs. "But even if it is a trigger, Ellie is safe. No one knows she's at the hotel. And no one can get to her—not with you around, anyway."

"We're not safe until he's behind bars," X says, looking out the window. "We can't let our guard down."

Sandy reaches into her bag and begins organizing her things, something I know she only does when she's nervous. I eye the blond wig, waiting for me on the floor, and sigh inwardly. When would this be over? I don't know how much more I can take. I feel a flare of anger take hold.

"Well, then let him lose his shit!" I shout. "He doesn't own me! I'm tired of making decisions to combat his craziness. If I want to date my bodyguard, I will damn well date my bodyguard!"

Even behind his sunglasses, I can tell X's eyes go wide at my words. I hear a small giggle from the backseat, and even the driver turns around and smiles. Embarrassment creeps in over the anger, but I try to mask it. "Why are you all looking at me like I'm crazy?"

"We're not. I support whatever you want to do. In fact, I think you and X would make a great couple." Sandy catches my eyes in the rearview mirror, and I glare at her. Way to make things awkward! The little traitor.

X's lips twitch when he looks at me, and I wonder if it's because my cheeks are turning bright red, per usual. "You know what I meant," I say. "I'm tired of letting this guy run my life."

"I know, E," Sandy replies, smothering a smile. "I was just kidding."

X runs a hand over his short-cropped hair and blows out a breath. "I know things must feel suffocating. It's been a long few days, but we have to make sure we stay two steps ahead of him at all times."

"Well, Sandy was right. He has no idea where I am, and I'm not afraid of him when I've got you."

The words feel good coming out of my mouth, mostly because they're true. I do feel safe with X. He started out as a huge—pun intended—abrasive annoyance in my life, but he turned into my lifeline. My face in that picture says it all.

As we ride back to Connecticut, several more articles go up with photos of X and me. Different angles, but same story. Eloisa Rae Morgan is officially rumored to be having a scandalous affair with her bodyguard.

I briefly think of Joel, and for the first time since we broke up, I feel a sense of peace. How could I ever have dated a man like him for so long? He wasn't my type at all. My eyes are drawn to X and his incredibly handsome face. He could have been a movie star with those looks. But here he was following after me.

I shove the wig on my head when we pull up to the hotel. We reach the back door without any problems, and once we get to the room, I flop on the couch, kicking off my heels. Bellatrix jumps on my lap, and I cuddle her close. Poor thing has probably been so lonely by herself in this unfamiliar place.

Sandy sits on the couch beside me, and X disappears into his bedroom.

"I can't believe you said that!" I hiss, referencing Sandy's comment about X and me in the car. "I've never been so embarrassed in all my life!"

Her eyes twinkle. "What? It's true. X is hot. You're hot. You would make a great couple. Don't tell me you haven't thought about it."

I decide not to lie. "I...sort of." She squeals, and I throw a pillow at her. "Be quiet! He'll hear you."

"Once this whole stalker thing is finished, I think you should go for it," she whispers.

"Um, you're forgetting something," I deadpan. "He's completely, one hundred percent not into me."

"Bullshit. Everyone is into you."

I roll my eyes. "They're not, and him especially. He's too hung up on being my employee." I tell her briefly about my drunken attack on him back at his cabin, and her eyes brighten.

"I bet he really wanted to kiss you but felt he couldn't. I bet that's what happened."

"Either way," I tell her, "I doubt it will go anywhere from here."

Which is depressing because of my crush, but I keep that thought to myself. I do, however, tell her about a couple of more humiliating incidents: X walking in on me in the shower; me revealing I haven't had sex in over a year.

She falls into a fit of giggles. "I think you like him, Ellie."

I sigh, not really wanting to say it out loud.

She leans in to pet Bella. "It's nice, you know. To see your attention directed elsewhere. Joel is such a dingbat. If we never see him again, it would be too soon."

I can't help but agree. "I thought the same thing myself in the car. It's weird I haven't heard from him, though. There's never been this much radio silence."

Sandy shrugs. "Let's just count it as a blessing."

I feel my stomach growl. "I'm starving. I wish we could go to Athens Restaurant."

"Why can't we?"

"I doubt X will let us leave the hotel."

"Not tonight."

His voice makes us both jump. He's standing over the couch, his face showing a hint of regret. "If the story about us having an affair dies down in the next couple of days, we can go. But we need to keep a low profile right now."

Bella, at the sight of X, jumps out of my arms and into his. She definitely likes him more than me.

X catches her effortlessly, as if her jumping into his arms is no big deal, and walks toward the phone. "What do you guys want?"

We end up ordering over a hundred dollars' worth of food. And it isn't just X with the large appetite. After all the drama of the day, I'm ready to feast. We order a chicken parm dish, a penne vodka dish, two Caesar salads, and a couple of appetizers with the intent to share. I also order a large bowl of chocolate ice cream for dessert. My number-one weakness in life.

When I used to do the fan brunches at my house, someone always brought a gift of chocolate ice cream. It was a well-known tradition. Everyone knew it was my favorite. I thought of those fan brunches and hoped they weren't a thing of past. I knew X would never allow one now. The thought was depressing.

X and I set up the table while Sandy kept us updated with what was going on with social media. Apparently there are some very unhappy reactions to the news that X and I are "dating."

"Can you catalog anyone that seems especially angry?" X asks as he makes his way to the door. "You never know."

Sandy nods and gives him a small wave as he leaves to get the food. "I think we need to put up another neutral picture of you—calm everyone down. They really loved the one we took in the lobby here."

"We'll take another one after dinner," I agree. "Maybe something that focuses on the performance today. I really want to bring it back to the music."

"Deal."

X returns a few minutes later with the food, and we all inhale it, exhausted from the long day. I can't wait to dig into that ice cream, so I grab it from the fridge when we're finished and walk over to the couch to enjoy it in full relaxation mode.

I put my spoon in and take my first delectable bite. Delicious. It isn't until my second bite that I begin to choke.

26

Xavier

I'm looking at my phone when E starts gagging. Sandy and I both look over in alarm and see that she'd dropped the ice cream all over the floor.

I run over to the couch, ready to pound her on the back if need be. But then...time seems to slow. I watch in horror as she puts two fingers inside her mouth and pulls a clump of God knows what from her throat, still gagging. What the fuck?

Sandy screams as the clump of something chocolate-covered drops on the couch. E runs out of the room, hand over her mouth.

I run around the couch and look closer at the clump, my heart seizing in my chest. Bellatrix is barking and goes for it, but Sandy scoops the little dog up and runs to follow E. I bend down to get a closer look, and my fears are confirmed.

A clump of hair. Blond hair. I grab the ice cream dish, and my hand touches a piece of paper. Taped to the bottom is a note with one word.

Bitch.

Anger and fear war inside me, and I just stop myself from smashing the bowl against the wall into a million pieces. The fucker is on a different level. How was he able to do this? How did he know where E was staying? How did he know about the blond wig?

I run into the bathroom, where E is currently throwing up her dinner into the toilet.

"Was that hair?" Sandy's shouting, her free hand rubbing E's back. "Tell me it wasn't hair!"

"Let's pack our bags," I say, my voice somehow staying level.

E, white as a ghost, turns her eyes to mine. "Why was there hair?" she chokes out. "Did someone...is it a joke...a mistake?"

"It wasn't a mistake. There was a note."

I have no desire to keep the truth from either of them, and both catch on to my meaning immediately. E's eyes fill with tears, and Sandy's hand flies to her mouth.

"How...?" E whispers, heavy tears dropping from both eyes.

Guilt pumps through my system, but I try to drown it out with reason. "I have no fucking idea. He must have followed us here and seen us enter the building."

E empties her stomach again, and I race back into the living room to grab my phone. I call the FBI immediately to update them on the situation, and then I call the local police. Then I get Joe and Big on the line.

"What the fuck!" Joe shouts. "Hair?"

"Human hair?" I hear Big demand from the background.

"I don't think so," I say, examining it again. "It looks synthetic. I think it's a nod to the wig she's been wearing."

"Fuck," Joe hisses. "This is bad. Do you think it's the same guy?"

"I do."

"How the hell was he able to get that into her food?"

"That's what I need you two for. Get here as soon as you can to meet the police. Somehow he got into the fucking kitchens, and I want to know how. Then I want camera footage pulled and sent to my phone." My heart's thumping angrily in my throat. It's almost hard for me to catch my breath, but I need to stay calm for the girls. "I'm getting her out of here, so I need you two to watch over Sandy, too."

"Roger that."

The phone goes silent for a second, and a question that's been plaguing me from the beginning slips out. "How did he know? How did he know the ice cream was for her?"

"Everyone knows Ellie loves chocolate ice cream," Joe answers sadly. "It's her thing. He probably assumed and got lucky."

I hang up with them a few minutes later, desperate for answers. I think back to when I got the food from downstairs, but the manager was only too happy to hand it to me. I want to go down to the kitchens myself and take all their heads off, but there's no fucking way I'm leaving E's side.

I walk back toward the bathroom and find E leaning up against the tub, her arms around her legs. Sandy and Bellatrix are both pacing the floor.

"I'm really scared," Sandy says, her small frame shaking. "How is this possible? How did this happen? He's fucking crazy!"

I give her a look and have her follow me out into the hallway. "We need to stay calm for E," I tell her. "I need you to take a few deep breaths and relax. Can you do that for me?"

She nods and swallows loudly. "Are we really leaving? Should I go pack our bags?"

"Yes," I tell her. "I want to leave within the hour."

She picks up Bellatrix and disappears into the master bedroom. Once she's gone, I put my head on the wall and take a deep breath, trying to gather myself before facing E. Why the fuck couldn't I keep her safe? This was all my fault! I bite my tongue until I taste blood and then manhandle myself into composure. Now is not the time for me to lose it.

When I walk inside the bathroom, she's running her fingers through her hair. I kneel down in front of her and fight the urge to grab her into my arms with an ironclad force of will.

"I know you have questions," I say quietly. "I sure as fuck do, too. But I want you to know both the FBI and the police are on the way, and we're going to leave as soon as our bags are packed."

She puts the back of her hand against her mouth. "I can still taste it," she whispers. "The hair. I knew it was hair the second it hit my mouth."

"I'm sorry," I say, unable to help myself, showing her a vulnerable side of me I haven't before. I can't help it; her face is breaking my heart. "I'm so sorry, E."

My words don't seem to comfort her, because she starts sobbing. Next thing I know, her arms are around my neck, and she's crying into my shoulder. Fuck it. I wrap my arms around her small waist and grip her tight, desperate to give her whatever comfort I can.

My hand runs in small circles over her lower back for a few minutes, and her cries quiet. I'm overwhelmed by her scent, her heated skin. She snuggles closer, and I shock myself when I realize I'm nuzzling into her hair.

Sandy clears her throat from the doorway, and we break apart.

"Bags are packed," she says, sounding unsure.

"Do I have time for a shower?" E asks.

I nod, even though I don't want her here for another minute. But at this point I don't think I'd have refused her anything. A loud pounding sounds at the door, so I leave the girls in the bathroom and shut the door.

Anxious as all hell, I check the peephole before yanking open the door to let the cops in. After demanding they show me their badges, I lead them over to the note and the clump of hair.

The hotel room is filled with people within fifteen minutes. Joe texts me that he and Big have just arrived and are heading for the kitchens. Goddamn, I wanted to go down there myself.

I hear a commotion at the door; it's someone shouting and demanding to be let in. I race over to see the manager of the hotel. His face is bright red, and he is nearly in tears. He blanches when he sees my face.

"I...I don't know what happened!" he stammers nervously. "Never in the history of this establishment! Is it true? Was there something in the food? Is everyone OK?"

"Let him in," I tell the cops.

The manager tries to straighten his tie as he walks over. I want to strangle him with the thing. "Everyone is fine," I force myself to say. "But there was something foreign in the food."

His eyes go wide, and he tries to respond, but I cut him off. "What do you know about this?"

"Nothing! Absolutely nothing! Our food is of the finest quality, and this is the first time something like this has ever happened, I assure you!"

My phone rings, and I glance at the screen. Joe.

"What is it?" I demand.

"Sketchy-looking motherfucker down here with a wad of cash. We saw him trying to sneak out the back. Not our guy, but he's guilty of something."

"How do you know he's not?" I ask.

"Old. Terrified of his own shadow. That sound like our guy to you?"

"Question him and get back to me."

"Already on it."

The line goes dead, and I direct my attention back to the manager. "You got drug deals going on in this hotel? Because if that's the case, I'll fucking have this place shut down faster than you can take your next breath."

A couple of the policemen come over to stand next to me, interested in the exchange.

"Absolutely not!" the manager replies, completely affronted. "I am insulted you'd suggest such a thing!"

"Anyone in your kitchens hard up for cash?" I ask, a picture of what might have happened starting to form in my head.

But it's clear the manager doesn't know how to answer that question, because his mouth opens and closes like a damn fish. Finally, he seems to find some courage. "I want to know what happened now! I have a right to know!"

My arms cross over my chest. "Who knows that Eloisa is here?"

A panicked look crosses his face. "I only just found out it was her myself! My assistant put the pieces together. I only informed the people who absolutely had to know!"

"Who absolutely had to know?"

"Well, my front desk staff, of course. And the kitchen staff. I wanted only the finest food prepared, so I made sure they knew who they were serving!"

Things were starting to fall together.

"Get him out of here," I say, walking back toward the couch.

My boss calls then, and I spend a few minutes getting him up-to-date before Joe beeps in.

"Dishwasher," Joe says when I pick up. "He knew Eloisa was staying here and which room."

"And?"

"Someone wearing a blond wig came up to him out back while he was smoking a cigarette. Offered him $1,000 for her room number."

"Fuck." My blood was boiling.

"Dishwasher Dan had a burst of conscience and said no, but he was unable to walk away from the cash, so he made a deal. He let the guy go into the kitchens and leave a note on her tray instead. Said today was his last day, so he didn't have to worry about losing his job."

"What a guy," I deadpan.

"My guess is he slipped it in then. He left immediately after."

"What did this guy look like?"

"Said he didn't get a good look at him. But said the voice was high and strange, as if this guy was trying to disguise it. Short. Dressed in a large hoodie and jeans."

I get off the phone five minutes later and go to update everyone in the living room. The action items become pulling the camera footage and taking dishwasher Dan to the station. I pray there's a solid image of the hooded stranger somewhere.

After all that is in place, I go to find E. She and Sandy are huddled on the bed, freshly showered and surrounded by their luggage. I take a few minutes to tell them what I've learned.

"He's desperate," I say. "The images today must have set him off, just as I thought. What I don't understand is how he knew we were here."

Sandy and E look at each other with guilty expressions. Sandy hands me her phone. "We were just talking about that. We think it was the picture we posted the day we got here. We made sure to keep her face out of it, but he might have recognized the lobby."

I remember then coming back from talking to the manager that first day and seeing the two of them looking at their phones.

I swallow my anger as I grab the phone and look at the picture. Sure enough, the image is of E's shirt and the lobby in the background. The huge chandelier, the paintings, the restaurant…a little research and anyone could have deduced where we were. Especially someone who was already in the area.

"I'm sorry," E whispers. "I didn't think. I knew enough to keep my wig out of it, but…I didn't realize."

"Someone is stalking you," I say forcefully. "This gave him a path right to us. No more damn social media photos."

They both nod, and I take a deep breath, willing myself to calm down. "This isn't anyone's fault. But you have to measure every move you make from now on."

Hopefully, the cameras will give us some answers, and we'll get this bastard, but while he's still out there, we have to be incredibly careful."

"So what now?" Sandy asks, her face filled with guilt.

"You're going with Joe and Big," I answer. "They're downstairs and should be up soon. E and I are leaving."

"Where are we going?" E asks nervously.

I pull out my phone. "My father's."

To say that my father was excited that E and I were coming would be an understatement. As I didn't take the time to explain the truth behind our visit over the phone, he wasn't aware of the situation and therefore could not contain his enthusiasm.

E and I leave the hotel room ten minutes later, bags in hand. She has a large jacket on with the hood pulled up to cover her face. She hasn't said a word since I told her that we're going to my father's. I have no idea how she feels about it, but it's a safe place for us both to regroup.

We just have to make sure we aren't followed.

E and I jump into one black SUV while Joe and Big jump in another. We ride the streets together for almost half an hour, switching lanes and trying to confuse anyone who might be following us. After I'm sure we're alone, I give the driver my father's address.

E is silent, staring out the window, her chin resting on her fist. A bottle of water perches precariously on her lap. I have never seen her look so defeated.

"Hey," I say, my voice carrying in the thick silence. "You OK?"

After a moment, she shrugs in response. "I honestly don't know."

"I want you to know something," I tell her seriously. "I know it may be hard to be believe, due to what happened tonight, but I would never, ever let anyone hurt you. Do you understand?"

She turns to look at me, and I feel a thump of yearning in my chest. I want to reach out and touch her face, wipe the streaks of tears I see. "I know that."

"I'm sorry," I say, staring into her eyes. "I wasn't careful enough, I—"

She shakes her head. "You're the only reason I'm staying sane, X. I know you'll keep me safe."

Her words echo in my brain and send warmth shooting to my toes. Her trust means more to me than it should. It's more than I deserve.

As we enter my father's neighborhood, I try to point out personal landmarks to her along the way. The place where I broke my first bone. The spot where I got caught climbing on the neighbor's fence.

She isn't really responding, but her expression becomes a little less heavy, and her eyes brighten as I tell her a few childhood stories. Her giggle when I tell her about my dog feels like a triumph.

We pull up to my father's, and I look at it as if seeing it through her eyes. Old. Built in 1900. Clapboard siding. A large wraparound porch with two cozy rocking chairs out front. This house holds wonderful and terrible memories for me, and the ever-present ache in my chest flares to life as we get out of the car.

E smiles as she takes in the place, bringing a hand up to remove her hood. Her long lavender-and-brunette hair spills out, and a burst of a wonderful scent reaches my nose. God, how I want to bury my hands in it. And damn me for having these thoughts with everything going on.

Tearing my gaze away, I head around back to grab our bags. I look over just in time to see the front window curtain open and quickly close again. I chuckle, swearing I can hear his footsteps running to the door.

Sure enough, the large red door swings open a moment later. My dad stands in the doorway with his hands on his hips, a jolly smile on his face. He looks as frail as ever, though. Bellatrix, as if she knows where she's going, runs up the steps to greet him.

My father's laugh carries as he bends down to pet the little dog. I walk around the car and gesture for E to go in front of me. She seems a little nervous, but I can't imagine why. She'll see soon that she has nothing to be afraid of.

"Hey, Pops," I call out when we get closer. "Lookin' good."

"Got on my new shirt!" he responds proudly. "Knew I had to look sharp when I heard the most talented girl in the world was coming over!"

E laughs as she walks up the steps. "I'm Eloisa. It's so nice to meet you."

"Donovan," my father replies, looking like the cat that ate the canary. "I'm sure you hear this all the time, but I am your biggest fan."

"Thank you," E says, her voice light. "I love your home. Is it as cozy on the inside as it is on the out?"

My father beams. "Well, what say we find out? Come right in. I've got the electric fire going."

He had more than just the "fire" going. There are snacks littered around the table, and it looks as if he's picked up a bit.

He follows E over to the sofa and fluffs her pillows before she sits down. "There now. Make sure you're nice and comfortable." He turns toward me. "Xavier, get the woman a drink, will ya?"

I send him an amused look before walking to the kitchen and grabbing three waters. I can't help but think how nice it is to see the old man so happy. When I walk back into the living room, the two of them are laughing like old friends.

"Don't let X scare you with his burly exterior," my father is saying. "On the inside, he's as soft as a kitten."

"I don't know about that," E jokes, settling farther into the sofa. "He seems pretty burly to me."

I roll my eyes and perch on the arm of the chair. "You must be getting senile in your old age, Pops," I say coolly. "E knows I'm as mean as they come."

She and I catch eyes, and when the tension flares between us, we promptly look away. My dad never misses a beat, and I'm sure he caught the exchange, but luckily he doesn't say anything.

"I've been telling Xavier here to bring you by for a visit, but I didn't think he'd actually do it, what with your busy schedule and all."

E narrows her eyes at me, relaying what we both already knew: I had told her no such thing. "Well, I'm happy to be here now," she says, petting Bella as she jumps on her lap.

She looks happy. She looks relaxed, and I'm so damned grateful. After everything that happened tonight, I wanted that for her.

My father pats her hand. "He knows that I've been following your music. I usually don't like what's on the radio these days, but your voice..." He whistles. "You sound like an angel. Rose and I were just listening to one of your songs the other day."

E grins. "Rose?"

"My girlfriend."

I nearly choke on my water. "Girlfriend, Pops?"

His chest puffs out. "Well, why not? I'm not dead yet, son."

The phrase shocks me, but I block out the pain and try to make a joke. "She hasn't tried your cooking yet. That's why she's sticking around."

"X has never had a girlfriend," my father continues, to my absolute mortification. "He's dated here and there, but never anything serious."

"Pops!" I cry, possibly turning bright red myself. "Can you not?"

E grins evilly. "That's not too surprising. He doesn't seem like the girlfriend type."

"Oh, that's where you're wrong, darlin'. X will make a fine husband one day."

ONE-WOMAN SHOW

I glare daggers at the old man. Already knowing what he's up to, I shouldn't be surprised he's trying to set E and me up, but it's making me really uncomfortable. Probably because I have no fucking clue what's happening between us.

"Hmm. I don't know," E replies stoically. "He needs to learn to laugh once in a while."

My father belly laughs at that. "Oh, he used to laugh all the time up until—"

He abruptly cuts himself off. Up until my mother died—that's what he was about to say. E looks confused at first but then realizes that it's probably something better left unsaid. Clearing her throat, she eases the tension hanging heavy in the room. "Well, I'd love to meet this Rose. If she's dating a man like you, she must have wonderful taste."

"Indeed she does!" he replies. "Now, how long are you planning on staying for? You're welcome as long as you'd like!"

E's eyes are sad as she looks to me for an answer.

"Our schedule is flexible right now," I reply smoothly. I don't want to talk about what happened tonight just yet, and I'm sure E doesn't, either. "E has some personal things going on that you and I can discuss later."

I can tell my dad knows something serious is up, but he doesn't push it, and for that I'm thankful.

He reaches over and pats Eloisa's hand instead. "How would you like to see some old movies of Xavier here? Did you know he only ate french fries and hot dogs when he was little? Couldn't get a veggie down his throat to save his life!"

E laughs out loud, her eyes twinkling. "I'd love to."

"Really?" I tease. I don't want to watch those old movies, but if it makes her smile like that, I'm up for anything.

My father hands E a blanket and prompts her to tuck in while he sets up the VHS. I watch as she does just that. Man, the scene in front of me feels surreal. I can't believe I'm here with E and my father—and even little Bellatrix—watching home movies like some kind of family.

For the first time in a long time, I feel at home.

27

Eloisa

I wake up early the next morning, and it takes a second to get my bearings. When I realize where I am, a blanket of peace washes over me. X's father is wonderful. He looks sick, true, but his zest for life is refreshing and impossible not to soak in.

I sift through the events of last night with a sense of detachment. Finding that clump of hair in my food, like some kind of sick warning, was one of the scariest things that had ever happened to me. The fact that someone who wanted to kill me had put it there deliberately—ugh. I snuggle farther into my blankets, trying to force away the sudden chill.

An hour or two later, I get up and pad downstairs, hoping for a cup of coffee. I hear X on the phone in the dining room and find Donovan in the kitchen with the Keurig going.

"Good morning, gorgeous," he calls out when he sees me. "How do you like your coffee?"

"Good morning. And black, please."

I sit on one of the stools around the kitchen island and smile as I watch him whistle happily and set up three mugs.

ONE-WOMAN SHOW

"It was so nice to wake up to a full house," he tells me. "With X's job, he doesn't get to visit as much as I'd like. Let alone sleep over."

I thank him as he hands me my cup and takes the seat beside me. "Does he have any brothers or sisters?"

"No," Donovan replies. "My wife and I had a hard time getting pregnant. Tried for years before Xavier. He's our miracle baby."

My first instinct is to ask about X's mother, but I decide not to, as it's clearly a touchy subject. But Donovan sighs heavily, warming his hands around his mug. "I miss her."

"She was very beautiful," I answer. "X and I were up at your cabin and I saw a few photos..."

"She was. She had her troubles, but...man, some days I really miss her."

Unable to help myself, I hedge, "He didn't really want to talk about her."

Donovan's eyes turn sad. "No. He never does. One thing to remember about X is that he takes everything personally. He internalizes things and blames himself for things he shouldn't."

"It is hard to tell what he's really feeling," I reply. "He doesn't show much outward emotion."

Donovan laughs without humor. "He's gotten pretty good at hiding his feelings." He turns to me with a sparkle in his eye. "You, however, are not."

I blush. "What do you mean?"

"I don't want to pry, but when you two showed up here yesterday, it looked as if you had seen a ghost."

"Oh," I say quietly. "There are some things going on..."

Donovan holds up a hand. "Don't feel as if you need to tell me. I know if Xavier is watching over you, it must be bad. They only bring him in if they need the big guns."

I nod.

"You're safe with him," he says. "I hope you know that."

"I do. He seems to have an instinct for danger."

Donovan suddenly looks sad. "I believe that stems from what happened with his mother."

"When did she die?" I ask, wanting more information if he is willing to give it.

"When Xavier was thirteen. Tragic accident..."

X's voice suddenly cuts through our quiet conversation. "Good morning."

We both jump, guilty. Donovan recovers first. "I've made you a coffee, son. Two milks—just how you like it."

X walks over and grabs the mug. "Thanks." His eyes fly back and forth between us as he takes his first sip. "E, can I talk to you for a moment?"

Uh-oh. He doesn't look happy. Did he hear our conversation? I'm dying to know what happened with his mother and can't help but be a little resentful that he interrupted us. I was so close to getting farther under that shell! "OK."

I get off the stool and follow him into the dining room. His eyes travel over my face before he speaks. "They've pulled the tapes."

I fight to remain calm. "And?"

"Can't get a clear shot. The sweatshirt he's wearing is huge, and the hood is pulled down low over his face. The video marks him at about five feet three."

Well, that information surprises me. I'd been picturing him as a hulking, scary monster, not someone who was the same height as me. "Really?"

"He was seen walking in and out of the hotel parking lot, so no car. But if he walked, that means he must live in the area. Cops are canvassing now for clues."

Sadness washes over me. "What about the indoor cameras?"

"Just prove that the dishwasher's story checks out." His face falls. "I'm sorry."

I think about what Donovan told me and wonder if he's feeling guilty. "It's not your fault. I'm just curious as to how this little man was somehow able to throw a rock at me on the red carpet, tape a knife to my door, and shove a clump of hair in my food without getting caught."

"He blends in," says X, his eyes flashing. "Doesn't draw a lot of attention to himself. Not to mention getting a few lucky breaks, so to speak."

ONE-WOMAN SHOW

I lean against the closed door. "I'm just worried about everyone. Are they safe? What if he goes after them?"

"Rob is in LA, but Sandy, Joe, Big, Jacques, and Michonne are all back at your house," X says. "And the rest of them, they're all fine. I hate to say it, but…it's probably the safest place for you right now. There's no way he's getting in there now or has the balls to come back."

"I don't know if I want to go back there just yet," I tell him quietly. "I just…"

"I understand." He nods. "We can go back to that later. But it's time we talk to the FBI."

I blow out a breath. "OK. We should at least tell your father what's going on. If there are going to be police coming over, he deserves to know the truth."

"I'll tell him."

"Should we also tell him about the rumors circulating…about us?"

X rolls his eyes. "He probably already knows. He's always on Facebook, so he must have seen it."

I laugh. "He has been kind enough not to mention it, then."

X chuckles. "He brings things up in his own way. If you didn't notice, he was trying to sing my praises last night."

I laugh harder. "Those movies were great. Don't worry. I won't tell anyone you weren't potty trained until four years old."

"I can't believe he got all that on video. Parents document the strangest things."

We both laugh quietly together, and it's the best and strangest thing ever. Despite everything, despite my confusion surrounding X, there's a genuine comfort growing between us, beneath the attraction and beneath the tension. I can't help but wonder if it's born from two souls who had difficult childhoods.

Once we quiet down, he clears his throat. "I'll go explain things to him. Then we can take Bella for a quick walk."

A few hours later, I'm sitting between X and his father, talking to the agents. They ask me all the normal questions, and I feel like an idiot because I have nothing of substance to give them.

"I don't know," I say for what feels like the fiftieth time.

"How is she supposed to know that? She has thousands of fans all over the world!" X's father shouts, coming to my defense for what also feels like the fiftieth time. "She's not spending her days looking out for madmen and vagabonds!"

"Pops, please," X says with a sigh. "They're just trying to help." He looks to the two male agents sitting on the couch. "Something is bothering me about his appearance, but I can't put my finger on it. Is there any way we can clear up that video?"

Agent number one, who has been the most aggressive so far, shakes his head. "Not soon enough. Just looks like a short, petite man to me."

I lean forward. "Is there something I can do? A restraining order I can take out or something?"

Agent number two makes a pained expression. "It wouldn't do much good. At this point, we don't even know if he's working alone."

"He's working alone," X interrupts. "Stalkers are independent. And he's getting away with all this shit because he's working on his own terms. Dual criminals have a completely different profile."

The agents, who are obviously outranked by X, nod. Agent number two looks at me with sad eyes. "I want you to know we have our best people on this. We're going to get this guy, because he's going to mess up. It's just a matter of time. As long as Xavier is here, try to live your life as normally as possible."

"Ha!" Donovan grouchily responds. "Easy for you to say! I doubt anyone's stalking you!"

X sighs loudly and stands up, holding out his hand. "Call me if you hear anything."

They leave a few moments later, with Donovan nearly slamming the door on their behinds. "Ridiculous!" he sputters. "How has he been able to get away with all this!"

"There's something I'm missing here," X says quietly, hands folded in front of him. "Something I'm not seeing."

Donovan runs over to me and pulls me into a hug. "I'm so sorry you're dealing with this, darling. What a way to start a day."

Sundays used to be my favorite day. When I'd have my brunches. When I was able to trust my fans. I tell Donovan and X as much.

"What a nice thing that must have been for them," Donovan says.

I laugh, lost in the memories. "I met the most wonderful people. One time this girl wrote me the loveliest poem about how I changed her life. It meant so much to me."

"Don't let one rotten apple spoil the bunch," Donovan cuts in. "You've got a week until this tour of yours. You're still making a difference in their lives, darling."

"Speaking of," X grumbles. "We've got a lot to do this week. And if the tour is still on—"

"The tour is still on," I put in hastily. "I can't run scared and let down all those people who bought tickets."

He nods, standing up and grabbing Bella on his way. "Well, then, we've got a lot to do."

The next week was insane—so insane I almost forgot there was a psychopath stalking me.

I recorded the new song I had just written and practiced it with the band. Went on photo shoots and staged dozens of social media posts. Perfected a few dance numbers. Met the tour staff. Talked to catering. Put the final touch on makeup and wardrobe choices. And interviews. So many interviews. The one good thing about that was I'd been able to take Bella to most of them, and she provided a lot of comic relief and distracted folks from the more serious things that had happened to me. Everyone unfortunately learned about her obsession with food when she tried to take the doughnut right out of a cameraman's hand. But other than that, things were running smoothly.

Everyone was caught up in the excitement. Even X, who had been by my side the entire time. It got to the point where I was completely uneasy without him around. He helped me with everything, gave his opinion, and generally made me feel safe.

But at the same time, it was extremely hard to be around him. My attraction to him was stronger than ever, and it extended past the physical. His quiet confidence, comforting presence, and no-bullshit attitude complemented and leveled my constant daydreaming, general uneasiness, and wishy-washy demeanor. I was a balloon floating toward the clouds, and he was the one making sure I didn't float away.

The rumors about us dating died down a little, as did the drama between Martha and me. Concocted stories were just a part of the business I was going to have to get used to. But I was happy to see that most of the news was focused on my upcoming tour. That was all that mattered. Sandy, as always, was really good at keeping me up-to-date with the latest. But she was acting a little strange lately.

"Are you OK?" I ask as we sift through my outfits in the wardrobe room two days before the tour starts. "You haven't spoken much today."

She frowns. "Yeah. I'm fine. Just nerves is all."

"Aren't I the one who's supposed to be nervous?" I joke.

It earns me the smile I'm hoping for. "I just want everything to go right for you. You...you've done so much for me, and you deserve it."

I turn and pull her into my arms. "I couldn't have done it without you, you know."

She nods, and I try to push again. "Are you sure you're OK? You'd barely touched lunch."

She looks around nervously and licks her lips. "I'm sure."

Hmm. I guess she'll tell me whatever is on her mind in her own time. I have a million other things to worry about, so I push it to the back burner.

"Your dad called again," she tells me. "Have you changed your mind about allowing him to come to the show?"

I shake my head. "He can come." I decided a few days ago that the urge to have him see what I'd made of myself was stronger than the need to never speak to him again. I wanted him to see that in spite of him—in spite of him leaving me homeless and lost—I had found a place for myself with my fans and with my music.

"And if he wants to see you after?" she asks warily. "He's been asking about it nonstop."

I sigh. "We'll cross that bridge when we get there."

ONE-WOMAN SHOW

Michonne, Jacques, and Rob burst through the door then, all with huge smiles on their faces.

"I don't want to jinx it," Rob says, his grin a mile wide, "but I think we're ready."

"Fuck yeah, we are!" Michonne chimes in, looking as stylish as ever in designer jeans and a glittery crop top. "First stop, Hartford, Connecticut!"

"My work on display for all to see," Jacques says dramatically, holding my face in his hands and admiring my makeup. "A dream come true for all of us!"

Sandy and I look at each other and burst into laughter. "You all are sure in a good mood," I say happily.

"And ready to celebrate," Michonne says. "Rob rented out the bar next door for some of the crew to let off some steam."

"No outsiders allowed," Rob quickly adds.

Out of everyone, Rob has been having the most trouble dealing with the stalker situation. I think he's been warring with himself constantly on whether to minimize my exposure or put me in the spotlight as much as possible to advertise the tour. Poor guy.

Everyone becomes subdued a bit at Rob's comment, which is what usually happens when *it* comes up. I know my crew's miserable over it, but they try to put on a brave face for me.

In a good mood, I decide to take some weight off their shoulders. "Well, what are we waiting for, then? Who's got first round?"

28

Xavier

Normally I'd be uncomfortable spending the evening at a bar, but it's worth it watching E unwind.

This past week had been a whirlwind. Never before had I seen someone work so hard. All the decisions she had to make for this tour were blowing my mind. All the song lyrics she had to remember...all the stage directions. A seemingly endless parade of people constantly wanting her attention, and she'd cater to each one. It was remarkable. It was admirable. Especially with all the crap we were addressing with the police.

So seeing her now, laughing by the stage and surrounded by her crew, felt good.

Something had happened between us these past seven days, and our relationship had shifted once again. When we talked now, we always looked each other in the eye, as people who were close tended to do. Because of this, I knew exactly how she was feeling most of the time, and I realized the opposite was also probably true. I couldn't help it. I wanted to offer my support, despite the fact I didn't have much insight into running a tour, but I found myself genuinely wanting to make things easier for her. I wanted to relieve the load that was no doubt on her back.

She told me once, after a particularly grueling run-through, that she had no idea what she'd do without me. She'd said it casually, but I couldn't get the image of her face when she said it out of my mind. I could tell she really meant it, and for some reason, I couldn't stop thinking about it.

I was getting to the point where I couldn't imagine life before her, either. She was the one I felt I could turn to, even though I was still scared to open up. That I would get to this point with someone was astounding, and all the new feelings were truly scary.

I'd never paid attention to celebrities before I started this job. Didn't think they had difficult things to deal with. After all, they were rich, beautiful, and happy. But man, how wrong I was.

Not about the beautiful part, of course.

I watch E take a sip of her wine, and our eyes catch over the rim of her glass. She sends me a big smile and waves me over.

I wade through the crowd to her side, where Michonne's lifting her own glass in a toast.

"To Ellie," she begins, her eyes bright. "To the most hardworking and talented woman I know. You truly amaze me. Inside and out, you are one of a kind. And I have to say, fabulously dressed, too."

Everyone laughs and then someone yells, "To a tour that's totally going to rock!"

Surrounding cheers ring out, and I stare at the oft-present blush rising on E's cheeks. Goose bumps surface on my arms when she leans into me to hide her embarrassment. She's so humble and barely lets anyone give her praise about what she's doing. I understand now it's because she doesn't think she deserves it. She's doing what she loves and doesn't think that warrants the thank-yous and the well wishes.

"Hell yeah, it is," Joe puts in happily. "Ellie, are you sure you don't want to throw in my dance number I told you about? I think the crowd would dig it."

"I'm sure," E jokes. "I don't think the world is ready for your twerking."

"I know I'm not," Sandy teases.

I'd noticed something different about Sandy the past few days. Couldn't put my finger on what it was, however. It's not as if she wasn't doing her job, but something about her seemed off. I chide my suspicious nature and try to stay in the moment.

She pulls E in for a hug. "This is going to be a blast. Thank you so much for this opportunity. I'm so happy for you."

"Here, here!" Big calls out, surprising everyone. "To the woman who turned my life around. I wish you nothing but health and happiness."

In the midst of all the glasses clinking, someone yells out, "Song!" And after that, everyone starts insisting E go onstage and sing. At first she resists, but after some persistence, she finally agrees.

Someone hands her a guitar, and she makes her way onto the small stage. I stand right at the front and a little off to the left to watch. I feel a few curious looks thrown in my direction—which has been normal over the last few weeks—but I ignore it. Not everyone is used to my presence, and I don't really make an effort to explain myself. The stalker situation has been kept within her immediate circle, and I want to keep it that way.

Someone brings E a stool, and she takes a seat, looking out over her crowd. "I wish I could explain to everyone how full my heart is. How thankful I am to each and every one of you for the time and effort you've put into making this tour happen. Your creativity and dedication to making this work...well...I'll carry that with me for the rest of my days. I am forever grateful."

Whistles and cheers ring out, and when the noise dies down, her eyes meet mine. She bites her lip—which I now know she does when she's nervous about something—and adjusts her fingers on the guitar.

"This song goes out to someone special. He told me it's his favorite song, and I want to play it for him here today."

And then she starts playing "Bridge Over Troubled Water." My heart squeezes in my chest as I hear the opening chords.

When you're weary,

Feeling small
When tears are in your eyes,
I will dry them all.

A thousand emotions rush through my body, and I'm unable to look away from her face as she sings. This song means so many things to me, and I haven't heard it in years. It means happiness, it means preserved memories, and it means guilt from events that I can never forget.

For a moment I feel as if I'm drifting.

I'm on your side
Oh, when times get rough
And friends just can't be found
Like a bridge over troubled water
I will lay me down.

Images of my mother fill my vision, and I have to look away. God.

The guilt of what I did was always going to be there, ready to be called upon and simmering beneath the surface of my everyday life. I'd never be able to escape it. Besides conversations with my father and my boss, I had never spoken about it to anyone, but here and now it felt as if E was sharing my pain.

Sail on, silver girl
Sail on by
Your time has come to shine
All your dreams are on their way.

I try to concentrate on her instead. Her face is tilted up, and her fingers are expertly maneuvering the strings. Her gorgeous, colorful hair, small, delicate face, and long lashes that lead to a body of absolute sin. It's able to distract me enough until the end of the song.

She takes her fingers off the strings, and amid the clapping, her eyes meet mine. I try to hide the emotion that must be shining through, but I'm not sure if I'm successful, as a nervous expression passes over her face.

Our connection is broken when Rob jumps onstage, yelling about adding that song to the lineup. I look away, eager to give my thrashing heart a break.

I work so hard every day to put on a brave face. I cocoon myself in a life of discipline and order, not leaving any room for surprises or mistakes. *My* mistakes. She nearly shattered all that hard work, and the realization is taking my breath away.

When I see E making her way toward me a few minutes later, I fight hard to put that face back on.

"Are you OK?" she asks, looking up at me with nervous green eyes. Innocent eyes. "That song..."

"You sang it beautifully," I interrupt, trying to get my bearings. It's hard when she's standing right there and the song is still echoing in my head.

"You looked like you'd seen a ghost. I thought it would be a nice surprise, since you said it's your favorite song."

"I do. I love that song, but...I hate it at the same time."

Her lips form a small circle. "Oh."

"It was my mother's favorite. She used to sing it to me before bed," I hear myself say.

Her eyes go wide at my admission. "I'm sorry. I didn't know."

"Don't apologize," I tell her sternly. "You shouldn't ever have to apologize. Especially to me."

"What does that mean? Especially to you?"

I have to stop this conversation. It's getting out of hand. "Let's just drop it."

"X, I don't want to drop it. What's going on right now?"

"Nothing. I'm fine."

"No, you're not. You can tell me. We're friends, aren't we?"

This conversation is making me want to crawl out of my skin, and I feel my armor come back in full force. "No, we're not. And I want you to drop it."

The lie feels like black tar spilling out of my mouth, and E rears back as if I've slapped her. Because we *are* friends. And there's something more between us, too. A red-hot chemistry I can taste on my tongue, even now.

How long can I keep denying it?

"I'm sorry," I tell her earnestly, desperate to get the hurt expression off her face. "It's just...don't ever apologize to me. I've done things. Bad things. I don't deserve any pity over my reaction to a damn song."

She leans in closer. "What have you done?"

At that moment, Michonne comes over and throws her arms around our shoulders. "Come on, you two! We're celebrating. Why the glum faces?"

She looks between us cautiously when we both don't respond. "Oh, no...did something happen?"

I pull myself together and shake my head. "No, nothing. Everything's good here."

Thankfully, E gets pulled away into another conversation, giving me time to recover from the one we had.

I can't let her get to me like that. There's something about her energy that has had me on edge from the very beginning, and it's only getting stronger with time. I've worked so hard to hide my past. I've worked so hard to distance myself from the person I was.

And she is dragging him out without even trying.

E and I don't talk again for the rest of the night. I know where she is at all times, of course, but I make sure to keep my distance, worried she'll try to talk again and ask me more questions.

We aren't alone again until the end of the night.

The tension between us on the ride back to the hotel is thick with unanswered questions. I stare at my phone, trying to ignore it. Bella, however, is not so easily ignored. She jumps onto my lap and circles three times before settling down. The little rat. I run a large hand over her soft fur.

"She loves you," E whispers.

I laugh, despite myself. "I don't know what I did to earn her affection. Well, besides all the food I slip her."

E shrugs. "Maybe she knows you're keeping her mom safe. I think she felt the job was up to her for a long time."

"How long have you had her?"

"About twelve years. When I was...living on the streets...I used to camp outside the animal shelter. The barking, for some reason, was comforting to me. Maybe because they were all trapped like I was. Anyway, one night a man brought in a box of puppies. He was in a hurry, and the box fell out of his arms. About five or six puppies got loose. Bella here ran right over to me. I'll never forget it. He eventually got all the puppies back into the box, but he didn't realize there was one missing."

I look down at Bella with new eyes, and as she stares back up at me, I can't help wondering what's going on in that tiny brain of hers. She's a little hero.

"We've been inseparable ever since," E adds. "I don't know what I'd do without her. She's literally my best friend."

Feeling like I should say something, I clear my throat. "Why the name Bellatrix? Is that Greek or something?"

To my surprise, she bursts into laughter. "Seriously? No. It's from Harry Potter. You know, Bellatrix Lestrange?"

"Le what?"

She laughs again, the rich sound filling the car. "That's it. We're watching the first movie when we get back to the hotel."

Her laugh cheers my mood considerably. "Isn't Harry Potter for kids?"

"Harry Potter is for everyone," she tells me, her voice playful. "I promise you're going to love it."

"If you say so."

"I can't believe you've never seen it. Wait, scratch that, I think I can. You seem more like a *Terminator* guy to me."

It's hard to look away from her bright smile. "I don't really have time to sit and watch movies. Once in a while I find time, but it's rare."

"Well, you have time now. What's your favorite movie, then? *Goodfellas*? *The Godfather*?"

I think for a moment. "I don't know. Maybe a Western."

She blanches. "A Western?"

"Yeah, you know. Kill the bad guy, save the girl. Simple."

She stares at me, and now I'm wondering what's going on in her brain.

"A tale as old as time," she finally says. "And here you are, saving me."

Maybe. But what is she doing to me in return?

29

Eloisa

The day of my first show dawns clear and sunny. To say I'm filled with butterflies would be the understatement of the damned century.

Scared to open my eyes and face the day, I curl up in bed, remembering the small girl with the guitar on the street corner. The small girl with the ratty hair searching for spare change on the side of the road to buy food. She has come so far. She has learned so much. And today, all of the hard work, the failures and the losses, culminate with one show.

I'm ready to sing my heart out.

The sound of Bella's nails hitting the floor let me know that it's time to get up. I have to let her out and have the largest cup of coffee this hotel will permit.

The accommodations this time around aren't as luxurious, but they're still pretty nice. The best thing about this place is that it's hidden away in the suburbs of Cromwell. Not as well-known. We'd gotten in and out with little fanfare.

I pad down the hallway, the smell of fresh brew hitting my nose and raising the hair on my arms in anticipation.

X is standing at the counter with his back to me, pouring out two mugs. Man, he is a sight for sore eyes. His large, muscular back is encased in a tight black T-shirt, and a pair of jeans hug his sinfully well-formed legs and ass. I can't help but admire it and daydream about what it would be like to touch him. To have him touch me.

My shiver at the thought must have been so loud that he heard me. He looks quickly over his shoulder. "Mornin'."

I swallow hard, the glimpse of his strong and handsome face dancing behind my eyelids. God, I have it bad.

But today is not the day to confront my feelings about my bodyguard, or look into what happened between us last night, so I take the cup of coffee from his outstretched hand and breathe the aroma in deeply. "Mmm, good morning. Thank you for this."

"It's the least I can do," he replies, crossing his arms and watching me take a few cautious sips. "How are you feeling?"

"Like I'm about to perform in front of seventeen thousand people."

He laughs. "Better you than me."

"I don't know," I tease. "I heard you humming in the car the other day. Do you have a voice you haven't told me about?"

His eyes twinkle. "I'll never tell. We men have to keep our secrets."

I can feel the shit-eating grin on my face, but I'm unable to wipe it off. Holy crap. I think we were just flirting. The easy banter between us feels good after the tension from last night. I really want to know what he had been so close to telling me. What awful things had he done?

I deliberately keep my voice light. "And what secrets are you keeping, X?"

"That I'm not a morning person."

I'm shocked. "I don't believe that. You're always up at the crack of dawn!"

"Because it's my job to be. But I'd love to sleep in one morning." He sighs, picking up Bellatrix, who had just begun to bark.

She settles into the crease of his arm, up against his hard and probably warm chest. I can't help but glare at her jealously. "Well, how about tomorrow morning? We have a two-day break in between shows."

He gives me a hard look. "Not while I'm on the clock."

I take another sip of coffee, a terrible thought suddenly occurring to me. When the psycho is caught, does that mean X will leave? I mentally slap myself. Of course he will! He dreaded this job from the beginning and is probably champing at the bit to return to his real life. The thought is depressing as all hell.

"What's the frown for?" he asks.

"I'm just going to miss you when you're gone," I tell him, not caring how it makes me look. Must be those first-show nerves. Why not put everything on the line?

He laughs. "Where am I going?"

"Well, once we catch the guy who's stalking me, you'll probably go back to DC..."

I leave the comment open-ended, obviously hoping he'll refute me. I can tell my words take a moment to settle in, and he looks at me over the rim of his mug. "Are you saying you want me to stay, E?"

"Yes." Damn, I'm feeling bold!

He opens his mouth to respond when the door bursts open. Michonne, Sandy, Jacques, Rob, Joe, and Big pile into the room like a herd of elephants.

"Good. You have coffee," Sandy says first. She has a pile of notepads in her arms and an actual camera.

"I can't believe the day is finally here!" Michonne cries, pulling me into her arms. "I am so proud of you, baby girl."

I hug her back. Rob catches my eyes over her shoulder. "Ellie, I need you to approve a few things, and you have a last-minute interview in ten minutes."

And so it begins.

I'd like to say that I remember every moment of that day, but in truth, it went by in a blur. Makeup and clothing choices, racing to the arena, calling one of the backup dancers because one of the regulars had gotten sick, microphone checks, a power outage, bursting into tears, holding on to Bellatrix for dear life...

And X. X standing silently by my side in support the entire time: helping me choose the best color eye shadow, helping me into my insanely high shoes, holding my hand on the way to the arena, handing me the number for the new dancer, checking my microphone, rubbing my back as I cried, and taking Bellatrix from me when it was showtime.

It was showtime.

When the chords of my introductory song begin, I'm so nervous I can't feel my legs moving as I walk onstage. I know I'm waving. I know I'm smiling. But other than that, the flashing lights and the deafening roar of the crowd rob all of my senses. Standing there, picking up my guitar from the center of the stage, feels like it's happening in slow motion.

Is this really happening? The moment is so out-of-body I can barely catch my breath, let alone belt out a song.

As I get closer to the center of the stage, I'm able to make out a few faces in the front row. They are raucous in their excitement—excitement for me! It's unbelievable. Some of them are crying as they try to get my attention.

A crushing wave of panic washes over me, and I put one hand on my stool to hold myself up. I don't deserve this fanfare. Why me? How did I end up in this position when thousands of other singers across the country never will? No one deserves to be this lucky. No one.

The faces of the crowd swim back into my vision, and another wave of panic nearly topples me over. Is he out there? Is he watching?

I look toward the curtains, fading fast. This is a nightmare. I can't control my own actions. No matter how much I tell myself to get it together, it's not working. Reality slams me hard back to earth. I'm not going to be able to do this.

X catches my attention from the side of the stage. He's just standing there, arms crossed, his expression one of determination. I wait for him to come get me. To carry me offstage away from all this, but it's clear he's not moving.

His eyes narrow, and he nods in my direction. I know what he's thinking. *Get ahold of yourself, E.*

I think of what he would do in this situation. He'd pull himself together, that's what. He's the most skilled human at hiding his emotions that I've ever met. He never lets on that he's not a morning person. He never lets on that he's carrying massive amounts of guilt on his shoulders every day. He never lets on that his dad is sick.

I have to do the same.

A deep inhale and a look to the heavens later, I hold both hands up and take a bow. I adjust the monitor in my ear and greet the crowd, just as I'm supposed to, and strum the first notes of my first song, like I'm supposed to.

And the show goes on.

The entire time, X doesn't move from his position in the wings. I feel his eyes on me, and I swear it's my lifeline. With X around, nothing bad will happen. With X around, I'm safe.

And my God, did I have a blast. My fans are incredible. Hearing them sing along with the music, watching them sway to the beat—I was so incredibly high on life, and when it was all over, all I wanted to do was press the reset button and start again.

When the lights go out after my second encore, I race into the wings and throw myself into X's arms. It's the only place I want to be. I don't care that I'm sweaty, and I don't care that I'm openly showing him so much affection. For me, he's made this show possible. I was able to take his inner strength and use it as a model for my own.

"Thank you," I whisper into his neck.

It takes me a second to realize he's holding me as tightly as I'm holding him. "I'm so proud of you," he whispers back.

His words settle over my heart, and I nuzzle closer to him, wanting his touch. I feel him tense in my arms, but the moment is lost anyway when the crew comes over and joins in a group hug.

Apparently my minor freak-out was barely noticed, because Jacques lifts me into his arms and tells me I didn't miss a beat.

"I couldn't have done this without you guys," I tell them seriously, tears filling my eyes. "Each and every one of you. Thank you for doing this for me."

"You were amazing," Michonne says, sounding teary. "I couldn't take my eyes off you."

"Pictures are already going up," Sandy puts in excitedly. "All good things. I think we can officially say this show was a success!"

I'm on cloud nine as I meet and thank my band and all the dancers that have been a part of the show, and whenever I meet X's eyes, he has nothing but a huge smile for me. I want to talk to him alone, but there's too much going on. I want to thank him again, as he was as much a part of the show's success as anyone else that had anything to do with it.

It feels great to get into comfortable clothes back in my dressing room and hug Bella. The next show is in two days—the one my dad said he would be going to—and I'm looking forward to a day or two of lounging around. The thought of him seeing this show no longer scares me. Let him watch. I secretly hope that it makes him regret what he has done: literally abandoning his daughter to the streets.

X is furiously texting on his phone when I step out of the room. Bella nips at his heels, and I hide a grin as he absentmindedly bends down to pet her. "Fans with access passes are waiting by the back door," he tells me. "I've got eight security guys down there, and they're giving me the go-ahead that it's safe to push through."

"I'll have to stay and sign autographs," I tell him, a little worried about his reaction. "They've already paid for it." X begins to shake his head, but I give him a pleading look. "Please? I'd hate to let them down. There should only be about fifty of them."

His eyes scan my face for a few moments before blowing out a breath. "Fine. Ten minutes, E."

Sandy's eyes meet mine behind X's back. "I'll hold Bella," she says.

I nod at X, knowing ten minutes won't be enough time but thankful he's even allowing it. There's no way I can leave those fans disappointed after they paid for a little time with me.

A part of me *is* scared that the crazy psycho could be among them, but when I walk outside and see everyone's happy, smiling faces, the fear dissipates. X is stuck to my side like white on rice as we make our way down the line.

I have lovely conversations with two families, a pair of frat bros, and girls here on a bachelorette weekend. One girl has a T-shirt with my face on it matched with a rose—my favorite flower—in her hair, and I smile a happy smile when she takes a picture of me. I'm smiling for a third picture when I hear Sandy shout Bella's name.

A woman and her daughter start talking to me at that moment, and I feel X shift beside me. "It's OK," he whispers. "Bella's just jumped out of Sandy's hands."

His words put me on edge, and I want to turn around and see where Bella has gone, but I don't want to interrupt the mother and her tearful daughter. When I see X still looking around a moment later, my heartbeat picks up. "Does she have her?"

I see Sandy on her hands and knees, searching through people's legs and calling Bella's name. That answers my question.

"Bella!" I call out nervously, trying to be heard over the cacophony of voices and screaming. "Here, girl!"

X puts an arm around my shoulder, and we walk over to where Sandy is still searching. His arm is a silent warning for me not to run, not to panic.

Sandy looks up at me nervously. "It happened so fast!" she explains. "I didn't even have time to grab her. It was like she got wind of something she wanted and there was no stopping her!"

I bend down. "It's probably all the new smells. Bella!" I call again, trying not to freak out. There's literally no sign of her. I keep hoping to hear a bell or something, or—

"Bella!" X calls out in a commanding tone only he can pull off. He's on his feet scanning the crowd. About five moments pass before I hear a bark. And then there she is, pushing between legs, looking as satisfied as a clam.

"Oh, thank God," Sandy and I say at the same time, watching as my damned dog jumps into X's arms. I lightly grab Bella's furry chin with my fingers. "Where have you been, girl! Don't you dare run off like that again!"

She licks me a few times before settling into X's arms. What am I going to do with her?

Sandy, X, and I jump into the SUV about five minutes later to return to the hotel. As expected, there are reporters waiting at the door, but we're able to bypass them and get to our rooms without any other problems. X had requested the fourteenth floor, so between that, the extra security, and the locks, I feel pretty safe.

Sandy goes to her room after another congratulatory hug, leaving X and me alone. I pour a glass of wine and sink into one of the chairs by the window.

I'm beat, but being alone with X is making my heart pound. What the *hell* am I going to do about him? He isn't even going to be sticking around.

"Thank you," I tell him quietly. "I don't know what happened to me up there tonight."

His eyes are understanding, the color like molten chocolate. He's beautiful and unique in every way. "Nerves. It's normal, I hear."

I laugh. "Oh, yeah, I forgot. You're not afraid of anything."

He looks at me with an expression I can't decipher, but I get the distinct feeling he wants to disagree with me.

"Seriously," I say. "You gave me that extra push. I can't thank you enough."

He nods. Even though he did nothing but stare at me from the wings, we both know something passed between us in that moment. And it had to do with the connection that was developing between us.

I slip off my shoes, groaning. My feet are absolutely killing me. I take a large sip of wine, savoring it with my eyes closed. I'm just about to speak again when I realize X is right beside me. Next thing I know, his hands are on my feet, rubbing tight circles into the sole.

I'm completely unable to stop the embarrassing moan that leaves my mouth. His touch feels unbelievable. It honestly seems as if he is circling magic healing powers into my skin.

I hear him chuckle, but I'm way too lost in the sensation of his hands to care. Visions of him taking me into his bedroom and rubbing down my whole body sear across my vision. I know it won't happen, but oh, how a girl can dream.

He gives me his attention for a full ten minutes, and when he stops, I miss his touch like I would miss my arm. I try not to pout as he takes a seat across from me on the couch.

"Thank you. You're a godsend."

A loud ping signals he's gotten a text, and when he looks at it, he chuckles. I have never seen him laugh at a text before, so I give him a curious look.

"My dad," he explains. "He's just discovered emojis."

I laugh along with him. "You're kidding."

"Nope," he says. "So for the past two weeks he's been texting updates about his day, but with emojis. Literally, everything he does."

"That is the cutest thing ever." I sigh happily. "You should give him my number. I'd be happy to text with him."

X gives me a look. "I wouldn't do that to you."

"Why? I wouldn't mind. Your dad's great."

"OK, I will, just because I know it will make his day. But don't say I didn't warn you."

As his hands fly over the keys, I feel compelled to ask, "How is he doing? You know...?"

I don't have time to finish the sentence. X knows I'm talking about the cancer. "Tough to say," he begins. "Doctors say he must be in tremendous pain, but I don't know, because he never complains."

"You're like him," I say quietly. "The suffer-in-silence type."

"Maybe." X shrugs. "I just...I wish I could help him somehow. I wish he would tell me what he's feeling. I'm afraid it's going to get really bad—bad enough for a normal person to go to a hospital—and he won't tell me."

"Have you told him that?" I ask quietly.

X nods. "I don't know how much good it did. He looked so frail when we saw him last week. I've never seen him like that."

He's scared. It's not written on his face, but I know him well enough now to sense the fear. It's in the tightness of his shoulders, in his eyes—in the way he keeps talking when he's usually a man of few words.

"And I don't know that he's going to chemo regularly. He won't tell me, and the hospital won't, either."

I fight the urge to walk over and pull him into my arms. "That must be scary. But even if he told you if he was going to chemo, or if he told you that he wasn't, he'd still make the same choice. You knowing doesn't make a difference or not. Your dad strikes me as a man of his own mind. I doubt you'd be able to change it if he's decided what's best for him."

"He's so damn stubborn," X says, wiping two hands over his face.

At that moment, my phone dings. We both look at each other. Me with excitement in my eyes and X with exasperation in his.

Donovan: *I hope you had a wonderful show tonight, darling! Make sure to celebrate and make sure Xavier celebrates, too. He needs more fun in his life.*

The sentence is followed by a line of party emojis and happy faces, and I laugh out loud.

"What did he say?" X asks.

"That's for me to know," I tease.

X rolls his eyes, but I can see that he's happy his dad's reached out. I text back, periodically looking up at X as I do.

"Your dad says you need to have more fun," I tell him in an innocent tone. "Is that true, X?"

He shakes his head and lets out a laugh without humor. "He doesn't know what he's talking about."

"I don't know," I say, my voice playful. "Right out of college you head straight to the secret service, then on to DC. You work for the president for eight years, then immediately after, you come to Connecticut to trail after me. Tell me you've taken a couple vacations."

He looks distinctly uncomfortable, so I know right away he hasn't.

"That's so sad, X!"

He leans back into the couch, getting more comfortable. "I've been plenty of places with the president...I just haven't had much time to explore."

"Where would you go?" I ask suddenly. "If you could go anywhere?"

"Norway," he tells me after thinking for a moment. "I'm a sucker for great views. I've always wanted to take a boat out there and get lost in the mountains."

So he had given it some thought. "That sounds beautiful."

"One day," he says. "I've got plenty of time to vacation."

"Well, you've got to take a day off for that to happen," I tell him.

"How about you?" he asks after a moment. "Where would you go?"

"Alaska. I've always wanted to see the aurora borealis. Maybe in one of those heated igloos you can rent."

"Sounds cold," X comments. "But one of my buddies went last year and told me it was gorgeous."

I want to keep the conversation going, as his mood is a lot lighter than usual. "Where would be the last place on earth you'd want go?"

"Wyoming," he answers immediately.

We both laugh at that, and the conversation continues on, just as I'd hoped it would. I don't know what's in the air, or if X was left feeling emotional after talking about his dad, but he is in the mood to share. He tells me about how he used to want to be a firefighter or an astronaut, and that he had a huge crush on the Winnie Cooper character from *The Wonder Years*. He tells me that he loves animals and wants to have a farm one day. He tells me about how much he hates the current president and is thinking about refusing to go back and work for him even if his boss asks. I learn his favorite food is Mexican and that he hates classical music, and that, without fail, he has dreams every night.

I want to ask about his mother, but after a couple of hours I can barely keep my eyes open. I must have fallen asleep, because I suddenly feel myself being lifted into a pair of warm, strong arms. *Heaven.*

I'm not sure if I mumble that out loud, but I feel his chest rumble underneath my cheek. When he places me in bed, I almost ask if he wants to lie down with me, but either I'm too tired or I'm not ready to put myself on the line like that.

But I almost did.

Almost.

30

Xavier

When I wake up, I know something's wrong. Call it a gut instinct or chalk it up to years on the job, but my radar is flying off the handle.

Thinking of E asleep in the next room, I throw the covers back, grab my gun, and go to her as quickly and quietly as I can. The clock in the hall reads 4:00 a.m. We had just gone to bed about three hours ago.

I turn the knob to her room carefully and walk to her bedside. Unfettered relief assaults me when I realize nothing is amiss. She's sound asleep, her arms up by her head.

But the feeling won't go away.

Even though I know no one is there, I check the closets and under the bed, and then head out to the living room. The coast is clear.

Then it hits me. Where's Bella?

She hadn't been in bed with me, and she wasn't in E's room. I would have expected her to hear me wandering around by now and be nipping at my heels, looking for those treats she loves so much.

Something isn't right. A sinking feeling pulses in my stomach.

Could someone have come into the room and taken her? I shake my head as I head to the bathroom. No one could have gotten into this suite. I'm the only one with a key, and I would have heard it.

Really worried now, I turn on the light in the bathroom.

Nothing.

Could she have jumped into the shower? It's low enough—

But when I pull back the curtain, she's not there.

It's when I'm turning back around that I see her. She's wedged between the toilet and shower, as if she'd tried to hide.

I know before I kneel down that she's dead. Her small body looks completely stiff, and her face is frozen in place. I take in the glassy eyes and wide-open mouth, trying to think over my stuttering heart.

Dear God. The poor little thing.

What could have happened? What the hell was I going to tell E?

Fuck!

I don't move for a few moments, resting my head in my hands. The dog was old—perhaps it was just her time to go. What shit timing, though. A wave of sadness passes through me.

I agonize for a few minutes over what to do. My instinct says to get the dog out of here as soon as possible, that E won't want to see her like that, but I can't decide, knowing that she will be in shock and might want to say goodbye.

I walk over to the connecting door and knock as softly as I can, praying Sandy will hear me. Maybe she'll have some insight on how to handle this. The stars are in my favor this night, as Sandy opens the door a few minutes later, her eyes sleepy.

"What's going on?" she asks, midyawn.

"It's Bella...she's—she's dead."

"She's what?" Sandy is now wide-awake, racing into the room. "Where is she?"

I point to the bathroom, and when she sees the small dog, she bursts into tears. "Oh, no...oh, Bella!" She turns to me. "What happened?"

I run a hand over my face. "I don't know. I noticed she wasn't running around, and then when I found her here, it was too late."

"Oh, no," Sandy keeps repeating. She reaches out to pet Bella's fur but immediately pulls her hand back, gasping. "Look at her gums!"

"Huh?"

Her gums are black!" Sandy whispers, tears still streaming down her face. She leans over to get a closer look. "Why are her gums black?"

My heart races. The thought that Bella could have ingested something toxic had crossed my mind, but what the hell did I know about that? "I don't know. I'm going to call emergency services, but what do you think I should do? Should I let E see the body before...let her say goodbye ?"

Sandy whimpers and buries her face in her hands. She sniffles a few times and then nods. "I think it'd be worse if we just took her away. If she just woke up and Bella was gone."

I was hoping that wasn't going to be her answer, but if that's what she thinks is best, so be it. I haven't known E as long as she has, so I'm going to take her word for it.

Sandy and I creep into E's room, and my heart feels as heavy as a ton of bricks. I turn on the light as Sandy goes to her bedside and shakes her awake.

As E blinks into reality and sees us both standing over her, she instantly comes alert. "What? What's wrong?" She takes note of Sandy's crying and scrambles out of bed. "What is it?"

"It's Bella," Sandy whispers, crying harder now. "She's...she's gone."

It's at that moment that I know E's reaction is going to be worse than I even anticipated. She goes stock-still, and her face drains of color. Her hands shake as she wipes hair from her brow, looking between Sandy and me. "What do you mean, she's gone? She's missing, you mean?"

I know E understood what Sandy meant but clearly doesn't want to believe it. And before Sandy can respond, E races out of the bedroom, calling Bella's name. Sandy watches her go and then sits down on the bed, sobbing.

I find E flying around the living room looking under the couches. "Bella! Come here, girl!"

I take a deep breath, trying to keep my emotions in check. "E, she's in the bathroom, but I have to warn you, she looks—"

Without waiting to hear the rest of my sentence, E flies past me and into the hallway. I give her half a second before following her.

When I turn the corner into the bathroom, E is staring down at Bella, her mouth twisted in shock. And when her eyes meet mine, I'm positive I've never seen such abject sadness. My heart lurches in my chest, and I reach out a hand. "E..."

E grabs onto my hand for dear life, dragging me into the bathroom toward Bella. We both fall to the ground, and E lets out a harrowing sob. "X, we have to help her! We have to call someone!"

I don't know how to respond, and when I make no reaction to help, she narrows her fists in anger, throwing away my hand she was holding. "Why aren't you doing anything? Why are you just sitting there?"

She kneels down and tries to pick up Bella, but pulls her hands back immediately, just as Sandy had. I know she knows then that nothing can be done. She falls back into the tub, her whole body shaking. She must be short of breath, because it looks as if her next words are painful to get out. "Why? Wha...why?"

Worried she's going to pass out, I stand up and try to get her to go with me. "I'm so sorry, E."

"Get off me!" she yells, pushing my hands away. She doesn't take her eyes off Bella as she says it. I'm worried now she's going to hyperventilate, as she's gone even paler, if possible. "I'm not leaving her!"

Sandy appears in the doorway, and I get up to tell her under my breath to call emergency services. She nods tearfully before disappearing back down the hallway.

When I turn back around, E has her head in her hands. God, I have never felt so goddamned helpless in all my life. I kneel back down beside her and put my hand on her back. I whisper *I'm sorry* over and over like an idiot, because I have no freakin' clue what else to say.

We sit there for who knows how long. E seems to be in a state of shock. I know that Bella was a best friend to E when she had no one else in the world. My heart aches in pain as I scramble for the right words. Nothing feels right to say.

I hear a knock on the door some time later, and Sandy rushes to open it. Normally I would have vetted anyone who came to the door, but I can't seem to move from E's side. When the two women appear in the doorway, E finally springs to life. "No," she whispers, clinging to me. "Don't let them take her," she begs. "Please don't let them take her."

"Come on," I tell her softly, trying to encourage her to get up. "We have to say goodbye."

"No!" she screams, beginning to fight me. "Please don't let them! Please!"

The two women skirt around me to take a look at the dog. "We're so sorry, ma'am. We understand how much pain you're in," one of them says sadly, kneeling down beside us.

I see the women exchange a look when they see Bella. Something is wrong here. I know it.

One of the women gestures for me to follow her out of the bathroom, and I get up reluctantly. Once we we're out of earshot, she looks at me somewhat suspiciously. "There's piles of vomit by the front door."

I hadn't even noticed. "What does that mean?"

"It can mean a lot of things, but after seeing the black gums, I don't have a good feeling. I've seen this before. It's likely she ingested something."

Bad thoughts swirl through my head like a deadly tornado. What could she have gotten into? "As I'm sure you saw, that's Eloisa Rae Morgan in there. I'd like a rush on the autopsy. We'll pay double. Triple if you don't leak this to the media."

The woman looks insulted but agrees. "You have my word."

We both head back into the bathroom. The other emergency services worker is whispering in E's ear and rubbing her back, just as I had been. After a few moments, the other woman pushes by me and kneels down beside the pair. "Let's say goodbye, " she says softly. "Let's let her rest in peace."

For the first time I see a tear trickle down E's face. The shock is wearing off, making way for a new, sad reality. She bends down and puts her face into Bella's fur and begins sobbing.

The two women look at me, and I know what I have to do. I give her a few more seconds and then walk over to her, scooping her up in my arms in such a way it leaves no room for argument. She screams as I drag her out of the bathroom.

Sandy is looking at us, her eyes wide.

"Give us some time. Make sure this gets sorted out," I tell her, nodding toward the women. "Give me an update when there is one." I start down the hallway, trying not to let E's wailing affect me.

Sandy watches E and me disappear into her bedroom. E's inconsolable now, sobbing out Bella's name and crying harder than I've ever witnessed anyone cry in my life.

I feel fucking terrible.

Going on instinct, I lay her down, pull my gun out of its holster and get in beside her. She curls into my arms immediately, her cries louder than ever.

I hold her close, my hands running up and down her back as I whisper in her ear. "It's OK," I tell her. "It's OK."

But it's not OK. E just lost her best friend, and I know how much of a blow this is. That dog meant the world to her, and I can literally feel her pain in every cry and jerk of her chest.

I don't know how long we lie there, but she doesn't stop crying until the sun starts peeking through the windows. Thank God she had a couple of days until the next show. Would she even want to do it? I couldn't give a shit. All I wanted was to give her a little relief.

I knew she'd fallen asleep when I felt her cries even out. But still, I didn't move. I didn't move when Sandy came in a couple of hours later and told me they were hoping to have results within forty-eight hours, or when she brought in water and some Advil an hour after that.

I didn't want to move. If this was the only comfort I could give, then I was damn well going to give it.

Around noon, I felt her come awake. She started sniffling, and every few moments her chest would shake, but she was otherwise silent. She made no move to get out of my arms, and I was thankful for that. I only hoped I was giving her an iota of comfort.

Ten minutes later she shifts so she can look at my face, and for a moment we just stare at each other. Her beautiful green eyes are filled with tears. Her face is red and sticky, and her hair is matted down with sweat.

I'd never seen anything so perfect in all my life.

Her bottom lip is shaking, and for the millionth time I search for the right words, but I can't think of a thing. What a failure I am as I just stare at her with nothing to say.

Then, something comes to me. I don't think; I just speak.

"My mom was an alcoholic," I start.

I see E's eyes widen, and I take that as a sign to continue. "She was a wonderful mother, and an even better wife. She and my dad, they were so in love. High school sweethearts." Images assault me, and I close my eyes. "I can truly say I had a fulfilling childhood. I did all the sports I wanted. We had dinner as a family every night, and we took vacations a few times a year. Growing up, I had no idea my mom struggled with depression."

I took a deep breath, unable to believe I was saying this out loud. But the need to distract her outweighed everything else I was feeling. "As I got older, I noticed the wine in her water bottle. I noticed her getting up to refill her glass several times a night."

E doesn't say a word—just watches me.

"And as I got older, thirteen to be exact, I got curious. I didn't understand the repercussions of what I was doing. All I knew was that when Mom drank this stuff, she laughed a lot. I remember thinking how much fun it must be."

This would be the hard part of the story. Because this was the part that haunted me my entire life. I'd never really spoken about it out loud. God, how had I gone all these years?

"I got into her liquor cabinet one night. Did like seven shots—something insane like that—and I passed out."

E's biting her lip, her eyes still spilling over in tears, but I can tell she's listening.

"My mom was the only one home—and she was as drunk as I was, I'd find out later. When she found me, I was unconscious, with a bottle in my hand. She tried to drive me to the hospital, but we went over an embankment about a mile from our house."

E gasped, and I felt her hand fist my shirt.

"She died instantly. I woke up without a scratch on me, with the hangover of a lifetime. It was so bad, they didn't even tell me about the car accident until a day later."

She stares at me now with a different kind of shock. I wonder what she thinks of me. A monster. A killer. I thought I'd share my own story of loss, but hearing it all out loud...how could she even want me around after this?

But I continue the story, not knowing what else to do. "My father has never blamed me. He's treated me the same my entire life—with nothing but love and understanding. He knows the guilt I struggle with daily. And there has to be some Freudian shit involved, considering the career I went into, but...I've never apologized to him. Can you believe that? I mean, I punish myself. I haven't had a drink since, and I never will. But I've never apologized to him. And now he's sick...and I'm still too much of a coward."

I stop talking, overwhelmed by my life and the terrible memories of what happened. God, my old man deserves so much more. I took his wife from him, and he's never blamed me. The opposite, in fact. And I can't even look him in the eyes like a man and tell him I'm sorry.

E must see all the emotions churning within me, because she grabs my face with one soft hand and directs my eyes to hers. And in that second, we're just two people dealing with loss. Me, stuck in tragic memories, and she, stuck in a nightmare.

Rational thought exits my brain at top speed. I can feel it happening, but I can't stop it. All I can think about is the understanding I see in her eyes, so far from the rejection I'd expected. It brings me to a state of disbelief. A state of disbelief mixed with a sense of peace from getting all that off my chest.

I knew what was going to happen a second before it did, and I couldn't have stopped it. Not even if I had possessed all the willpower in the world.

Her lips meet mine in the sweetest, saddest kiss I've ever experienced. Just a small, brief touch that sends calm over me like a warm blanket but desire through my blood like a storm. A thousand bolts pass between us as we lie there, our lips touching for a second time, a third.

I can feel her short, staccato breaths in my mouth every time we separate, and it spurs me on to hold her tighter.

It feels like giving in. It feels...amazing. There's such an overpowering relief on my end, because holding myself back and keeping myself in denial have been so hard.

I want this woman. I want her just like this.

But there's so much going on externally between us. So much sadness and uncertainty. I feel it all, bubbling underneath the surface. After a fourth kiss that I'm desperate to take farther, I pull away. I press my lips to the top of her head and hold her close while I catch my breath. I can feel the puffs of air against my neck as she does the same.

As the seconds tick by, my mind swims with thoughts of *What next?* What did this mean for us? What did it mean for me working for her? Was it a moment of weakness for us both? No...no, that wasn't it. Because the truth was that I wanted more. More from her. More with her. And no matter what, I knew I wasn't leaving her side with that bastard still out there.

E falls asleep a few minutes later, and I'm able to get up without waking her. I take a long, hot shower before I check on her once again to make sure she's still asleep. Then I head into the living room.

Michonne, Joe, Big, Rob, Jacques, and Sandy are all there waiting. I feel a surge of panic that they know what happened between E and me, but I tamp it down and keep a straight face.

Michonne has tears in her eyes. "How is she?"

I sigh, grateful for the cup of coffee Joe hands me. "Sleeping."

Rob looks torn. "We have to get on the road tonight...Do you think she's..."

"I don't know," I snap. "She's hurting right now."

The room goes quiet before Jacques breaks the silence. "Poor Bella," he says, wiping under his eyes. "I'm going to miss that little doll."

Sandy is sitting at the table, her head down. "She seemed fine the last time I saw her. It just feels so sudden."

"It was sudden," I say. "The vets are doing an autopsy. We should expect results soon."

Rob's voice is cautious as he addresses the room. "I don't mean to sound callous, but we really can't afford this interruption. Our next show is in less than two days."

I know Rob means well, but the comment annoys me. "Her well-being comes first," I tell him sharply.

He gives me a look but doesn't say anything. I wonder again if any of my emotions regarding E are written on my face.

"This fucking sucks!" Joe spits out. He's standing behind Sandy's chair. "On top of everything else she's going through, she loses her dog. How much can one person take?"

I understand his frustrations. "We'll have answers in a little while. I think we need to give her some time."

Rob sighs. "Fine. We're supposed to leave by eight tonight. Keep me updated...and give her my best." He grabs his briefcase, gives me another look, and then starts herding everyone up to head back to their rooms. "It's business as usual for the rest of us. We have a few things to get done before we take off."

Everyone but Sandy leaves. "Is she OK?" she asks. "I can't imagine what's going through her mind. She loved Bella so much."

"She's a strong woman," I respond. "She'll be all right."

Sandy looks incredibly tired. The dark circles I've noticed under her eyes this past week are more pronounced than ever. I take a shot in the dark. "Are *you* OK?"

She shrugs, but when she looks up and catches me studying her, her eyes go wide. "Just, um...just tired. I should probably try to get a nap in before tonight."

She pushes up out of her chair, gives me a small wave, and then leaves the room through the connecting door. There's definitely something up with her, but I can only worry about one woman at a time. So with that thought, I grab a water bottle and head back to E's bedroom.

I stop short of the door and decide to make a quick phone call. The person on the other end of the line is so happy to hear from me, and even happier to hear what I have to say. E will hopefully cheer up when she hears this news. And whatever I can do to help E and make her feel better, I'll do. It's a scary thought.

She's awake when I go in, staring into space and clearly lost in her thoughts. I'm unsure of what to do. Am I supposed to just get back into bed with her? Am I supposed to keep my distance? Am I supposed to pretend like this never happened and go back to putting up my social wall?

I feel lost, but when she sees me standing there and opens her arms, I find I can't resist. She wraps herself around me as soon as I settle in the bed, and another surge of relief pushes through me. Relief born from acceptance. If she's inviting me to lie with her again, that must mean she doesn't regret what happened. Because even with all my reservations, I can't get myself to regret what happened. Not the kiss—or telling her about my mother.

I felt more comfort in those moments than I'd felt in years doing anything else. It was like a warm bucket of water had been thrown over my head, bringing me back to a reality I had forgotten about.

I run my fingers through her hair, half amazed to be in this position with her and half aching for her pain. "How are you?"

Her shoulders move imperceptibly. "I just...she was OK when I went to bed."

I don't want to mention anything about my suspicions until I'm absolutely sure. "We're going to find out what happened. We'll have answers as soon as we can."

She doesn't respond, but I feel my T-shirt grow wet again. Man, I wanted to stop her tears more than anything. I decide to tell her about my phone call.

"So, I called Harold just now."

She tenses. "Harold?"

I blow out a breath, still surprised at my actions. "Gave him his job back. If he goes through some regulatory training courses. We can't afford any more mistakes."

There's silence, and I wonder if she's not as pleased as I thought she'd be, but when I feel her staring at me, I look down and see a small smile on her face. "Thank you," she says. She leans in and—bold as can be—presses another sensual kiss on my lips. I'm rendered speechless. Is that how it's going to be between us now? If so, I need time to catch up. I've never been in a position like this—where I wanted something so much, but at the same time was so scared of it.

That's why it takes me completely by surprise when she shifts her body until she's lying directly on top of me. Her long hair is like a curtain around my face, and when she pushes up on her arms and looks down into my eyes, I groan aloud at the view. The sensation of her weight, the smell of her skin, and the intense heat she's emitting is an intoxicating combination.

We just stare at each other. Me because I have no clue what the hell to do. I search for my iron will, my black personality that I always have on hand, and it's nowhere to be found. Instead, I feel myself grow hard as a steel rod beneath her. I knew she feels it, too, because her eyes go dark and she clamps her legs around me, grinding softly into my erection. I don't have a chance.

Without warning she bends down and smashes her lips to mine. This kiss is different than what happened between us earlier, and my mouth opens instinctively when I sense her urgency. She takes full advantage and sweeps her tongue in, stealing my senses and all my rational thought. Her taste isn't anything like I had imagined but just what I'd dreamed. She tastes like strawberries and the essence of her smile, if her smile had a taste.

It only takes me a half a second to overcome the white-hot shock blasting through my system and respond the way I want to. And then I become frantic.

I wrap both arms around her back, lift my knees up to rest my feet on the bed and pull her into me, running my hands through her hair to cup the back of her head. Our mouths fight for dominance, in and out, up and over. The cadence of it is deadly, the chemistry between us unreal. It's as if I had kissed her a hundred times before, we're so in sync.

She starts rhythmically grinding into me, making me half-mindless. I can feel the heat between her legs, and I run my hands down her back to cup her bottom—whether to stop her or keep her going, I have no idea. I start to feel like I'm completely losing control. She's literally running this show, and that makes me short of breath for more reasons than one.

I don't even realize until my hands hit bare skin that I've reached down into the back of her shorts. The feeling of the soft, smooth skin of her ass is my undoing. She's so perfect. I suck in a sharp breath, my thoughts reeling.

Should this be happening?

I know that a part of her is doing this for comfort, but what about the other part? I'm so confused, turned on more than I've ever been in my life and...what is she thinking right now? Could she possibly need me as much as I need her? Panic starts to grip my chest.

"Stop thinking," she whispers over my mouth. Her hands are threaded through my hair. "Keep touching."

I pull away and grit my teeth. This has gone too far. The panic was building, clashing with desire. At this point I'd probably listen to whatever she told me. Do whatever she wanted me to do. I couldn't let that happen.

"What are we doing?" I whisper back. I hold her cheeks in both my hands and lift her face away from mine. "What are we doing?" I repeat.

At first she looks angry that I stopped her, then she looks confused. And then, before I have a chance to prepare myself, she bursts into tears.

"I'm sorry," she sobs. "I don't want you to think I'm using you. I just...needed..."

"Comfort," I sigh, feeling low as hell. Maybe I did have it all wrong.

She shakes her head against me. "No. I needed you." She lifts her head. "I've wanted you. For a while now."

She's looking at me with clear, shiny green eyes that are begging me to tell her the same. That I want her, too.

I'm not sure if I can give her that control, but I can't lie anymore. I'll figure out the rest later, but I can't deny her this. I don't have any flowery words, but..."Me too."

31

Eloisa

I wake up in a daze. My face feels swollen and my body achy. What…? Then I remember. My poor, beautiful, life-saving little Bella is gone. My best friend and confidante spent her last moments alone, probably scared, squeezed in next to a toilet.

My chest seizes painfully, and more tears come. I miss her so much already. I reach out toward the bed beside me, to her spot, but feel nothing there. It's like my right leg is missing.

But then I remember something else…moving over X's rock-hard body. His soft lips pressing against mine, his solid, strong arms holding me close. A burst of awareness has me sitting up in bed. Did that really happen?

I put a hand to my lips. Holy crap. It did happen. I fooled around with my bodyguard. I kissed him after he told me what was probably the darkest secret in his life. The poor man was carrying around so much guilt.

Did I regret it? The answer was instantaneous. No.

I wanted X. I wanted to do more than just kiss him with my clothes on. I was tired of denying myself his comfort, his strength. I didn't know how this whole thing was going to play out, but I wasn't going to let it go. I was a red-blooded woman attracted to a perfect-looking man, and I wasn't going to run away scared.

I lie back down in bed, overcome with desire for X and a deep sadness for Bella. The mix of feelings is exhausting. The window outside tells me the sun is going down, and I know we're probably late for leaving for the next show in Massachusetts.

The door opens a few minutes later, and I see X peek his head in. I lift mine infinitesimally so he knows I'm awake. His eyes never leave mine as he comes to kneel beside my bed.

How was he going to act? What was he going to do? The X I knew wasn't one to show emotion. He kept everything locked up tight to his vest, but...looking at him now, he seemed lighter. Had talking about what had happened with his mother helped? Speaking of...

"Thank you for telling me about your mother," I whisper, reveling in the fact that his face is only inches away from mine. Just his presence makes me feel good.

His jaw flexes. "Thank you for listening. I understand if you feel differently about me now—"

I put a finger to his lips. "Don't. You're blaming yourself for something that wasn't your fault. I think deep down you know it, and I think if you talked to your dad, he'd tell you the same thing. It was a tragic accident. You have to allow yourself to let go."

He takes a deep breath and then looks away. He's a smart man. I know he knows I'm right. But I also know that forgiving oneself is easier said than done. And it doesn't happen overnight. I can only hope this is a first step for him.

"Besides," I continue boldly, "if I feel differently about you now, it's because you gave me the kiss of a lifetime."

His eyes flash. "I'm sorry...I shouldn't have taken advantage of you when you were sad about Bella."

I would have laughed if I wasn't so heartsick. "I'm pretty sure you were the victim here." He doesn't say anything—just scans my face. I'd never seen his eyes look like they did now. As if in wonder. As if he was staring at something beautiful. "What do we do now?"

He sighs, looking to the ground. "I don't know. My first priority has to be the job. Until this guy gets locked away..."

I nod, understanding. Now is not the time to explore what is between us. I can't help but want him, though. And right now he's so close. I haven't had sex in a year, and I'm feeling desperate. "Does that mean we can't...?"

He knows what I mean and puts his forehead to the bed in response. "Don't tempt me." But oh, how I wanted to. The thought made me squirm, and he definitely took notice. "We both can't afford to be distracted right now," he finally says.

I pout, and he shakes his head, laughing under his breath. "You're something else." He pauses, as if trying to find the words. "I'm not used to...I don't know what..."

He's scared. He isn't a man used to giving up any sort of control. I can understand that. The man I see before me now is nothing like the man I first met only a few short weeks ago. I'm taking him out of his comfort zone. "Good."

He sighs, giving me another one of his hardened looks. Unbidden, thoughts of Bella swarm back in, and all the good feelings X just brought out in me dissipate. "Have you heard from the vet?"

He shakes his head. "Not yet."

"Is Rob freaking out right now?"

"An understatement."

I groan and try to blink away the tears that come to my eyes. The last thing I want to do is wreck a tour everyone has worked so hard for. But how can I perform when I feel like I do now? "I can't do it."

He puts a finger under my chin so I look at him. "Yes, you can. There's no *can't* for you. There never has been. You lost your mother, you were abandoned by your father, and you lived on the damned streets. Through sheer talent alone you were able to not only survive, but also live out your dream of playing music to the world. And even now, even when you've made it, you're still dealing with forces of antagonism. The media and their outrageous stories, Martha Mathers and her petty bullshit. Your douchey ex and his drama...and some fucking psychopath that someday soon I'm going to rip limb from limb. You can do this. You're the strongest, most courageous woman I know. You put me to shame."

His words creep around my chest like a vine and squeeze the breath out of me. A burst of emotion, like an exploding heart, erupts between us.

It's then I realize we're more alike than I thought. I've spent my life fighting an uphill battle, and he's spent his trying to come down that hill after the battle he had, but it's the same kind of fight.

"I don't put you to shame," I finally respond. "We're meeting in the middle. The middle of the hill."

He looks at me curiously, and I briefly explain to him what I mean. And as if by magic, we meet in the middle for a different reason, both drawn together for a kiss.

I travel to my second show in a haze of sadness.

I can only assume the loss of Bella feels like the loss of a beloved family member. Thinking of her little face saps me of my energy, and it's all I can do to keep myself together. The poor thing. How I wish I could have been with her when she passed on. She was always there for me, and I wasn't there for her in her time of greatest need.

But X is right. I can't let my fans down and cancel. This show is just as much about them as it is me. Not to mention this is the show my father plans on attending. Who knows if he actually meant it, but...I don't want to appear weak in his eyes.

Sandy, Joe, and Big all accompany us in our SUV while the rest of the crew rides in one of the tour buses. It's nice to have the extra company, but a part of me wishes it was just X and me.

They do their best to cheer me up, exchanging stories about Bella and shedding a few tears. The vet still hasn't gotten back to us. At least X didn't mention it, if there was word. What could have happened to my little girl?

It was my main question as we made the three-hour ride to Boston.

When we get to our scheduled hotel, there are fans lined up outside the door. I know X tried to keep the location a secret, but sometimes things have a way of revealing themselves, no matter what you do.

I can't get myself to sign autographs or engage. I feel so disconnected from everything, and all I can think about is getting in bed and trying to escape reality with sleep. That's my plan until the show tomorrow night.

Luckily, the team understands, and they escort me through the crowd without question and into the lobby, where I'm eventually shown to a private suite and a large, comfortable bed.

I guess I pass out right away, because when I wake up, someone is crawling into bed next to me.

"Is this OK?" he asks into the darkness.

I don't answer. I just wrap my arms around him, so grateful for the comfort. I feel him relax in my hold, sensing that he's gaining just as much comfort from me. We hold each other, both squeezing once in a while as if reveling in the feeling. So much for now not being the right time.

"I couldn't help coming here," he explains. "You looked so sad all day. I...I couldn't help."

I nod, understanding. Being with him gives me a feeling I never knew existed, and one I have no idea how I ever did without.

⁓⁓

"You ready?" X asks, the cacophony of a screaming arena nearly drowning out his voice.

I stand in the wings, about to make the entrance to my second show. I know he's worried about a repeat performance—me freezing the second I get onstage—but I'm confident it won't happen this time. "I'm ready."

Sandy had come up to me earlier and let me know that my father was in fact here. It lit a fire under my ass like nothing else could. He wanted to see a show? I'd give him a show.

"Good. Good luck."

"You're supposed to say 'break a leg.'"

"Why the hell would I say that?"

"Because it means good luck!"

"That's the stupidest thing I've ever heard."

"You've never heard that before?"

"No."

I laugh, enjoying the playfulness that has sprung up between us in such a dark time. "Well, now you know. It's what all performers say to each other before heading onstage. It's tradition."

"I'm still not saying it."

I sigh. He's so handsomely adorable, I stand on tiptoes and place a small kiss on his lips...and he tenses, but he lets me. I have no idea if that's allowed or not, but I don't care. He held me last night, but I'd barely seen him today with everything going on. But when we get together, it's almost like we can't help ourselves.

Which is completely and utterly surreal. Me with the intimidating and angry storm cloud. Hearing my cue, I turn away to head out onstage. I see Sandy watching us from the corner of her eye, and I make a mental note to tell her about X and me. I don't want her to feel like I was lying to her.

Walking onstage this time feels different. This one is for Bella.

And all in all, the show goes as it should, despite the fact that I cry during a few of my ballads. I'm still able to get through all my songs and let the crowd chalk it up to a passionate performance.

I can't see him there, but I can feel him. My father. The one who abandoned me and basically left me for dead. I hit my highest note of the show with that thought in mind.

Goddamn it. I was proud of myself. I'd been able to push aside the devastation I felt over losing Bella and the nerves over my father in the audience and put on a show that was even smoother than the last. My fans bolster me, as they always do. And thoughts of X and what is developing between us make my heart sing.

It's so uncertain, but once again, when the show is over, he's the first one I run to. Even with everyone watching, he lets me fly into his arms. I catch the team's questioning looks—and Michonne's grin—over my shoulder. Apparently our embrace looked as heady as it felt.

I'd thought X might be nervous to outwardly show affection toward me, but I shouldn't have been surprised. He had always been a man who didn't care what people thought, basically doing whatever he wanted.

When we let go, he smiles down at me. "I'm proud of you."

"Thank you."

"Everyone is watching us, aren't they?"

"Yup."

He sighs and turns around, a dark expression on his face. When he does, Rob, Big, and Joe look away awkwardly, like they hadn't been watching us, but Michonne, Jacques, and Sandy walk over the few feet to where we're standing.

"Come here," Michonne says, holding out her arms for a hug. "You were amazing, just as I knew you'd be. I want to suggest upgrading your outfit for the second act, though. How would you feel about hot pants?"

"She would look amazing in hot pants!" Jacques puts in, taking his turn with a hug. "But no blues, please. The color makes her skin look washed out."

"No more outfit changes," Rob chimes in from afar. "We just got everything figured out!"

"Blue in general does not make her look washed out—only dark blue!" Michonne says back.

"Ellie looks great in blue!" Joe calls, genuinely confused. "Who doesn't look good in blue?"

Jacques sniffs and waves his hand as if swatting the comment away. "What would you know about it?"

Big shrugs. "Blue's my favorite color." I notice X roll his eyes at the comment and can barely suppress a grin.

Sandy stands a bit off to the side, her face tense. I still haven't asked her what's been wrong with her lately, as I've been so distracted by my own drama. She seems especially troubled now. I gaze at her for a few seconds, and she looks away.

"Everything OK, Sandy?" X asks, picking up on the exchange.

Sandy runs a hand through her ponytail. "Your father. He texted me...he wants to come backstage and see you."

There's an awkward silence, but we had all been expecting this to happen.

"Hey, you don't have to see the bastard," Joe says, walking over with Big and Rob. He stands by Sandy, and they share a look. "I mean, it's up to you."

Rob clears his throat. "He made a big stink outside the arena today. Telling everyone he was your father and carrying around old photos of you two. There's some pictures on social media of him posing with your fans."

Ugh. The nerve. Stealing my fame to make himself feel less guilty over the hell he put me through as a child. But a part of me, the little girl who still feels a sense of abandonment, wants to see him.

"It's fine," I finally say. "I've been avoiding him for a year. I might as well face the music."

"Are you sure?" X asks.

"I'm sure."

Everyone goes quiet, and I can tell they aren't happy with my decision.

I look around at all their glum faces. The faces of my family. "Look, thank you all for your support. But please don't worry about it. It's not like I'm inviting him back into my life."

"Damned right," Joe said. "We're just worried about you, that's all."

"But we support you," Jacques says stiffly.

"Thank you," I tell them. "I love you guys."

After a few sappy moments, I smile and look at Sandy. "You can bring him to my dressing room in about ten. Does that work?"

She nods. And then, almost as an afterthought, she says, "Oh, amazing job, Ellie. You were beautiful out there."

I watch her walk off, her face in her phone.

32

Xavier

Ten minutes later, E and I are in her dressing room. She's pacing around nervously while I stand off to the side, looking at the pictures fans posted with her father earlier that night. There are tons of them. The bastard.

When E begins fixing her hair in the mirror, I can't stand it.

"Hey, stop that. You look gorgeous."

My voice is a little rougher than I'd intended, and I know E picks up on it. She stops fixing her hair and looks at me over her shoulder in the mirror. In another life, I'd take her away. Somewhere far away from all this bullshit. But she's famous, and I'm...me. I'm not the man who can do that for her.

The problem is, I can't help wanting her. I can't stop myself from touching her when she wants it or needs it. Like after the show. One taste of it, one taste of her, and I lost everything I'd worked so hard for...but it didn't feel as bad as I thought it would.

"You think I'm gorgeous?"

I stare at her. Is she serious? She's the most beautiful woman I've ever seen. "It was the first thing I thought when I first saw you."

Her mouth drops open. Literally. "I thought you hated me!"

I shrug. "I didn't know you. I thought you were just like all the other celebrities I had encountered. But I still thought you were gorgeous."

She turns around, leaning against the vanity. She has a devilish smile on her face. "I still can't believe you walked in on me naked."

"Best day of my life," I tease.

She smiles, biting her lip. "So far."

A knock sounds at the door, cutting the moment short.

Sandy pushes her way in, followed by a man I recognize from the photos as E's father. I bristle as I watch E do her best to pull herself together.

Sandy comes to stand by my side as E and her father size each other up. His face is etched in what looks like a mix of sadness and awe. E's looks blank.

I think I'd been expecting an evil monster, but E's dad is just a regular old man. Shorter than average, balding. He has her clear green eyes, but that's where the resemblance ends. Everything else about him is completely average.

"Eloisa," he begins, fidgeting with his hands. "Your show was so much fun. I'm so proud of you."

"Thank you."

He takes a step closer. "I'm so happy I got to come. And thank you for letting me back here. I've been calling..."

"I know. I've been busy."

Her father apparently isn't deterred by her short answers. "You... you reminded me so much of your mother up there. You look so much alike."

"So I've heard." E runs her eyes over his face. "I also heard you were taking photos before the show."

He nods. "I hope you're not mad...I'm just so proud of you I could burst. I know you're probably ashamed of me."

"I'm not ashamed," E tells him, her arms crossing defensively. "I just...I don't know you."

There's a moment of silence, and then...

"I thought your aunt was going to take you!" he tells her desperately. "I was a coward. I was an alcoholic, depressed coward! I never knew you were on the streets. If I did—"

My stomach sinks when I hear alcohol was involved. Damn. She was surrounded by it. And here I was, adding my own shit to her plate.

E put up a hand. "We don't have to go over this again. What's done is done. Let's just...What did you think of the show?"

I watch the scene, anger and frustration bubbling beneath my skin. Her father is waxing poetic about her performance when all I can think about is punching his bum face. How could he leave his little girl on the streets to rot? Anything could have happened to her. He didn't deserve to bask in the air she breathed. Watching him snivel at her feet, desperate for her approval, was the only thing that made me feel any better.

I look over to see Sandy with the same expression. She seems to hate E's dad as much as I do.

My phone signals a text, and when I see it's from the vet, my heart skips a beat.

Vet: *Poison. Bromadiolone. She had enough in her system to kill a dog three times her size. What the hell happened?*

My stomach sinks like a block of concrete.

I stare at the phone, unsure of what the hell to do. When could she have gotten poisoned? Who could have given it to her?

What the fuck was I going to tell E?

I show the text to Sandy, and the second she sees it, her eyes widen. Her breath picks up, and the next thing I know, she bursts into tears and runs out of the room.

E doesn't notice Sandy's hasty exit, as she's still dealing with her father. I want him the hell out of the room so I can get to the bottom of what's going on and break the news to E. I send a quick text to Joe and Big, asking them to come to the dressing room as soon as possible.

Her father is taking pictures out of his back pocket, and when he does, a slew of letters come with it.

"Oh!" he says, bending down to pick up the pile. "Messages from your fans. They asked me to give them to you."

I burst into action. "Give them to me."

I snatch the few he has in his hands and bend down to grab the rest. I have a terrible feeling. I don't know if it's from the news I was just given about Bella or if it's something else, but I'm not taking any chances.

Big bursts into the room a moment later.

"Where's Joe?" I demand.

"X, what's going on?" E asks. Her face looks scared.

"He's talking to Sandy. She's really upset," Big replies. He looks around, eyes landing on E's father. "Everything OK in here?"

"I told them I would give those to her," her father says, gesturing toward the pile in my hand.

I ignore him, handing them to Big. "Can you look through these and let me know if you see anything?"

He nods, bringing the stack to the side of the room to begin sifting through them.

My heart is going a mile a minute. "Are we done here?" I ask E. "I need to talk to you."

Rob walks into the room then, his face pale. When he notices E's dad, he regroups. "X, we need to talk. Now."

At that moment, my phone starts ringing. It's the police. *Holy fuck.* I take a deep breath, trying to keep my head on straight. My mind is buzzing in a million different directions. I send them to voice mail to deal with later.

"We're going to have to finish this visit on a later date," I tell her father. I walk out of the dressing room and gesture to one of the guards. "Can you escort Mr. Morgan to his car?"

I feel E's hand on my arm. "X, what's going on?"

My phone starts ringing again. This time it's the colonel—a call I can't ignore. I hold up a finger to tell her I'll be right back and walk down the hall. "What is it?"

"Martha Mathers was found dead this afternoon. Note was stuffed inside her mouth. It read, 'For Eloisa.' They had trouble between them, didn't they?"

I sink against the wall, trying to process the news. I try to keep the shock out of my voice. "They did. Do you think it's the same guy?"

"Has to be," the Colonel replies. "Who else?"

"Any leads?"

"Not yet. I'll keep you updated."

"Do that. I'm dealing with some things here right now. I'll call you back."

"What things?"

I briefly tell him the situation before I hang up. I stride back into the room to find E's father being escorted out by Rob.

"What did I do?" he asks me nervously. E is trailing behind, her eyes troubled.

"Nothing," I tell him. "I'll have E call you later."

He turns back to her, as if looking for a hug, but she just stands there with her arms wrapped around herself.

"Come on," Rob says. Then he turns to look at me. "We need to talk. It's about Martha."

I nod. "I just heard."

Big comes up behind E then, his face hard. He holds up a letter silently behind E's back.

Shit. One fucking thing after another.

I grab E's hand, needing to hold on to her. "We're going back to the hotel."

I turn to Big. "Find Joe and Sandy. We all need to talk."

He exits behind Rob and E's father.

I take a deep breath, trying to gather my thoughts. I text the vet back and then look at E. "Grab your things. We're leaving. And don't look at your phone."

The door of the hotel room closes softly behind Sandy. E's core team is scattered around the room, quiet and unsure about what's going on.

I have no idea what to deal with first, but I decide to tackle the news about Bella.

I walk to E's side and put a hand on her shoulder. "I talked to the vet today. Bella...she was poisoned."

Audible gasps fill the room, and Rob jumps to his feet. "Poisoned?"

I don't take my eyes off E's face. She's incredulous. "What do you mean?"

"The vet found bromadiolone in her system, which is a rat poison."

I let that sentence sink in. A few moments pass before everyone begins talking at once.

E, with tears streaming down her face, sits down on the couch a few minutes later. "Who could have done this?" she asks sadly.

Rob clears his throat, his face drawn. "Could it be...could it be the stalker?"

"It's the same person," Big cuts in to respond. He draws a letter from his back pocket, and I'm happy to see it's now encased in a plastic Ziploc. "He must have found E's father outside and sent a note back."

"What does it say?" E asks quietly from beside me.

"It says, 'I didn't want to hurt Bella. I only hurt Bella because you hurt me.'"

"What the fuck!" Michonne shouts, pulling E into a hug. "How did he get to Bella? Why the fuck can't we find this guy?"

"This is horrible," Jacques says, wiping his eyes under his pink glasses. "We have to cancel the tour until we find this maniac."

Rob turns white but doesn't say anything. Just takes a seat on the couch and puts his head in his hands. Big slaps a meaty paw on his shoulder, his face contorted with sadness.

The room dissolves into angry conversation and tears.

"This situation is getting out of control," Rob finally says. "The red carpet incident. The knife on the door. The chocolate ice cream, Bella, and now Martha? Who the fuck is this guy?"

"What happened to Martha?" E asks, her voice shaking, as if she knows what's coming.

I guess it's time to drop the next bomb. I have the group sit down as I tell them what the police just told me before this meeting. Martha was found dead in her New England home, a gunshot wound to the chest. I explain about the note and tell everyone the police are on their way.

Without another word, E runs into the back bedroom, slamming the door. I know her well enough to know that she's feeling intense guilt. Sandy is now sitting on the couch between Joe and Michonne, crying hysterically.

The police and FBI arrive a few minutes later to get statements and to make sure we're all up to speed. Because of Martha's celebrity, the homicide case is escalated to priority one.

Everyone is on the search for this asshole, but no one more than me. It was going to take all my willpower to not wring his neck when I found him, and I *would* find him.

The problem is the media. After a long debate—in which I ultimately get my way—we decide to keep this whole thing under wraps for as long as we can. My fear is if it gets out to the world, the perp will go into hiding. I want the fucker feeling as if he'd gotten away with it.

After the smoke clears, I tell the team members to go back to their rooms and get some sleep. There's another show in two days in New York, and as of now, it's still on.

I head into the kitchen and pour myself a glass of water, thinking that I could really use a drink. I don't even remember how drinking alcohol felt, but I have a feeling it would really do the trick right now and calm my nerves.

E, who only came out once to talk to the police, is back in her bedroom. She's been quiet since hearing the news about Martha, her demeanor ghostlike. I need to talk to her.

I open the door and find her sitting up on the bed, her phone in her hands. She's staring out the window when I sit beside her.

We don't say anything for a few moments. I have no idea what *to* say. I'm so damned sorry she's going through this. Going through this at a time that should be one of the happiest in her life.

"I talked to Joel," she whispers.

I seize up. Did she turn to him for comfort?

"I wanted to warn him...just in case." She wipes an errant tear. "If this guy went after Martha, maybe he'd try to go after him. He's the only other person I'm publicly connected to."

Relief sweeps away the jealousy. It makes sense, and she has a point. "I don't want you to worry about the team. Security is airtight. No one is going to be able to get to you or them."

She nods sadly. "Joel told me you talked to him."

At first I'm confused, but then I remember picking up her phone that night at the cabin. She looks at me, and I shrug innocently. "You told me I could handle him. I didn't want him calling you anymore."

She sighs heavily. "He's in Barbados with his new girlfriend. I'm sure he'll be fine."

"Why did you guys break up?" I ask, finally allowing the question to come out after so long.

She bites her lip nervously and can't seem to meet my eyes. "Well, he cheated on me. The man I met in the beginning of our relationship is long gone. When he got famous and the groupies started coming around, he changed into a different person. He also had serious alcohol problems."

Damn. Another one. I try not to let the news bring me down. I'm nothing like him. I want to tell her that, but it doesn't feel like the time. "Yeah?"

"He cared about getting his next drink or lay more than he cared about me. I think he's sober now. I just hope he's changed, for her sake."

I can't help but wonder if she's upset over his new girlfriend. I hope not. She goes quiet, resting her head on my shoulder, and I put my arm around her.

"What's going on between us?" she asks, staring out at the moon. It's not the first time the question has come up, but it feels different this time.

"I don't know," I tell her honestly, watching the shadows the moon is making on her face. I wish I had a better answer.

"Please," she says, her voice breaking. "Tell me something good. I need...I need to hear something good. I feel so guilty."

I squeeze her tight to my side. "This isn't your fault, E."

"It is. Indirectly," she says, moving her face into my chest. "It is."

"So, what, if you were never born, this wouldn't have happened? I know it's awful that the guilt is heavy, and it hurts."

"What can I do to stop this?" she asks quietly. "I feel so helpless. He...this person must hate me so much."

Her words swim in my brain. Something about her wording strikes a chord, but I can't put my damn finger on it.

"This isn't about you; it's about him," I tell her. "And you know I'm right." She doesn't say anything, so I push on. "Didn't we just talk about guilt the other night? Didn't you tell me not to blame myself about what happened to me?"

"That was different."

"Yes, but it's the same idea. And you were right. What happened with my mother was tragic and terrible, but it wasn't my fault. And what's happening now is not your fault. You hear me?"

She sits up and looks directly at me, and we stare at each other for a few moments. I feel the bond between us crackle. It's there, holding us invisibly by our emotions. She must feel it, too. "What's going on between us?" she asks again.

I stare at her lips, remembering how they feel against my own and dying to feel it again. But this—I feel like I need to give her a real answer. "All I can think about is you. All I see is you. And it's not for the reasons I was hired for. Here I am, brought in to protect you, and I can't find the man who's hurting you."

"I don't want you to leave," she says, leaning in. "When this is over, I don't want you to go."

"I don't want to," I tell her, surprising myself, but unable to take it back. "Whatever's happening between us—I don't want it to stop."

"Why?" she asks, pressing her cheek intimately against mine, starting a fire. The heat burns through my body, damn near feeling like it's opening up my soul.

I swallow hard. "I've lived such a lonely existence before this, before you. Work, diligence, order...I never let anyone else in, not even my father. You're breaking that curse I live with. You're breaking it down inch by inch, because you force me to see that my false bravery is for nothing, and you force me to see what real bravery looks like. You inspire me. I can't imagine meeting anyone else...in the middle...like I've met you."

She takes a short breath—surprised, I know—at how candid I've just been.

Feeling vulnerable as hell, I force myself to stay still. Damn, I had just bared the inside of my heart to this woman. But just as I did when I told her what happened with my mom, I feel lighter. I want to know, though, what does she see in me? I know what everyone else sees. A hard, mean, and angry person. And I know how I see myself. Does she too see the weak, emotionally challenged man who sits before her?

As if she can read my thoughts, she takes my face in her hands. "I want you to stay. I want you to stay, because you make me feel safer than I've ever felt in my life. You give me a peace like I've never known, a home, and you are the strongest, most selfless man, and you don't even know it. You've lived your life repenting for something you shouldn't have. And now that we've met in the middle, all I want to do is move forward. That's what I want."

Despite everything we're dealing with, she's still able to fill me with light. And I know I'm doing the same for her.

"And there's one more reason," she says lightly, crawling onto my lap and forcing me down to the bed. "Because you're so fucking hot."

Our mouths meet in a clash of teeth and desperate hunger. A low moan sounds in the back of her throat, and the sound vibrates through my body. The events of the day along with both of our confessions have me as electric as a live wire, and she's so amped up I can barely keep my hands on her, seemingly able to feel the need pouring from her skin.

The darkness of the room outlines her body in shadow and gray light, and every time I open my eyes, it feels like a filtered dream.

Her mouth moves from my lips, and we both take a desperate breath of air, but a split second later she starts raining kisses all over my face, moving down to my neck and causing me to involuntarily push my erection into the space between her thighs. I've never wanted anything in my life as much as I want her. The feel of her body on mine is literally driving me insane.

I knew I wasn't going to hold back this time, and once I felt her chest rub against me, I put my hands on her beautifully curved hips, run them up the sides of her waist, and take her shirt with me until it's all the way off. She isn't wearing anything underneath, and my eyes blink rapidly, anxious as a thirteen-year-old boy to look at her, to take her in.

She sits up as if wanting me to look my fill. My eyes feast on the gorgeous sight before me. Perfectly formed, perfectly sized, pale-white breasts with small pink nipples are all I can see. My fingertips are drawn like magnets, and when I cup her, running my thumbs over those nipples, we both moan.

She moves to take off my shirt, and we spend long minutes exploring each other's bare skin. Her little hands are all over my chest, squeezing my muscles. At the same time, she's rubbing up against me in a rhythm as old as time. Her skin is incredibly soft, and I lean up to kiss every freckle that I'm able.

I need more. I push up against her more forcefully, sending a message that she reads loud and clear. Rolling to the side, she undoes her jeans with shaking hands. I help pull them down her legs, my eyes glued on what her white underwear is hiding.

Staring into her eyes, I shift her up on the bed and move over her. "I can't believe we're here right now," I tell her.

"We made it to the middle," she whispers back, hands still roving over my upper body, making me shiver.

I lean down, taking one flawless breast in my mouth, wondering if some God out there made her body and her mind just for me. Her skin feels incredible under my tongue, especially the underside of her breast, and I take my time nuzzling her there.

She's worked up; I can tell by the heat of her skin. I lower my head and pepper openmouthed kisses across her stomach, trying to infuse how much I feel for her into every touch of my lips.

When I get to the top of her underwear, I don't even have to ask. Her legs spread wide open, and her hands go to the top of my head as if wanting to force me to stay put.

I look up her, my eyes no doubt filled with emotion. Hers are molten with heat. "Sorry, it's been a year," she tells me, her voice hoarse.

Nothing else she could have said could have turned me on more. "Let's fix that."

I put two fingers in the sides of her panties and drag them down her legs, my mouth watering at the vision before me.

"Fuck," I growl under my breath. Pulsing waves of heat unfurl inside me. "This is...you are..."

"Stop talking," she tells me, her voice husky.

"Yes, ma'am."

I lower my head and get to work, sliding my tongue eagerly through her folds. Her taste explodes on my tongue, and I close my eyes, savoring her and anxious as hell to get her off.

I don't have to wait long. Her knees clamp around my head, and she bucks up off the bed, crying out my name and scouring her nails on my scalp. Best. Feeling. Ever.

I don't want to stop, but her hands are tugging me up, so I move up her body and soon we're kissing again. After that it's a scramble of hands and wet kisses, and I fumble to unbuckle my belt and slide off my pants.

"I'm on the pill, and I've been tested," she whispers to me, cradling my face in her hands. "Please don't stop."

"Me too."

She pulls back to give me a strange look, and I shake the cobwebs out of my head. "Wait, not the pill thing."

She laughs beautifully. "I figured."

Finally, finally, I'm positioning myself between her legs. I close my eyes and take a mental snapshot of the moment and of how she looks right now. It's an image I never want to forget. She's more than I ever imagined and more than I deserve. Her long hair is splayed around her head, her green eyes are dark and hooded, and her mouth is parted and glistening from my kisses. I stare an extra second longer at those lips, a part of me still unable to believe she's even letting me kiss her.

Without warning, she moves out from under me and straddles me like a damned cowboy. "I want to be on top the first time."

I can barely find the words—or the air—to respond before she grabs my cock, sending lightning through my body, and presses the tip inside her.

Time stands still as inch by inch she slides down on top of me. Her warm, soaking-wet heaven has my eyes rolling in the back of my head, and I have to mentally snap myself out of it before I leave the moment completely. Grabbing her hips, I push up at an angle inside her and gyrate my hips, rewarded when she throws her head back and cries out my name again.

Her hands go to her breasts, and she tugs on her nipples as I try my damnedest to keep up a rhythm. It's incredible. This is incredible. She's incredible.

She places her palms flat on the bed beside my shoulders and starts moving up and down in time with me, and I've never felt more in sync with anyone. We're connected in so many ways, physically and mentally, and my balls tighten as I try to hold on and not blow it too soon.

Our mouths connect again, and my hands slide around her back to hold her close. Her skin is moist, or maybe it's my palms.

An immature sense of pride overwhelms me that out of all the millions of men in the world who probably fantasize about her, it's me that she's chosen. If they only knew that their fantasies pale in comparison to the real thing.

She leans up again and starts moving faster, and I bring my hand up to her clit, rubbing in small circles to try to get her to go off again, knowing I won't be able to last much longer.

I don't want it to end. I want her in so many different ways, in so many different angles. I want my hands on every millimeter of her skin, but I'm fading fast. She leans into my hand, helping herself along and then just like that, she hits her peak. I feel her inside walls clenching around me, sucking me dry, and I grit my teeth, forcing myself to last through her release. The second she lets out a breath, I explode inside her. A white-hot shot that overwhelms me in its enormity, guts me with its intensity.

I hold her tightly in my arms, trying to ground myself.

Long seconds tick by as we catch our breaths. Her arms are tangled around my chest and shoulders, neither of us making any attempt to move.

When she finally looks up at me a few long minutes later, her forehead is damp, her eyes gleaming. "Wow."

We share a look, and I'm sure she can see the awe in my gaze. "Wow."

"I needed that," she says, nuzzling back into me.

I laugh, unsure whether or not I should be offended. "Well, glad to be of service."

Her eyes are bright with laughter as she rubs a hand across my chest. "What? You were hired to protect my body, weren't you?"

I pretend to be offended. "Seriously, E? This is your idea of pillow talk?"

She giggles. "I'm not in the mood for pillow talk."

"What are you in the mood for?"

"I want to do that. Again."

"Good God, woman."

She sits up, straddling my hips. "I told you. It's been a long time."

I'm fascinated by the fact that I'm getting hard again. I've got stamina, but it usually takes me twenty minutes or so. When she feels me rising against her, she presses against me erotically, reigniting the heat between us.

While I'd love to spend the night getting lost in lust with E, a lot has happened tonight. A lot of terrible things.

"Wait," I say. "Can we...can we talk first?"

She gives me a look and then puts her hands above her head, winding her hair into a ponytail. It gives me an amazing view of her breasts, and my mouth goes dry. I close my eyes to block the view. "Are you OK?" I force myself to ask. "There's so much going on and—"

She presses a finger to my lips. "I know there's a ton of shit I have to deal with, X. And I will. But not right now. Please?"

"But—"

"I appreciate you trying to be a gentleman, but you're one of the only good things I've got right now. I need to enjoy it. I need to enjoy you."

"I still don't feel right about it. I feel like we need to have a rational conversation, not to mention figure out our next move with the tour and—"

"You're thinking too much." She smiles devilishly as her hand snakes down my stomach to grab hold of my dick. Arousal zings through me, and I feel myself pulse in her hand. She lifts a brow, the saucy minx. I roll over on top of her and rub my hardness against her stomach. Her eyes close, and her lips part. Two can play at this game.

As I take her again, all I can think is that I want this pain-in-the-ass beautiful celebrity with a heart of gold and a voice to match to be mine. I've never wanted anything like that before.

We stare into each other's eyes, enjoying the small moment of happiness while we can. But dark thoughts inevitably drift in.

I need to catch this fucker.

The fucker who wants to steal this from me.

I lean down to kiss her slowly, and we cling to each other in the darkness, both unsure of what the morning might bring.

33

Eloisa

When I wake the next morning, I feel strange.

Strange because my heart is bursting with emotion after my night with X at the same time as it's breaking because of everything else.

I think about Martha and how I'll have to live with the weight of her death on my shoulders. I won't exactly miss her, but she was an icon in the music industry—now a legend. I think about Bella, and how she saved me that day long ago, and I think about Sandy and my crew and how I have no idea what I'd do if something happened to them.

And I think about X. I think about how my annoying, invasive bodyguard is now a source of pure happiness. We've unexpectedly connected on a level I would have never anticipated, and I know he sure as hell didn't see it coming, either.

But here he is, naked and tangled in my sheets.

I know his alarm is set to go off at any minute, and I want one more moment with him before the sun comes up and he's back in bodyguard mode. For a few seconds I just admire his body. He's a perfect specimen, and hell if he isn't taking some sort of growth hormone for his nether regions.

I sigh inwardly and decide not to climb on top of him like I want to. I'm pretty sure we had sex five times last night, and I need to give the poor man a break. Easier than it sounds, I think, as my gaze roves over his rock-hard abs and chiseled face.

I press my lips against the skin above his ear instead. "Good morning."

He turns to me and blinks a few times. Then he pauses, as if remembering everything that happened the night before. I know I have to be careful, as what's happening between us is probably even scarier for him.

Is he going to jump out of bed and run out of the room? Does he regret it?

Those worries are dismissed when he tilts my chin up to kiss my lips. "Good morning."

He rubs a warm hand down my back, squeezes my butt, and rests his forehead against mine. Then he jumps out of bed, and I get an amazing view of *his* backside as he heads for the shower. I sigh, but I know better than to mess with his morning routine.

I may have broken down some of his walls, but he's still a man of discipline.

I decide to get up, too, and I'm surprised when I find Sandy standing in the kitchen. It looks as if she didn't get a moment of sleep.

"Hey," she rasps out.

"Hey." I walk over to her and put my hand on her shoulder. "What are you doing up so early?"

She shrugs. "Just reading social media. Everyone's talking about Martha. No one knows about the note, though. The police are keeping it quiet, as they said they would."

I nod, reaching behind her to open the cabinet and grab three mugs. "That's good."

"How are you holding up?" she asks quietly.

ONE-WOMAN SHOW

I sigh, not sure if I've even processed all my thoughts. "I feel guilty. Sad. Scared. No, terrified." I turn toward her again and cross my arms over my chest. "You?"

Her face crumples. "Not so good."

"Hey." I pull her into a hug. "It's going to be OK."

She lets out a tearful, sarcastic laugh. "Right."

Something is bothering me, though. Sandy was acting strange even before all this happened. I want to ask her if anything else is going on, but there's a knock on the door.

Before I can answer it, X comes racing out of the room, a towel around his waist. "Stay there," he commands.

He looks through the peephole and growls before throwing it open. Joe, Big, Michonne, Jacques, and Rob stand in the hallway. When they see him in the towel, their eyes widen.

"Ooooweeee! Talk about a wake-up call," Jacques says with one brow raised as he sizes X up.

"Good morning to you," sings Michonne, giving me the eye over X's shoulder.

"Bad time?" Joe asks, spotting Sandy and me and throwing a shit-eating grin in my direction.

I roll my eyes. "No, you guys can come in."

Everyone pushes into the room and starts talking at once.

"E, I've been thinking about you all night," Michonne tells me, her dreads now pink. She must have been stressed if she had Jacques do a late-night dye session. For her, a bad day means a new hair color. "I know you must feel terrible—"

"But nothing is your fault," Joe cuts in. "I refuse to let you mope around."

"We're going to catch this guy," Rob says, his voice determined. Well, I had certainly never seen him so riled up.

Everyone clearly has a lot of unspent energy. I look to X, who's quiet, leaning against the door, obviously not caring that he's in a towel. My gaze rakes down his body, amazed that I had that man inside me last night.

The warring emotions inside me come to a head. "Can I say something?" I ask loudly to the group. Everyone goes quiet as they prepare to hear what I have to say. I can tell some of them are thinking I'm going to cancel the tour. And maybe I should. I don't know.

"It's been a trying few days," I begin. "And, yes, while I do feel a lot of guilt"—I hold up a hand to quiet any response—"I do want to continue on with the tour."

"Thank God," Rob says, putting a hand to his heart. Michonne shoots him a dirty look. "What? We shouldn't be bowing down to this animal! He's got the force of the FBI, the police, and X on his tail. His days are numbered."

I can only hope.

"We're behind you, Ellie," Joe says as he stands next to Sandy. "Whatever you decide."

"We've got your back," Big tells me. "Right, X?"

When I look in X's direction, I can tell he's been watching me the whole time. He gives me a small nod, as if in approval of my decision. "Right."

And so it went.

The next three shows went off without a hitch. There were no scares, no letters, no drama, and no sign of the crazy psycho who had been wreaking such havoc in my life.

Things almost started to go back to normal. I knew the investigation was carrying on as intended, but I wasn't privy to all of the details. X was on the phone a lot, though, talking to his boss, the police, and the FBI in turn—frustrated with the lack of progress. I knew he wanted to go out and start looking for this creep on the ground, but I also knew that he wouldn't dare leave my side.

After our first time together, the next two weeks flew by. X and I spent every night in each other's arms, talking well into the morning about everything under the sun and touching each other until exhaustion forced us to close our eyes. If I had been able to see all the layers he had hiding underneath his rough exterior from the beginning, I probably would have fallen in love with him on the spot.

ONE-WOMAN SHOW

I found out that we agreed on politics, which surprised me. I found out that we both had dreams of backpacking across Europe, carrying nothing but the clothes on our backs. We both wanted a big house in the country somewhere one day, and we both hated watching reality TV.

The biggest surprise of the two weeks constantly in his company was discovering his sense of humor. It existed! Surprise, surprise—X loved to make funny faces, and the first time he did, it was so unexpected I fell into hysterics. If things got too sad or too serious, he'd throw me a funny face, and it would instantly brighten my mood.

We also couldn't keep our hands off each other. That man's talent in bed was mind-boggling and like nothing in even my wildest daydreams. Where he found the time to hone those skills over the years was beyond me. He always seemed to know exactly how to move, exactly where to touch next to send me gallivanting off into another life-changing orgasm. And the things he'd whisper to me at night as we stared into each other's eyes—"Thank you, E." "I can't get enough of this body." "Don't ever stop being who you are." "Your face is the best face."—would always put me over the edge.

It didn't take long for everyone on the tour to get wind of our relationship. Some people were surprised, mostly the men, while the women seemed to nod knowingly. They saw it coming, they told me. Michonne said she knew the second she saw X that it was inevitable for two beautiful people like us to get together. Rob was a little wary at first, but X had a conversation with him and his boss to put everything on the table. I'd been so proud of him for doing that. A risk so far out of his comfort zone. I'm not sure how the conversation went, but I'm pretty sure both men understood that X was not going to leave my side even if it was a conflict of interest.

I didn't know what I would do if he had to leave. I was completely dependent on him being there. Now, us being together felt as natural as a sip of water. It was hard to look back on where we'd come to where we were now.

I tried not to dwell on anything but the tour. I tried to block out the media as much as I could. Especially because of the show—the sixth one—that I had tonight.

I was especially looking forward to this show, because it was at Madison Square Garden, a place I'd only dreamed of performing.

As I stand backstage, admiring all the pictures on the wall, I feel someone come up behind me. I whirl around, nervous, sensing that it isn't X.

"Picture for Instagram?" Sandy says, a tight smile on her face. She hadn't really bounced back like the rest of the crew, and I wasn't sure she was totally into continuing on with the tour after everything that had happened.

"Sure," I say. I pose next to a framed photo of Whitney Houston, pasting a silly grin on my face as she snaps a few pictures.

"Got it," she says with a smile in her voice. "Thanks, Ellie."

She goes to turn away, but I grab her arm. "Hey? You OK?"

She doesn't meet my eyes. "I'm fine. Just can't shake everything, I guess."

I sigh. "I know it's hard. Thank you for standing by me. But...you've been my assistant for a while now. I can tell when something is off with you. What is it?"

She shakes her head. "I...I don't know if I can tell you."

My stomach seizes. What is she hiding? "You can tell me anything. You know that."

"I know."

She looks over my shoulder at that point, and I feel X's presence behind me a second before he appears. "Jacques needs you," he says. He nods to Sandy before pulling out his phone. When I look up, Sandy is walking away.

"Wait!" I call out. "Can we talk later? At the hotel?"

When she gives me a short nod, I let out a sigh of relief. I'll get to the bottom of things. I hate seeing her walking around like this.

X is still busy on his phone, so I slip my arms around his waist, kissing the pulse point at his neck, which I know he likes. I'm rewarded with a low growl. "Hey, watch it now," he whispers. "You don't want to start something you can't finish."

"Ellie," Michonne says, coming up behind us, "we need you in hair and makeup stat. Jacques wants to try something new."

I give X the eye. "You're in trouble later, mister."

He throws me one of his saucy faces, and we all laugh as we make our way to the dressing room.

34

Xavier

I stand in the wings, watching E sing her last song of the night in Madison Square Garden. I'm so proud of her. I know this night is special to her, and that she's pulling off the performance of a lifetime. I have so much respect for her, for the journey she had to take to get here.

The last two weeks have been eye-opening. I've never spent so much time with a woman before, and I'm at the point where I can't imagine my life without her. Waking up to her face after a night of intense passion, watching her fall asleep after an intimate conversation, is new for me.

She's under my skin. She's in my blood.

I never want it to end.

What that meant, I didn't know. But I did know that I was comfortable and 100 percent satisfied. She was mine, and I was hers. I didn't care who knew it, and that was the part that shocked the shit out of me the most. I had never been more vulnerable in my life. I would have never allowed such a thing before, but with E, it was inevitable.

I watch her move across the stage, her eyes closed in passion as she belts out the lyrics of one of my favorite songs of hers. A song about things she hates. A song that she tells me I inspired her to write. It's her standing up for herself. Her letting herself be vulnerable about her past and what happened to her. I'm more turned on than I should be.

But emotion comes with a price. As the days pass and the stalker—now possibly a murderer—continues to walk free, my worry grows. The chase is consuming me. How is this person able to get away with so much? Get away with murder? If something ever happened to her...I shake my head. I can't think of it. It would destroy me.

She was the only person I'd ever been able to open up to, and since I had, I felt stronger than ever before. Funny how that works. I'm also beginning to feel comfortable in my own skin. If someone took that away, if someone took her away—

I'd die before letting it happen.

My phone rings, and I look down to see an unknown number. I pick it up anyway.

"X."

"Xavier Cannon?"

"This is he."

"This is Dr. Shannon. Your father was admitted to the hospital this afternoon. He had a seizure."

My pulse gallops. "Is he OK?"

A sigh comes over the line, and then a pause. My heart seems to disconnect and sink into my stomach like a bowling ball. And then the doctor says, "He's conscious but...the cancer is...the cancer has...I think you should come to the hospital as soon as possible, Mr. Cannon."

I put a hand against the wall to steady myself. "Is he going to be OK?"

Another sigh. "In complete disclosure, I'd be surprised if he made it through the night. I'm so sorry."

I think I answered her after that. Said I'd be there right away, but I'm not sure.

Sheer sadness warps my system, nearly knocking me off my feet, and all the guilt I've been battling with E comes rushing back in like a freight train.

I never told him I was sorry.

Lost in a haze of disbelief, I don't even notice when the show hits its halfway point. E's five-minute break. I don't even notice when she appears at my side until she gently shakes me. "X. X, what's wrong?"

I look into her eyes, feeling too scared to speak, but knowing I have to get the words out. I have to tell her. "It's my father."

Her face drains of color. "What? What happened, X? Is he OK?"

"The doctor doesn't think he's going to make it through the night."

She gasps, her hand flying to her mouth. "Oh...oh my God...where is he?"

"Stamford Hospital. I...I have to go."

She nods, her head moving rapidly, her hands holding my arms. Tears fill her eyes, and to my utter shock, she reaches up to wipe a tear from my face. "Of course you do. Leave right now. I'll be fine."

Her words break through the black cloud and make my heart pound. "No. No, I can't leave you." Fear lances up my spine, making me dizzy. I could lose them both.

Joe and Big come over, looking worried. I think they ask what's wrong. I think E responds, but I'm too lost to keep up with the conversation.

"Hey," Joe says firmly, putting a hand on my shoulder. "We got this. Go see your father."

"I'll leave right after the show," E tells me then. "I'll come to the hospital. I want to be with you. It's only an hour away. Leave now."

My emotions are at war inside me. I'd just vowed to myself that I wouldn't leave her. If something happened to her while I was gone, I'd never forgive myself. I couldn't live with that type of guilt for a second time. But my father—thinking of him lying there and leaving this earth without ever hearing an apology from my lips absolutely guts me.

"Nothing is going to happen to her," Big assures me. "You need to go say goodbye to your father."

"Please," E begs. "Please don't stay on my account. Maybe I can leave the show now—"

"No," I tell her. "Don't do that. Finish it out, and I'll see you afterward." There's no way I was letting her walk out on what might be the biggest show of her life.

It was only a couple of more hours.

I repeat that in my head as I look at Joe and Big. "I'm trusting you." I try to infuse the fear of God and the devil in them with my stare, and I think it works. They both nod profusely.

"We've got the whole team watching her; she's going to be fine."

I search my pockets for my keys. He might not make it through the night. I inhale deeply before pulling E into my arms. I have no words.

"I'll see you soon," she says, holding me tight. "I'll come right there after the show."

I nod, feeling the desperate pull to get to my car quickly. "Call me if you need me. I mean it."

Everyone agrees, and with one last look at E, I take off down the hallway and out to my SUV.

I'm pretty sure I break the law on my way to the hospital, because the hour-long drive takes me about forty minutes. Thank God there isn't any traffic. I barely even remember the ride, as I was being assaulted by images and memories of my father. He was such a patient, kind, and understanding man. Everything good I had inside me was because of him. And I hadn't even given him the courtesy of an apology for fucking killing his wife. The love of his life.

I break down. Or at least I'm sure I do, because when I park the car, my face is sticky with tears. Jumping out of the car, I run into the emergency room and stop the first nurse I find. It takes about ten minutes for me to get to his room.

He's awake, but seeing him lying there, tubes everywhere, wrecks me. I walk slowly over to the bed, get to my knees, and press my forehead into his hand.

"Xavier," he says, his voice hoarse. "You made it."

I can't waste another minute. "Dad, I'm so, so fucking sorry about Mom. I ruined your life. I didn't mean to. I was young and didn't know what I was doing." My voice hitches, and I fight to catch my breath. I can barely see out of my watery eyes, but I look up at him anyway. "And it's not OK. I've lived my life without ever telling you what was in my heart. I love you, Dad. I love you so much. And I'm so sorry."

He smiles, resting a hand on top of my head. "My, that girl is good for you."

"She is."

"I'm so happy to see you happy," he croaks. "To see you open up to someone. Finally." He pauses to cough, and I rush to get him some water. "But Xavier," he continues a few moments later, "I've always known how you felt. You may not have told me in words, but you told me in actions. And I want you to know I've never blamed you—not once—for what happened with your mother. Her issues were no one else's but her own. It's not your fault. I'm sorry I didn't do more to relieve you of that guilt."

I wipe a stray tear from his eye. "No, no. Please don't do that. Don't put this on yourself. You've done nothing wrong. You're the best...you've been the best..."

"You're the best thing that ever happened to me," he chokes out. "Not your mother. I loved her, yes, but you were the true love of my life. And I thanked my lucky stars every day that you walked away from that crash. I wouldn't have been able to go on without you."

Hearing those words, words I had longed to hear for a lifetime...it was like cold water for a dying man. But God, I didn't want to let him go. "You can fight this, Pops! You can hold on. It doesn't have to be the end."

He smiles sadly, rubbing a hand over my scalp. "Take care of that girl. Let her into your heart. Tell her I think she's perfect for you, and that I said thank-you."

I think I nod, but I'm unable to form any more words. I climb into the bed like a little boy, and wrap my arms around him.

About twenty minutes later, I say my final goodbye.

35

Eloisa

I have no idea how I got through the second half of the show. I phoned it in—messed up the lyrics a few times. I didn't want to be there. My heart was with X and his father, and I was counting down the minutes until I could see him. It was all I could do not to run offstage and follow him. I prayed silently that he'd make it in time. That he'd get to speak the words he needed so badly to say. My heart seized, overwhelmed at the thought of what he must be feeling.

I run offstage after my last song, having already decided that I'm not doing the encore. I nearly run Sandy over in my haste to get to my dressing room. Her face, clouded with worry and anguish, stops me.

"I heard from X," she tells me sadly. "His dad...his dad passed about half an hour ago."

Oh, no. I sink down on a nearby crate, my heart and hands shaking. "How is he?"

She shakes her head, her eyes watery. "I don't know. He just sent a text." She hands me her phone. "He's going to wrap things up there and meet us at the hotel. He told you not to come to the hospital."

I read the messages with a heavy heart. I quickly dial his number, but he doesn't answer. I put my head in my hands, feeling absolutely miserable. Poor X. I have to go to him, make sure he was OK. Did he make it in time? Did he get to say goodbye? I send him a quick text to let him know I'll be waiting for him. I need to hold him. Talk to him and give him my condolences. Sadness washes over me when I think about Donovan, too, and what a loving person he was. I only met him once, but he left a mark.

The crew packed up, all of us down and out. This was just something else to add to the pile of shit we'd been dealing with. I even let Joe and Big take extra precautions with me, leading me through the back door of the hotel. I didn't want to do anything else to worry X and add any stress to his plate.

I kept checking my phone, but he still wasn't answering. The desire to hear his voice was becoming overwhelming.

Rob walked me up to my room, an arm around my shoulders. He assured me security around the hotel was crawling and in place and that I had nothing to worry about. They were going to vet any guy who stepped foot in the door! I wasn't worried about myself, though. All I wanted was X.

Inside the room, I had no idea what to do with myself. Sandy and Joe invited me to dinner in the lobby to talk, but I refused, unable to think about eating. I could barely stomach the thought.

Alone and pacing, I think about my own father. I think about his face as he left my dressing room a couple of weeks ago. He doesn't deserve anything from me, but...how would I feel if something happened to him? Had I said all I needed to say?

Making the quick decision, I pick up the phone and dial a number I've never dialed before.

He picks up on the first ring. "Eloisa?"

"Yeah, it's me." Oh, God. What have I done?

"Is everything OK? You've never called me before."

"I know. I just felt bad the way things left off."

"Don't feel bad. I understand." There's a quick pause. "I know you must have so much going on. I didn't follow what was happening that night, but...I hope you're OK."

I wasn't OK. But could I live my life without giving him a chance to repent for what he had done? I learned with Joel that alcoholism was a disease. The man I was talking to now was sober, as far as I knew. He told Sandy he wanted to ask for my forgiveness, but I'd never given him the chance. Lost in thought, I don't respond, but then he surprises me and gets my attention.

"Your show was amazing tonight."

"You were there?"

He sighs. "Yes. I've got tickets to several more, too. I'm so proud of you, E. Watching you up there...it brings me so much joy. I know I've been a terrible father, and I don't deserve anything from you, but...I can't keep myself away."

I make another quick decision. "Are you still in New York?"

"Yes, I'm staying at the Motor Inn."

It's right down the street from where I'm staying. "Do you want to come over and talk? I'm at the Marriott. I...I'm not sure where our relationship can go from here, but I'm willing to finally hear you out."

I hear what sounds like a soft cry before he says, "I'd love that. Can I...can I come now?"

I don't know where X is, but I figure I have enough time to get in a small talk with my dad before he gets back. "Sure. Just...security is really tight. Find Big in the lobby, and when you get here, call me. They'll never let you up otherwise."

We get off the phone a few minutes later, and as soon as I hang up, I get an alert for a text message. It's from Sandy.

Sandy: *Hey, Eloisa. What room are you in?*

Huh. That's weird. I could have sworn she was around when I got my room number in the lobby. She probably wants to talk, as we planned earlier. It's not the best time, but perhaps I can fit that in, too, before my dad arrives. I want uninterrupted time with X when he gets here.

I quickly text back: *Room 224.*

36

Xavier

I splash some water on my face in the bathroom, leaning heavily against the sink, unable to look at myself in the mirror.

He's gone.

The man who raised me, shaped me into the person I am today, is gone.

The pain is so sharp it makes my body tremble, and I walk out of the bathroom feeling like a zombie. They wheeled him out of the room just moments ago, and the room feels as empty as my heart.

I look to the heavens, not sure what the hell is up there, but so thankful that I was able to get what I needed to off my chest. I only wish I had done it sooner. I have E to thank for that. She opened me up like a damned sieve, and I was beginning to feel like a new man.

The nurse cleaning the room has her back to me, so I clear my throat to get her attention and to let her know I'm leaving. I'd call someone tomorrow about the plans for the body. I just can't deal with it right now. She apparently doesn't hear me, so I walk closer. "Ma'am?"

When she spins around, I realize that the she is a he. "Oh, um. I'm sorry."

He waves away my concern. "Don't worry about it. Happens all the time. Comes along with being short."

I laugh awkwardly, and we talk for a few minutes before he moves on to the next room.

As I leave the hospital, I pull my phone out of my pocket. I have several missed calls and text messages from E. I can't wait to get to her. There's literally nowhere else I'd rather be than with her right now.

As I approach my car, something about the nurse clicks into place. I thought he was a woman, but he was a man. I think E's stalker is a man, but...

Holy. Fuck. I think back to the hotel video of the stalker—the short stature and high voice. I think back to all the times this person has gone unnoticed. I think back to the hearts above the *I* letters in the note.

I don't know for sure, but my instincts tell me I'm spot-on. My brain had been fighting to tell me this from the beginning. Something never felt right.

All this time we've been searching for a man. But the stalker is a woman.

I run to my car, step on the gas, and fly out of the parking lot, dialing E on the way.

37

Eloisa

I hang up the phone after letting Big know my father will be arriving. He wasn't thrilled with the news, but after I promised he could escort him up and stay for the duration of the visit, he agreed. Dad would definitely have to go through a full pat down, but that was the price he was going to have to pay.

A knock signals Sandy's arrival. I hurry toward the door, looking forward to what she has to say. What could be bothering her that she doesn't want to tell me?

I swing open the door, but it isn't Sandy standing in front of me.

A short girl about my age with a bright-red bow in her boyishly cut black hair stands in front of me. Before I can even ask, there's a small pistol in my face.

"Get inside," she says. Her voice is eerily high-pitched, and her small, fairylike features strike a chord somewhere in my brain. I've seen her before.

I back into the room, trying to figure out what I can pick up and throw at her. I look around out of the corner of my eye, but it must be obvious.

ONE-WOMAN SHOW

"Don't even think about it," she growls, eyes lit with anticipation. She looks wild, and it smells as if she hasn't washed in days. I watch in terror as she shuts and locks the door behind her, trapping us in.

Oh, God. X is going to blame himself for this when it's really all my fault. How did this girl know my room number? How did she get past security? Why didn't I look through the peephole to make sure it was Sandy? Could she be my stalker? Surely not.

I back away until my legs hit the coffee table, nearly causing me to fall over. I right myself quickly and run behind the couch, just to put something between us. She isn't saying anything. She's just staring at me with a sick sense of fascination as she makes her way toward me. I have to stall her.

"Who are you?"

She scoffs. "You don't recognize me?"

I rack my brain, desperate, because I can't remember who this girl is. But someone must be looking out for me from above, because a hazy image arrives from the far reaches of my memory. It's the bow that ultimately gives her away. I've seen it before. "You came to one of my brunches."

She smiles sweetly, as if lost in the memory. "I knew you'd remember me. You told me I was your favorite."

"You are my favorite," I choke out, playing along. At least I think playing along is what the crime shows tell you to do. Then I remember something else. "Oh my god. Darla's doggy treats."

She comes closer, a crazed look in her eye. "Right again."

I'm at a loss for words. I've been accepting packages from this woman for months.

"Darla's doggy treats! Darla's doggy treats! Box after box sent with care. How could you?" she scoffs, pulling at her hair with her free hand. "How could you betray me?"

"How...how did I betray you?"

"You didn't say hello. At the red carpet. Sorry about that rock, by the way. But I just got so mad when you didn't recognize me."

"There were a lot of people there," I say carefully, trying to defend myself. "I didn't see you."

"Bullshit!" she screams. "You looked right at me! I took a damn picture of you! We locked eyes, but you looked right through me! That's what everyone does! No one ever notices me. If they did, I wouldn't have gotten away with throwing that rock at you in the middle of a crowded red carpet. But no one saw a thing!"

Her face twists in anger, and she raises the gun, so I fight to placate her. "If I had known who you were, I definitely would have said hello. I appreciated all those packages you sent me. I'm...I'm sorry!"

She sighs loudly. "I'm trying to forgive you, Eloisa. I'm really trying, but you make it so hard. Especially all that bullshit with your bodyguard. I wanted to die when I saw those pictures."

At her words, a flash of a girl in a bow springs to my memory from that day. Oh, God. It was her. "You were at the *Crenshaw* show, too." I remember seeing her in the audience, behind the woman with the child.

She shrugs, the gun held casually in her hand. "I've been a lot of places. Your house, your hotels...behind your SUV. I followed you that day. But you didn't notice. Sometimes you look me in the eye, sometimes you don't. You've been playing games!"

This bitch is crazy. I had to keep her calm. "I haven't! I swear! I...I'm happy to see you. But how did you...how did you know my room number?"

She reaches into her pocket, and I freeze, terrified that she has another weapon, but it's a phone. Sandy's phone. Oh, God! She sent that text asking about the room. "What did you do to Sandy?"

She scoffs and throws the phone on the coffee table, where it clangs loudly. I notice then that she's wearing gloves. "Sandy's fine. She was making out with some blond-headed monster in the corner of the restaurant downstairs, so I stole her phone from the table. Can you believe my luck? I planned to knock on every door until I found you, but I didn't even have to. Not a very keen assistant you've got there. Bad taste in men, too. But all those security types are idiots. They let me waltz right in here without even blinking."

Something she said stuck. Making out with...Joe? It had to be. Sandy was with Joe? Was that what she was scared to tell me? That must have been what she was hiding. She was probably worried about my reaction, how I would handle it. She was such a stickler for the rules. My heart bangs in my chest as her behavior falls into place.

"I've been very lucky these past few weeks, you know. It just proves that I'm on the right path. Everything I've done has brought me closer to you. I've been so close." She cackles, and my heart squeezes in fear. "And now, here we are," she muses.

I stare at her in horror and confusion. How can it have been her who was behind everything? How could this small girl be filled with so much hate? What did I do?

"What do you want from me?" I ask, inching around the couch as she gets closer. "Why are you here?"

"Eloisa, you know why I'm here." She waves the gun around in the air. "At the brunch, when you hugged me before I left, I knew what you were telling me. I knew you wanted us to be together."

She's insane. But while she's holding the gun, she's in charge. "You're wrong. I wanted to be friends, that was it."

"Friends? *Friends?* After that brunch, you never called! You just kept ordering more and more treats, but you never called! I was...crushed. But even then, I supported you. I've never stopped supporting you! I even killed that bitch Martha for you! I did have to teach you a few lessons along the way, of course. Poor, poor little Bella. No more treats for her!"

My breath caught. "How did you get to Bella?"

"When you were signing autographs at the show that night, I brought some of the doggy treats. I was hoping you'd recognize me and say hello if you saw the box. So I made it really pretty with my signature bow and the hearts. But, of course, you looked right through me again. But Bella remembered me! Bella got a whiff of my treats and came right to me. She really loved those, didn't she? Didn't you write to me one time and tell me she could smell them a mile away? Well, that was true. The greedy little bitch. Gave her one of my special ones."

Every instinct was telling me to defend my dog, but I bit my tongue. Pain shot through me as I remembered the events of that night. I knew Bella always ran for those treats. Why didn't I put that together?

She started coming toward me. What the hell was I going to do? I had to keep her talking, but I was scared witless that I'd say the wrong thing and she'd kill me. I had to ask, though. "Why Bella? Why would you kill an innocent dog?"

"Because you loved her more than you loved me."

My phone rings then, startling us both. X's name flashes across the screen, and I swipe my finger to pick it up.

She cocks the gun. "Give me the phone."

A fresh wave of terror runs through me, but I refuse. "No. I'm asking you to leave. We can talk about this tomorrow, after we've both had a good night's sleep."

She throws her head back in laughter. "Do you think I'm an idiot?"

I can hear X's voice shouting at me through the phone, but I don't dare put it up to my ear for fear she'll shoot me where I stand.

She narrows her eyes. "We're going to talk now, damn it! I didn't want to say this just yet, Eloisa, but I love you."

X's voice—if possible—gets even louder. I imagine the phone vibrating in my hand. I grasp it like a lifeline. "You don't love me."

"Don't fucking tell me how I feel! Your music...it speaks to me. Isn't that what you wanted, Eloisa? Your fans to love your music?"

I shake my head. "Please, my bodyguard is on the way—"

That was definitely the wrong thing to say. Her face turns bright red. "Tell him not to come. That we need to be alone." I gape like a fish, trying to find the words to refuse her. "Tell him!" she screams. She holds the gun up until it's pointing at my face. She's about six feet away, so if she pulls the trigger, I'm done for.

I put the phone up to my ear, my hands shaking like leaves.

"X," I squeak out. "You...you don't have to come."

"Big and Joe are on their way to your room now. They'll be there any second, you just have to hold her off until then! Do whatever she wants! Tell her I agreed not to come!"

I nod jerkily, even though he can't hear me. "He...he's not coming."

She looks around nervously. "We should leave anyway. There's somewhere I want to take you."

"Distract her, E. Tell her whatever she wants to hear. You're doing great. Just keep calm."

"I'll go wherever you want," I say loudly. The phone is still glued to my ear, and I'm finding it hard to look at her face.

"It's going to be OK, E. I promise. I'll be there soon."

"I love you."

The words come unbidden out of my mouth, and she must know I'm talking to X and not to her, because next thing I know, she's flying toward me. I drop the phone, putting my hands out as we both tumble over the couch and onto the floor.

I feel her grab hold of my face, her nails raking across my skin as I try to pull away. Blood from her hands falls into my eyes, blinding me. I cry out in pain, grabbing for her wrists and then squeezing them as hard as I can to try to get her to let up.

She knees me in the groin, and I groan, ribbons of pain shooting up my spine. "It doesn't have to be this way," she grits out, trying to hold my arms down. "I don't want it to be this way."

Since she's so small, I'm able to roll her over with the force I have left. I put my hands around her neck, straddling her waist, scared as hell. I have no idea if I can actually go through with choking her! My face is dripping blood, and when I notice her hand reaching out to the side, it's too late.

The gun goes off, but the bullet hits the ceiling, missing me by a few inches.

In the split second she takes to get her bearings, I grab my phone off the floor and run into the hallway, knowing I won't have time to make it to the front door. I hear her footsteps in the hallway just as I slam the bathroom door.

"Eloisa," she screams. "Don't do this! Don't fucking hurt me again!"

"X," I say again, putting the phone to my ear. "Are you still there? Please hurry!"

The phone slips out of my hand because of all the blood, and I hurry to scoop it back up before climbing into the bathtub.

The gun goes off again, and the doorknob falls to the floor. She's going to kill me. They aren't going to make it in time.

I put the phone up to my ear. "I love you," I tell him again, closing my eyes and wishing I could tell him in person. "I love you, X. You're the best thing that's ever happened to me. I don't care if you think it's too soon. It's now or never."

His voice hitches on the line. I can hear the rev of the engine as he speeds to get to me. "E, don't. It's going to be OK!" I hear him tell me sternly. "I...I love you, too."

"I'm sorry," I tell him, my voice breaking. "This is my fault."

"Don't! Don't, E! I can't...I can't bear to hear you say that! Hang on for me, Eloisa. Hang on. I'm on my way. I'm coming to you."

I hear the door slam open, and I clench my eyes together in fear. My face is throbbing.

"I can't lose you, too!" X cries into the phone. His words have my eyes opening. What the hell am I doing? I'm a sitting duck in this tub. No way I'm going down without a fight. I know I only have seconds, so I gather my courage.

When I pull back the curtain, several things happen at once. The girl is standing in the doorway, her eyes wild as she cocks her gun again, pointing right at my heart. But a loud slam in the living room startles her, and I take that second to charge her where she stands, both of us falling out of the bathroom and into the hallway.

There's a scramble, and I see three faces come into view as I'm fighting her off. My father's face is at the front. I look once more into the girl's face, and it feels like I'm looking at the devil. Her eyes are deranged and angry as she brings the gun toward my temple. I barely register my father reaching down and grabbing her off me, but I hear the gunshot ring out loud and clear.

I scream as I watched my father fall against the wall, a hand over his heart. The bullet that had been meant for me went into him. Joe and Big are shouting as they wrangle the girl and drag her away from the scene. Her screams are now mingling with the police sirens in the distance.

I crawl on my hands and knees to my father. There's blood gushing from his chest, and try as I might, I can't stanch it.

"Dad!" I scream. "Dad!"

He jerks a little, then lets out a long, slow breath. His voice is choppy, and I have to lean in to understand him. "That's the first time you've called me Dad in over twelve years."

I'm sobbing uncontrollably now, still trying to stop the flow from the gaping wound in his chest.

"I'm sorry, Eloisa," he croaks out. And as soon as the words leave his mouth, the life leaves his body.

That's where X finds me fifteen minutes later. Covered in blood and slumped against my father's body. I refused to leave his side for anyone else, but the second X comes barreling into view, I lift my arms for him to pick me up.

His skin is ice-cold, his face is drawn, and I've never in my life seen the desperately frightened expression on his face. I cling to him something fierce, and he clings to me with the same intensity. We sway on the spot for long seconds as the chaos unfolds around us. A few people try to talk to me. I can't lift my head away from his neck.

"I'm OK," I whisper in his ear when I notice he's shaking. "I'm OK."

He pulls back, his face wet with my blood. He moves his palm gently over the scratch marks on my face. "I don't know what I would have done. I was thinking the worst...I...I couldn't have gone on without you. I knew it before, and I'm positive of it now."

"You don't have to," I tell him, pressing my lips against his. "I'm so sorry, X, about your father."

His breath hitches. "I'm sorry about yours."

We come together for another kiss, and from that point on, we don't let go.

Epilogue

Ten Months Later–Xavier

"Happy birthday, Eloisa!"

The boisterous cacophony of cheers startles the girl at my side. So much so that she grabs hold of my arm in surprise. I laugh as slow realization plays across her face.

She turns to slap my arm playfully, "Oh my God! X! You said we weren't having a party!"

"I lied," I tease, leading her into our new living room, which is filled to capacity with all of our friends. I take a second and admire the vast countryside that can be seen through the large window. I still can't get used to it. "It's not every day a girl turns twenty-six, after all."

We're immediately assaulted by Michonne. "Happy birthday, Ellie! Wait until you see what I got you. Come to think of it, it's actually the perfect party outfit if you feel like changing..."

E laughs. "Thank you! I'm so surprised! I can't believe you are all here!"

"X is good at keeping secrets. He planned the whole thing," Jacques chimes in, giving me a smile.

"Thank you," E says, grinning up at me.

Man, I was so lucky I got to see that grin every day.

We closed on our new house three months ago. It's smaller than her old one, but perfect for us. There are still plenty of security measures—I insisted on it. She's still a celebrity, after all.

Sandy comes over then with Joe close behind. I watch as E embraces her gently, oohing and ahhing over her pregnant belly. We haven't seen them in a couple of weeks, as Sandy is due to pop any minute. I couldn't wait to have her back as E's assistant. No one kept the team as organized as Sandy, and E and I were going a little nuts without her.

I still couldn't believe she and that big doof were together. My mind goes back to that night, as it often did. Their relationship *had* been what Sandy wanted to talk to E about. She'd been scared to lose her job—fraternizing with a coworker and all that—and it had been heavily weighing on her mind.

At first I thought they were going to be doomed to fail, Sandy being such a straight-edge, no-nonsense type of girl and Joe...well, Joe being Joe, but I guess opposites do attract, because they seem happier than ever.

He slaps my hand in greeting. "Nice job, sir. Never seen Ellie look so surprised before."

I give him a nod. "Where's Big?"

Joe leans in close. "He's with the box in the back room. Damn thing won't sit still."

"OK, great. I'll make the speech sooner rather than later so he can join the party."

Rob and the colonel come over next. My former boss looks incredibly well rested. He has on a Hawaiian shirt with khaki shorts. Will wonders ever cease? Retirement looks great on him. He's currently the antithesis of Rob, who is as immersed in work as ever. Rob nudges me. "Think this is a good time to bring up her second album?"

I shrug. "She's taking her time. We're enjoying traveling for the moment. We've got a trip to Norway coming up, and then we're on to Alaska. Maybe when we get back."

He nods.

Eloisa's tour—she didn't miss a show—concluded with a bang. And she won a Grammy for what we liked to refer to as her hate song. It sat in a place of honor on our new mantel. Feeling like her goals had been accomplished and she needed a break, she didn't rush to make a second album, but knowing her, she'll be back in the studio eventually. I plan to be there next to her every step of the way—as I was in the middle of opening my own private security company.

We spend the next twenty minutes greeting everyone in the room. Most of the folks are from her tour and security team—including Harold. When he catches my eye, he holds up his ID before falling into a fit of laughter. The old man still likes to mess with me, but I think he has a soft spot with my name on it deep down. He's retired as well, and he and the colonel have become good friends.

There are a few celebrities in attendance, and they make me think of Pops. Man, I would do anything to have him here to celebrate the occasion. A pang—one I'm used to by now—zings through me at the thought of him. I wish he could see me now, too. Happy and so in love.

I've been making progress, opening up more. It hasn't been easy, and I rely on E's help a lot, but we are both working to put the past behind us. Put what happened last year behind us.

Our fathers passed away on the same day, both with words of love as their final goodbyes. E still doesn't talk about her father much. I know she wishes she could talk to him again. If only to thank him for taking that bullet for her. He might have been a shitty father, but his dying act was one for his daughter. It's something neither of us will be able to forget.

Feeling overcome with love as I watch her laugh with friends, I decide it's now or never. I find a break in the conversation and, without a word, lead E to the center of the room. Sandy hands me a microphone. She's the only one I've trusted with my bigger secret.

"If I could have everyone's attention," I begin. I wait a minute or two for the chatter to die down before I continue. "Thank you all for coming out to celebrate with us today. And thank you especially for keeping it a secret from this one!"

Everyone laughs, and E sends me a chiding look, a smile on her face and a blush on her cheeks. "This party actually serves two purposes. The first one is to celebrate the life of the influential woman I have the honor of calling mine. Happy birthday, E."

Cheers resound, and I give the signal for Joe to get Big, who's watching my gift in the other room. As he appears in the doorway, I turn to E. "My first gift to you."

Her eyes catch on Big carrying a big cardboard box—without a bow—and her face lights up with confusion and delight. "Oh no. Another gift, X? Wasn't the trip enough?"

I shrug, giddy with excitement for her to open the box. When Big places it down at her feet, a loud bark echoes through the room. While everyone laughs, E's eyes fill with tears.

She bends down slowly, lifting the flaps. A small white puppy, the same breed as Bellatrix, jumps into her arms.

"I've named him Dumbledore," I tell her gently, bending down beside her. "I looked through all the characters, and since he has such white hair, I figured it was a good fit."

She's speechless, and I'm unsure if that's a good sign or not. I didn't know if it was too soon, but once the idea caught hold, I couldn't talk myself out of it.

"Do you like him?" I ask, watching the small puppy lick her face. "We can find another home for him if you're not ready—"

"I love him," she whispers, burying her face in his fur. "X...this is the best gift I've ever gotten. Thank you."

Relief fills me. If that hadn't gone well, it would have totally messed up my next surprise. "Well, I hope you'll change your mind about that, because I have something else for you."

She looks at me curiously, her eyes full of love and her arms full of puppy. She stands up, smiling as the puppy pants with exertion in her arms.

I don't want to wait another minute. The second she's close, I drop down on one knee. She gasps.

"Eloisa Rae Morgan, you've made me a better man, and I want to spend the rest of my life with you. Loving you, honoring you, and cherishing you. I want to spend my days watching you onstage and rubbing your damn feet. I want to travel the world and make as many silly faces as I have to, to make you laugh. I want to do so many things, but I need just one thing from you: Make me the happiest man alive and be my wife?"

I—and the audience, I'm sure—can't breathe.

She's crying now. "I think that's the first time I've ever heard you call me by my real name."

I laugh, nervous as hell. "I thought it would be appropriate. But it's a onetime thing."

She puts the puppy on the floor and runs into my arms. "Yes," she tells me. And then shouts louder for everyone else to hear. "Yes! Yes! Yes!"

The crowd goes wild—this time for both of us—as I hold my new fiancée against my chest.

This is just the beginning—the opening act of our two-person show.

Made in United States
North Haven, CT
30 March 2023